LADY BUCKAROO

LADY BUCKAROO

Suzanne Lyon

GUNSMOKE

First published in the US by Five Star

This hardback edition 2013
by AudioGO Ltd
by arrangement with
Golden West Literary Agency

ISBN 978 1 471 32148 1

This is a work of fiction. Names, characters, places and
incidents are either products of the author's imagination or
are used fictitiously.

British Library Cataloguing in Publication Data available.

Printed and bound in Great Britain by
TJ International Limited

Lady Buckaroo

Chapter One

The sun was a huge red ball sitting squat on the horizon as fifteen-year-old Eulalie Buckley turned into the drive that led to her family's ranch. Ambling toward the large, two-story frame house, every muscle of the girl's body made its presence felt in the kind of sweet, tired ache that was the aftermath of adrenaline-burning exertion. Dismounting, she led her horse to the barn and bedded it down for the night, following the time-honored Western tradition of seeing to her animal's needs before her own. As she headed for the house, walking backwards so as not to miss the sight of the sun melting away into the endlessly undulating dunes of the Nebraska Sand Hills, she almost tripped over Wally, their old collie dog, who nosed her enthusiastically. Laughing, she ruffled the old dog's fur. A vee of geese honked above her head, and she followed their flight pathway into the distance. It occurred to her that this evening was no different from hundreds of other late summer evenings she had witnessed in her lifetime. But she would always remember, always savor, this particular one, for this day had been a sort of beginning. Today, she had discovered . . . *rodeo!*

When she and her older brother, Johnny, had left the ranch this morning, headed for the Sheridan County Fair of 1917, Lael had had no inkling that her life's calling was about to be revealed. But almost by accident—responding to a dare from her scamp of a brother—she had found herself entered in the ladies' steer-riding event. And she had won!

Twenty-five dollar bills bulged out the pocket of her dust-covered jeans.

Not that she really cared about the money; no, she was hooked on the high of rodeo itself. Unbelievably she had sub-dued a massive, angry steer, at least fifteen times her own weight, and had looked good doing it. Closing her eyes, she thought back to that moment when the snubber had boosted her onto the steer's back and yanked on the flank strap. The ground had exploded through the top of her head as the angry animal bucked and leaped, landing with tremendous force and then taking off again, leaving her stomach somewhere in the general vicinity of the moon. Too shaken to think, she had reacted instinctively, leaning way back and throwing up her legs in an effort to keep balanced. Hanging on with both hands, it had felt as though her arms might get yanked right out of their sockets. One of the steer's kicks had whip-lashed her head, and her teeth had clamped down painfully on her tongue. Then the monster had started spinning, all the while still maniacally kicking its back legs so that Lael had had no idea where the ground stopped and the sky started. And then, remarkably, it had stopped in its tracks, its sides heaving in defeat. The crowd had come to its feet for the petite, blonde cowgirl with eyes the color of summer sagebrush.

True, her body ached and her tongue was awfully sore, but her discomfort was a small price to pay for the thrill of that ten-second ride. Although Lael, like other girls who grew up in the Sand Hills, could not remember having learned to ride—she had just always been on the back of a horse—and, although she could throw a loop or cut an ornery cow from the herd as expertly as her father and brothers, it had never occurred to her to do any of those things competitively. Oh, she had heard about rodeo cowgirls before, like the famous Prairie Rose Henderson who had first ridden a bucking broncho in the 1904 Pendleton Roundup. But she had assumed, if she thought about it at all, that women's competition was strictly limited to the glamorous, big-time rodeos, like Pendleton or Cheyenne Frontier Days. Now here she was—the winner of the ladies' steer-riding contest at the Sheridan County Fair!

Smiling secretly, Lael pushed open the screen door and found her mother at the kitchen sink, drying the last of the supper dishes.

"There you are! Pa and I went ahead and ate since I wasn't sure when you'd be getting back, but I saved plates for you and Johnny. Is he coming?" Nellie Buckley dried her hands and, using the dish towel as a pot handler, removed a plate from the old, black oven.

"Not for a while yet. He's seeing Emily Olsen home. He bid on her pie at the fair and won it." Lael washed her hands and dropped in front of the huge, pock-marked pine table. All of her ten older siblings but Johnny had left home. Regardless, Nellie still cooked enough for an entire branding crew.

Serving the warm plate, the older woman snapped the dish towel over her shoulder and sat down next to her daughter. "So, now it's Emily Olsen? I declare, that brother of yours has more girls on the line than I do clothespins on wash day!"

Lael chewed gingerly, favoring her sore tongue. Not really hungry, she forked the food around on her plate as she considered whether to tell her mother about the steer-riding contest now, or later when her father would be there to hear the news. Of the two, she figured her mother would object more to her new-found interest in rodeo, on the basis that it was a decidedly dangerous activity. Her father's displeasure, on the other hand, would most likely be tempered by the fact of her first-place win and twenty-five dollars in prize money.

Rising slowly, Lael awkwardly carried her plate to the

sink, her sore muscles having stiffened as she sat.

"What's wrong?" Nellie asked, her sharp eyes missing nothing.

"Just tired. Think I'll have a hot bath and go to bed." But any hopes Lael had of saving the steer-riding news until morning were dashed when Howard Buckley banged into the kitchen, his arm around Johnny's shoulders as they shared some private male joke.

"Uh-oh. Ladies present."

"Oh, for heaven's sake, Howard. You're worse than a teenager." Nellie disgustedly worked the hand pump at the sink, drawing water to put on the stove for Lael's bath.

"Don't go jumping to conclusions now. Johnny and I were just discussing the merits of strawberry rhubarb pie. You used to make a hell of a good rhubarb pie, sweetie. Why ain't you made me one lately?" Winking broadly at his son, he sidled up behind Nellie and nuzzled her neck until she pushed him away.

"Get on out of here," she scolded, although her lips twitched with a smile. "Johnny, are you going to eat any supper, or are you too full of pie?"

"I'll always eat your fixin's, Ma." As Johnny swung one long leg over the kitchen chair and plopped down, he glanced at Lael. She could tell by the mischievous look on his face that he was going to spill the beans about the rodeo. She sighed. Brothers. It was hard to love them when you were so busy hating them.

"Guess what I did today?" she began lamely.

Howard filched a piece of bread from Johnny's plate and gave her an inquiring look.

Taking a deep breath, she blurted out: "I won the ladies' steer-riding contest."

The silence lasted a full beat, then drew out even longer.

Lael looked from one to the other, a hopeful little smile on her face, while they stared back, not comprehending. Finally her father finished his bite and swallowed. "Ladies' steer riding? You're telling me you rode a steer? In a rodeo?" His voice was so soft that Lael missed its edgy undertone.

"Yeah, and I won too! Twenty-five dollars. Pretty good, huh?"

Howard turned a furious face to Johnny. "What were you thinking, letting your sister do a thing like that? Ain't you got a lick of sense?"

"Don't blame me." Johnny threw up his palms. "She'd gone and done it before I knew a thing." Lael glared at him, knowing it was pointless to explain her brother's rôle in what she had done.

The older man suddenly turned and kicked the chair all the way across the room. It banged into the screen door and set Wally, perched just outside, to barking wildly.

"Now, Howard," warned Nellie, "calm down. It's not so bad. She was just having a little fun, weren't you, honey? It's not like she's going to make a career out of it, for heaven's sake."

"Yes, I will!" Even as she said it, Lael knew it was the wrong thing to say at the wrong time. But she couldn't help it. She would not let her parents forbid her from doing this. "It was . . . like nothing I've ever done before . . . like flying and falling at the same time. And the crowd loved me, didn't they, Johnny?" In desperation, she turned to her brother who, God bless him, shrugged and nodded in agreement.

"I don't care if the entire state of Nebraska loves you. You ain't going to ride no more steers!" Her father advanced on her, his eyes the same gray-green color as hers but darker now with anger. "Why do you think your mother and I break our backs on this place? So you can grow up to get trampled to

11

death or get that pretty face of yours smashed in? I've known plenty of rodeo folk in my time, and not a one of them's still in one piece."

"I didn't get hurt," Lael protested, rolling her wounded tongue around in her mouth.

"Then you're god damned lucky. If it didn't happen this time, I guarantee it will the next."

"Lael, honey, your father's right," said Nellie Buckley. "Rodeo is so dangerous. But it's not just the likelihood of getting hurt. It's the whole way of living . . . wandering from town to town, no place to call home, having to rustle up work in the off-season. It's no life for a woman. I'm sure some rodeo folk are fine people, but they're not, well, our kind of people."

"I can't believe you'd say that, Ma. What makes us any different from rodeo people? Money? It's not like we ever have any extra cash floating around this place. But look at this!" Lael dug in her jeans pocket and came out with twenty-five crisp, new bills. "This is more money than I've ever had at one time before in my entire life, and I earned it in ten seconds flat!"

"Sure, you came up a winner today, so you think that's how it'll be everyday. Well, I got news for you, missy, it ain't that easy. Nothing worth having in life comes that easy." Howard turned away and ran his hands through his graying hair, his anger changed to something else, something sadder and deeper.

"But Pa," Lael said gently, "it *was* easy. It was easy for me, and I loved it. That's all I want to do and I want to do it all . . . bronc' riding and calf roping and bulldogging and everything."

Howard Buckley turned and fixed his daughter with a gaze so stern it made her insides twist. "No rodeo, Eulalie Buckley, and that's final."

Chapter Two

The hands on the clock stood stock still. Lael forced herself to look away for what she thought was at least five minutes, but, when she looked back, the big hand had only ticked twice. She closed her eyes and groaned inwardly, hating with all her being everything that surrounded her, starting with her uncomfortably tight clothes—blouse, skirt, pantaloons, stockings, high button boots—and including the rock-hard chair she sat on, the rows of desks on either side of her, the pasty-faced students that sat at those desks and finally, most of all, Mr. Snively, the bespectacled, pockmarked instructor who stood at the front of the classroom and tortured her in an unbearable monotone with some gibberish about the correct way to post accounts receivable.

Squirming in her seat, Lael purposely knocked her pencil on to the floor just to have an excuse to bend over and lift her aching bottom off the wooden chair. Had she not been so miserable, she might have giggled at the spectacle of a seventeen-year-old girl, practically a woman, pulling the same sort of shenanigans she had as a grammar school student. But there was nothing funny about her situation—her exile, as she thought of it. At least, her parents had not sent her somewhere far removed from the rodeo circuit. Strangely they had sent her to Texas, the very heart of rodeo. To attend business school, of all things.

Two years ago, when her father had flatly forbidden her participation in rodeo, Lael had cried, argued, berated, and thrown tantrums, to no avail. Howard Buckley stood firm.

No daughter of his would waste her life pursuing the dangerous and uncertain world of rodeo.

But Lael had not been able to leave it at that. Her one taste of rodeo competition had awakened a passion she had not known she had inside her. A passion that had to be satisfied, at any cost. So, on the sly, she had entered a few small rodeos in tiny towns where the Buckley name was not known. And she had continued to win, not just in the steer riding event but on bucking bronchos as well.

Regrettably she had had to lie to her family in order to carry off the deception. Like the time she had come home with a shiner because the broncho she had been trying to mount had pitched into her, driving the saddle horn into her eye. She had told everyone she had stumbled against the barn door. Then there was the time she had sprained her wrist when her hand had caught in the rigging. She had managed to conceal that injury completely from Nellie and Howard. Only Johnny had caught on, and, when he had confronted her, she managed to bargain for his silence.

Of course, in a community as insular as the Sand Hills, it was inevitable that she would be found out—the wonder was that it hadn't happened sooner—and the upshot of being discovered was exile to Fort Worth, Texas to live with her brother, Roger, and his wife and children and to attend classes at the local business college.

School had started two weeks ago, and, were it not for the fact that Roger escorted her to the door of her classroom and her sister-in-law waited to pick her up at the end of the day, Lael would have skipped every day, so much did she despise the lifeless subject of accounting. As it was, she had yet to crack the spine of her textbook or turn in an assignment.

At long last, the minute hand clicked over to twelve. Lael slammed her book shut, interrupting Snively in mid-sentence. While the rest of the class wrote down the next day's assignment, Lael stuffed her book and papers into her satchel and was the first one out of her chair when the instructor finally dismissed them.

"Miss Buckley," came Snively's reedy voice, "a word with you, please."

Reluctantly Lael walked to the head of the classroom. Snively regarded her disdainfully from behind thick, wire-framed glasses.

"Miss Buckley, I've detected a certain lack of enthusiasm on your part for this class. Not only have you failed to turn in any of the assigned work, but you seem to lack . . . focus, shall we say, during the lectures."

Lael shifted from one foot to the other, itching to follow her classmates into freedom. "Yes, sir," she said meekly.

"May I expect that attitude to change? Otherwise, I'll have no choice but to fail you, you understand."

"Yes, sir." Of course, that was exactly what Lael wanted. She would endure anything, including her own humiliation and her parents' wrath, if she never had to set foot in this place again.

That night, Lael was especially quiet at the supper table, pushing food around her plate while her brother Roger and sister-in-law Amy kept up a steady patter with their two young children. Finally Roger attempted to bring her into the conversation.

"How was school today, Lael? Did the charming Mister Snively bowl you over with his scintillating discussion of debits and credits?" Roger Buckley, ten years older than Lael, was himself a graduate of the business college and was employed as an accountant at the Fort Worth stockyards. Unlike most members of his profession, however, he possessed a fine sense of humor that complimented his typical Buckley good

looks. It was a mystery to Lael how, with his ranch upbringing, he could endure the daily office grind, but he seemed
content enough.

Tonight, however, Lael was not to be jollied out of her
funk. Throwing down her fork, she glared at her brother.
"Snively's awful, and you know it. If he ever, just once,
changed the pitch of his voice, I think I'd faint. And the students aren't any better. They all look like miniature Snivelys
with their coke-bottle glasses and pinched little faces. I
mean, this is Texas! Don't these people ever get out in the
sun? Ride a horse? Plant a garden? Or just take a walk, for
God's sake?"

"I imagine most of them are too busy studying to spend a
lot of time outdoors. Something that doesn't seem to have occurred to you to do, little sister." Roger's tone was gentle but
contained an unmistakable barb.

"Roger, I'm never going to be a bookkeeper. All those
numbers are just gobbledygook to me. It isn't like I couldn't
figure it out, if I wanted to, but I don't want to. I want to do
something different with my life."

"Now, Lael," Amy broke in, her sweet face pleading for an
end to the unpleasantness, "you don't have to be a bookkeeper. You could switch to stenographic classes. And, realis-
tically, you won't have to work in an office for long. Some
good-looking young man is bound to snap you up in a year or
two, and then you'll be set."

"I don't want to be set . . . at least, not like that. Excuse me
for saying so, Amy, but being a wife and mother isn't the life
for me, not yet anyway. I've got a lot of things I want to do before I get caught in that trap!"

Amy drew a quick breath and dropped her eyes to her
plate. Lael was sorry to have hurt her but she wasn't going to
take back any of it.

"What do you want to do, Aunt Lael?" piped up five-year-old Molly.

Lael caught Roger's eye across the table. He knew, of course, why she had been sent to Fort Worth, and Lael assumed he had told Amy. But the children, Molly and the baby Benjy, knew nothing of her rodeo experiences. *Oh, for heaven's sake,* Lael thought, *it's not as though I committed a crime.*

Leaning close to the little girl, Lael said: "Sweet pea, what I really want to do is ride bucking bronchos in the rodeo."

Molly's eyes went wide, and she looked to her parents for confirmation of the fact that Aunt Lael had gone crazy. Wordlessly Amy rose and began to clear the dishes, snatching away Lael's half-eaten dinner. Roger sighed and placed his carefully folded napkin next to his spoon. "Pa would never forgive me, if I let you get back into that business, Lael. Don't put me on the spot."

"I didn't put you in any spot. Pa did by sending me down here thinking it would change my mind. Well, nothing's going to change my mind. I'm going to join the circuit, and, if you forbid me to do it while I'm living in your house, then I'll leave! I'm sorry if I seem ungrateful to you and Amy, but I'd rather fend for myself if it means being able to rodeo." Lael's voice shook, but her eyes were clear and her jaw was set.

A moment ticked by, and then Roger smiled and leaned back in his chair. "Can we go back to the beginning of this conversation, right before I asked you how school was going, and start all over again?"

Lael returned his smile and the tension left the room, but she refused to be deterred now that her wishes were out in the open. "Oh, Roger, I don't mean to cause trouble, but I'm not cut out for business school or any school for that matter. I just want to be a cowgirl. Please don't try to stop me."

Glancing at his wife, Roger gave a small shrug, and then winked at Molly who was still taking it all in, wide-eyed. "Tell you what. I'll make you a deal. You keep going to school, and I won't stand in the way of your rodeoing. At least, that way I'll have kept half my promise to Pa."

Lael hesitated only briefly. She would rather not go back to school at all, but, if that was the price to be paid, so be it. Besides, she'd probably flunk out pretty soon anyway. Grinning broadly, she slapped her palms on the table top. "Deal!"

Chapter Three

Louise Morris hung over the rail, taking in the last of the steer-riding contestants. As she watched, the rangy animal effortlessly tossed its rider to the ground. The hapless cowboy curled and rolled to his right but still managed to get tangled in the steer's scissoring hoofs. The crowd gasped, but Louise didn't even flinch. How many times had she seen this happen, and, like as not, the man would come through OK. Oh, he might be banged up a little—a bad bruise, a broken rib perhaps—but he would live to ride again. Rodeo folk were a tough lot.

She should know. She could hardly remember a time when she hadn't been swinging a rope or busting a broncho for someone's entertainment. First for her father and all his highfalutin' friends and then in public, at Wild West shows and rodeos across the country. She had performed for presidents and kings, at world's fairs and European stadiums. Yet here she was, feeling old and tired at thirty-four, strutting her stuff for a few hundred sodbusters in Garden City, Kansas.

Well, so be it. At least, when all was said and done, she could honestly say she was doing what she loved and doing it on her own terms. Being the first female rodeo producer had not been easy, even for "America's Cowgirl," as she was known, and her timing had been lousy. Just as her business was getting started, the war had erupted and suddenly she had found herself seriously shy of contestants as every able-bodied cowboy got shipped overseas. But she had persevered and with the help of her partner, George Early, had managed to stay afloat, producing rodeos in small to medium size towns across the Midwest and West.

In the arena, the fallen cowboy rose, clutching his side but signaling his OK to the crowd.

Unhitching herself from the rail, Louise intercepted him. "You OK, Harley?"

"Yeah, I reckon." The cowboy drew away his hand to reveal a torn and blood-soaked shirt. "Bastard's hoof sliced my side, but it ain't too bad. Too bad about the shirt, though."

"Better have the doc take a look at it. Might need a couple of stitches." Louise clapped him on the back, relieved that the man was ambulatory. Although Harley, like all the other contestants, had paid an entry fee in order to compete in the steer-riding event, he was also one of her employees, working as hazer and pick-up man, and she would need a full and healthy contingent of workers for next month's rodeo in Fort Worth. Louise and George had landed the contract to produce the Fort Worth Fat Stock Show, only slightly less prestigious than Cheyenne Frontier Days or the Calgary Stampede, and they were hoping the job would vault them into the ranks of big-time rodeo producers.

As Harley limped away, Curtis, Louise's brother, strode up, leading her horse Cancan. It was time for the show's finale where all of the contestants, contract performers, and Louise herself, of course, paraded around the arena, led by one of the local girls on horseback, proudly bearing the American flag. The latter touch had been George Early's idea, and Louise thought it was brilliant. What better way to garner good will, and thereby increase ticket sales, than prominently to feature one of the community's pretty young ladies? George had also distributed souvenir steer-head pins to the shops in town. Their purchase entitled a person to free admission to the show. Not only did this increase attendance, but it pleased the shop owners, for the pins had proven to be popular items. With marketing techniques like that, Fort Worth was sure to be a success.

For the first time that day, Louise smiled. She took Cancan's reins from her brother and toed her fancy riding boot into the stirrup.

"You look like the cat that ate the canary," Curtis said, tightening the cinch for her as she settled into the saddle.

"Just looking forward to Fort Worth. I got a feeling we're going to do all right there."

"We did all right here. Better than all right. This is a damn' good crowd for Garden City. But then I didn't expect anything less. Who wouldn't show up to see Louise Morris's All-American Rodeo?"

Louise gazed at him fondly, grateful for his support. Theirs was an odd family, separated by vast differences in age. Yet, through it all, she and Curtis had remained close. They needed each other, allies against the force that was their father, Big Jack Morris. Growing up with Big Jack had been a lesson in how to use manipulation and fear to get what you wanted. Although ten years older than Curtis, Louise had always felt a bond with the boy and had taken it upon herself to shield him from their father's blinding rages as well as from his deceptive affability.

Louise had been more mother than sister to Curtis for their own mother had retreated from life about the time of Curtis's birth, victim of some unnamed mental disorder that kept her hidden behind closed doors and shuttered windows. The poor woman used to summon Louise to her room where the girl would sit at her feet and nervously prattle on about her studies, her horses, her life, while the empty presence that was her mother nodded absently. Never once did the woman ask to see Curtis.

When their mother had come home from the sanitarium where she had spent the months leading up to Curtis's birth, she was accompanied by the young woman who had attended her there. According to Big Jack, his wife had become so attached to the girl, Alice by name, that she insisted he hire her to be her personal nurse. Eager to do whatever he could to please his ailing wife, so Big Jack said, he invited Alice to join their household although he already employed domestic help who could see to Mrs. Morris's needs. It was clear from the moment of her arrival, however, that Alice was not just another hired girl. Her status was several steps up from that of their cook, maid, or ranch hands, many of whom had been with the Morris family for years. Alice took all her meals with the family although her charge ate off a tray in her room. She seemed to have no set duties although she occasionally visited Mrs. Morris to take her blood pressure or administer medication. Mostly she entertained Louise and Curtis, taking them on outings into town, fixing picnic lunches for them, letting Louise pour over the fashion magazines she ordered.

At first, Louise had resented Alice's intrusion into their family, but resentment soon gave way to affection, for what ten-year-old girl would not enjoy the company and attention of a pretty young lady not that much older than herself? Too, Alice took on much of the care of Curtis, leaving Louise free to ride and rope.

About a year after Alice's arrival, Big Jack did a strange thing. Over supper one evening, he announced that because Alice had no family of her own, he had decided to adopt her. Alice was henceforth Alice Morris, Louise and Curtis's sister. Although Louise was mystified at this turn of events—how could one adopt a nineteen-year-old woman—she accepted

22

the news with equanimity.

And to this day, Louise and Alice maintained a close relationship. Alice, now forty-two years old, had stayed on at the ranch in West Texas, never leaving to marry or pursue other interests. Over the years, she had evolved into Big Jack's personal secretary, a position that she seemed to enjoy and that enabled her to travel with him on his numerous business trips. Meanwhile, Louise's mother still lived on at the ranch, feeble in mind if not in body.

Louise and the other riders lapped the arena, spurring their mounts into a full gallop as they headed out the gates. She put up Cancan and headed for her tent on the rodeo grounds. Gone were the days of staying in hotels at each stop. Now, to conserve money, most of the gang camped out when they were on the road.

Fixing herself a cup of tea on her little camp stove, she had just started going over that night's receipts when Curtis scratched on the tent flap.

"Knock, knock."

"Come on in. I'm just checking to see if we made any money tonight."

"Did we?"

"Same as usual. There's only so many people to come to a rodeo in Garden City or Hays or Lamar or any of the other rinky-dink towns we play." Louise sighed and pushed the book work away from her.

"You could cut costs if you eliminated some of the events, you know. There were only three contestants in the ladies' bronc' riding. Only three entry fees, but you still paid out a good size purse. It doesn't add up."

"Can't do it, Curtis. These gals depend on me. Do you realize that last year there were only ten rodeos that included women's events? That's not near enough to keep a gal riding

23

the circuit. If they can't make a living in rodeo, they're going to bail out . . . go to Hollywood and make those silly Westerns."

"Nothing wrong with that, if you ask me. It's a darn' sight better money, and it's got to beat humping your tail across the prairie in a broken-down buckboard from one crummy town to the next."

Louise narrowed her eyes at her brother. What had gotten into him tonight? He was not usually much of a complainer. "You got a hankering to leave, Curtis? You're not obliged to stay, you know. There'll always be a place for you here, but if you got the itch to move on, that's all right."

Curtis gave her an exasperated look. "I'm not going anywhere, Lou. It's just . . . well, you're always bad-mouthing Hollywood, telling everyone how only gunsels and greenhorns would want to be in moving pictures. The way I see it, most of those fellas are damn' good riders who just can't make a living riding the range any more. What's so bad about letting Hollywood pay them to be in the saddle?"

Louise leaned forward on the cot and flashed her brown eyes at Curtis. "I'll tell you what's so bad about it. You ever seen the way they do those stunts, like when a horse gets shot out from under its rider? Well, I have, and it's one of the cruelest things you can imagine. They wire up his front feet and then pull his legs out from under him when he's going at a dead run. Breaks the poor thing's legs half the time. No self-respecting cowboy would be a party to that in my book. I don't care how much money he makes."

Curtis pursed his lips but decided not to challenge his sister. It was a sore subject with her and not just because of her disdain for the movie industry's treatment of animals. Some years ago when Louise had been appearing in a Wild West show, she had met a young cowboy named Tom Mix. They had hit it off and for a while carried on quite a torrid romance. But then Mix had moved to Hollywood and become the star of Western films, and, somehow, Louise had gotten left behind. Curtis had never been sure whether that had been his sister's choice or whether Mix had simply dumped her, but, in any event, one could hardly mention Hollywood around Louise without getting a sour reaction. It pained him because, truth to tell, Curtis was fascinated by the movies and would give his eyeteeth to try his luck in Tinseltown.

Curtis slapped his hands on his thighs, preparing to leave. "Well, Lou, I'm not going to argue with you. Just remember what I said about cutting out the less popular events as a way to save money."

"Just because there aren't that many gals competing doesn't make their events any less popular," Louise said huffily. "The crowds love watching the ladies, and you know it. Besides, I don't think we've got anything to worry about. George telegrammed from Fort Worth, and it looks like we're going to get a lot of the top names. This one should really put us on the map!"

Curtis turned back from the tent flap and gave his sister a soft smile. People said they looked alike—they both had Big Jack's strong features and thick eyebrows accenting wide-spaced dark eyes—but Louise was certain her smile never looked as engaging as her little brother's. *Maybe that's because I haven't practiced it enough,* she thought grimly.

" 'Night, Lou."

"G'night. See you in the morning."

Louise stacked her bookkeeping materials and put them away. She was too tired to deal with them tonight. They'd be in Fort Worth in a few days anyway, and then she could turn all the book work over to George. He knew how she hated the business end of things and usually tried to spare her the drudgery of dealing with numbers. "You just do what you're good at, Louise, lining up the acts and giving the crowd a bang for its buck, and I'll worry about the rest," he had said early on in their partnership.

Tiredly Louise undressed, stuffing her soiled clothes into a canvas drawstring bag already filled to the brim. Tomorrow she would have to find a laundry in town. It wasn't easy living on the road, but where else could she be? Still living on the ranch like Alice, a slave to her father's whims? No, never. But if things had turned out differently, she might be. . . . Quickly Louise put a brake on her thoughts before they careened out of control. Slipping under the blankets, she lay listening to the sounds of night camp—horses blowing, low laughter from cowboys gathered around a card table, crickets in the fields. Sounds she normally took comfort in. But tonight she turned her face into her pillow and silently wept.

Chapter Four

The deal Lael had struck with her brother sounded good at the time, but she soon discovered it would have little, if any, practical effect on her ability to get into the arena. For one thing, back in September, rodeo had just been heading into the off-season, and, although Roger had given her the green light to compete, she found that she would have to wait until next spring for the season to get started again.

An even bigger concern was money, or the lack of it in Lael's case. Soon after her discussion with Roger, as she began writing to various rodeo committees, requesting programs and schedules for the upcoming season, it dawned on her that she had no money to pay for train tickets, hotel rooms, entry fees, all the expenses of riding the circuit. She could be darn sure her father would not pay her way, and she could not ask for help from Roger who had enough on his hands caring for his own family. Her only option was to find a job.

For two weeks, Lael floundered, bound by her promise to continue attending school, yet desperate to quit and earn enough of a nest egg that, come spring, she could hit the trail. Help came from a most unexpected quarter. A notice went up at the college that Mr. Snively was looking for a paid assistant to help grade papers and perform other administrative tasks related to his position as department chairman. Figuring she had nothing to lose, Lael applied for the job.

During the next week, Lael studied as she never had before, burning midnight oil to make up for all the work she had previously failed to complete. In the interview, she fed Snively some cock-and-bull story about how difficult it had been to adjust to her new home and that her schoolwork had suffered as a result, but that she was now ready to buckle down, and that being Mr. Snively's assistant surely would only increase her desire to excel. He bought it, no doubt persuaded as much by her frequent use of the Buckley smile as by her artful words. She started work the next day.

To her surprise, the winter flew by. Newly motivated and with a definite end point in sight, she found school and work to be bearable. When classes ended in May, she had saved enough to stake her for a month or two on the circuit. She counted on winning enough at those first few rodeos to get her through the season.

Roger and Amy reluctantly agreed to her plans, although they insisted that she stay only in hotels while traveling. No outdoor camping for a beautiful, unprotected young woman such as herself. Roger also agreed to refrain from telling their parents about Lael's rodeoing. Although it made him sick at heart to deceive them, he saw no point in upsetting them when it was clear he could do nothing to change Lael's mind.

So on a bright, clear day in the first week of June, 1920 Roger saw his little sister to the train station. She had wanted to wear her riding boots and newly purchased divided skirt, figuring she would have no use for street clothes where she was going, but Amy had protested.

"I think you should look like a lady when you're traveling, dear. Who knows who might try to take advantage of you, if you look like some itinerant cowgirl."

Lael fought the urge to remind her sister-in-law that, for the next few months, that's exactly what she would be. No matter—she would get to her hotel room and pack away her long skirt, frilly blouse, and lace-trimmed hat for the duration.

"Now you be careful, Lael," Roger said as he handed her up the steps of the passenger car. "Don't speak to anybody on the train and, when you get there, go straight to your hotel. You already registered and paid your entry fee by mail so you shouldn't even have to go down to the rodeo grounds until the time for your event."

Lael gave him an *oh, please* look from under raised eyebrows, and they both broke into laughter. "OK," Roger admitted, "I'm overdoing the big brother bit. But use good sense, Lael. If anything happened to you, I'd never forgive myself. And Pa would come all the way from Nebraska to personally tan my hide!"

"I'll be fine, Rog. Don't worry."

Roger removed a twenty dollar bill from his wallet and folded it into Lael's hand. "Here. If anything goes wrong, don't hesitate to catch the next train back."

"Rog, I can't take this. I know you can't spare this kind of money!"

"Pay me back someday when you're queen of the rodeo!"

The train blew its departing whistle, and with a last hug and a wave Lael stepped into the car bound for Abilene, Texas and the Taylor County Fair and Rodeo. As the train picked up speed, Roger's final words reverberated in her head, keeping time with the pounding wheels. *Queen of the rodeo, queen of the rodeo. . . .* Could she do it? Was she good enough? Could she get by on her own? Could she stick with it? The farther west she headed, the more she began to doubt herself. Why had she left her family and a secure future to go chasing a pipe dream? The odds of success were so long that, like as not, she'd be back in Fort Worth in a month, her tail between her legs.

Feeling miserable, her stomach knotted and her hands twisted in her lap, Lael leaned against the window and looked out on the flat Texas prairie. Ahead, she could see the train coming to an intersection with a dirt road. A figure on horseback waited on the road, and, as the train approached, the rider spurred the horse into action, galloping alongside the speeding engine. Lael could now see that the rider was a young girl, maybe fourteen or fifteen years old, and that she was laughing and calling to her mount as she leaned into the wind, racing the train. The girl's hair streamed out behind her, and the horse's hoofs kicked up dust soundlessly.

As she came abreast of the pair, Lael stared out the window at them, her lips parted, feeling vicariously everything that girl was feeling—the wind in her face, the power between her legs, the jolting ground racing by. With a sudden laugh, Lael flung the window open and leaned out as far as she dared, waving wildly to the young rider. The girl slowed her horse, stood in the stirrups, and waved back, tossing her tangled hair from her face.

Smiling, Lael sank back in her seat, feeling unaccountably better. Queen of the rodeo? Darn right! One of these days.

A hot, dusty wind swirled across the wooden planks of the station platform in Abilene. Gripping her valise, Lael shouldered her way into the wind, her long skirt plastered against her legs. She turned at the sound of a heavy door sliding open behind her. A tall man, wearing faded Levi's, a window-pane checked shirt, leather vest, and a sweat-stained Stetson, hopped down from a livestock car and slid out a wooden ramp. He disappeared back into the car and a moment later emerged, leading a sturdy, white-socked bay by its halter rope. He secured the rope to a nearby hitching rail and went back for another horse, this one a tall sorrel that had the lines of a Thoroughbred.

Lael paused to watch, always attracted by the sight of good horseflesh. The man came out leading a skittish palomino that balked at the ramp. He stroked its neck and leaned forward to whisper in its ear. It started down the ramp. At that moment, a strong gust of wind lifted Lael's hat off her head and sent it skidding across the palomino's hindquarters. Wild-eyed, it side-stepped right off the ramp, plunging into mid-air. Desperately, the man grabbed for the rope, but too late. The horse rolled onto its side, clawed its way back to its feet, and took off for the open prairie at a dead run.

Lael stared in horror, her shocked gasp carrying on the wind. The man gave her one quick furious look and then sprang into action, unhitching the bay and swinging up on its bare back in pursuit of the runaway palomino. Dropping her valise, Lael grabbed her hatless head with shaking hands. How could she have let such a stupid thing happen? Mortified, she watched the man give chase. He was falling behind, the little bay no match for the feisty palomino. *Why didn't he take the sorrel?* Lael wondered. Clearly that was a horse made to race.

Suddenly, before she could think twice, she untied the sorrel, led it beside the ramp, hitched up her skirts, and hoisted herself up. Digging her knees in, she whipped the animal around, following the path of the runaway. The sorrel was a beauty, smooth and swift, and Lael found herself smiling despite her embarrassing predicament. She caught up with the bay horse, glimpsing the man's shocked expression as she flew by. Ahead, the palomino still ran, the halter rope trailing along its withers. She came up beside it and gently kneed the sorrel over, reaching for the palomino's halter. Grabbing it with her left hand, she held on for dear life. With no stirrups

31

to hook her heels into, she felt as though she would be dragged from the sorrel's back and flung onto the hard ground. But, somehow, she stayed aboard, and, as she steadily pulled back on the sorrel's reins, both horses came to a stop.

Breathless, tingling all over from the adrenaline surging through her body, Lael slumped over the neck of the heaving sorrel. "Good boy, good boy," she murmured, rubbing her cheek against his wiry mane.

"What the hell do you think you're doing?"

Lael jerked around. The wrangler had come up beside her on the bay. He glared at her with eyes so deep blue they were only one shade lighter than black, the color of the eastern sky just before the sun slips below the horizon. His stubbled jaw clenched, and then, slowly, deliberately, he lowered his gaze, taking in the whole of her disheveled figure. Lael reddened, conscious that her skirt was hiked up to an indecent level, that her blouse had come untucked, and that her hair had come loose from its pins and tumbled wildly about her shoulders. A few strands stuck to the corner of her mouth.

His eyes lingered on the space at her throat where a button had torn off and then swept back to her face. His expression conveyed no hint of what he was thinking, but Lael was unnerved by the hardness in those obsidian eyes.

She had been prepared to apologize, but something about the man's demeanor prompted her to stiffen her spine and declare: "I think I'm returning your runaway horse to you, sir!"

He stared a moment longer, then turned to scan the horizon. His profile was all angles and lines except for his mouth that seemed generous even when set in lines of irritation as it was now. A tiny scar pulled at the edge of his lower lip. Lael jumped when he turned and caught her staring at it.

32

"You had no business hijacking Pegasus even if it was your own damn' fault the horse got loose."

"I don't know why you didn't take him yourself," Lael shot back. "You'd never have caught the palomino on that little bay."

The man's eyes narrowed, and for a moment Lael got the impression of power barely held in check although he had not moved a muscle. Pegasus tossed his head and nervously backed up a step or two. Lael kneed her mount to one side and brought the palomino up next to the angry cowboy.

"Here," she said, handing him the runaway's rope. "I'm sorry my hat blew off, and I'm sorry your horse spooked, but mostly I'm sorry I tried to help you get it back!"

With that, she dug her heels into the sorrel's side and loped back to the train, heedless of whether he followed or not. Clutching her valise, she marched into the station, found the ladies' room, and leaned over the sink to splash cold water on her face. *What an awful man*, she thought. *What if everyone here is like that?*

Gradually her trembling ceased. She raised her head and stared at her wind-blown visage in the mirror. Slowly she traced the outline of her lips with her little finger, pausing at the same place where the scar had started on his mouth. The memory of his flint-like eyes brought her up short. With a little snort, she yanked out her remaining hairpins and twisted the tangled mess into some semblance of order. *Forget it*, she told herself, and started to leave. At the door, she turned around for one last look in the mirror. She smiled and winked at her reflection. *At least you caught the damn' horse!*

Chapter Five

The next day, Lael rode in the opening day parade down Main Street. She had dressed in her new divided skirt with fringe along the outside leg seams, a white shirtwaist, and a bright yellow bandanna tied around her neck. Her scuffed boots and stained Stetson undercut the spiffiness of her new outfit, but she figured she'd replace those items with her soon-to-be-won prize money.

After the parade, she checked the stock assignments and saw that she had drawn a steer called Sambo. From her previous limited rodeo experiences, she knew it was helpful to know a thing or two about an animal before getting aboard, so she looked around for someone to ask. Nearby a seasoned-looking cowgirl stood, pulling on a pair of riding gloves.

"Howdy!" Lael walked up to her.

The woman barely glanced at her, then looked again, and frowned. Her eyes dropped to Lael's throat. Raising her pencil-thin eyebrows, she said: "Yeah, what is it?"

Lael shifted on her feet, put off by the woman's unfriendly manner. "I just wondered if you'd ever ridden a steer called Sambo. I drew him for today's go-round."

The woman put her hands on her hips and gave Lael a disgusted look. "Do I look like a steer rider to you?"

For the first time, Lael noticed the woman's costume. Instead of the typical divided skirt, she wore silk bloomers that fastened with elastic just below her knees. She was hatless, and on her feet she wore low rubber-soled shoes.

"Um, I guess not," Lael stammered.

Rolling her eyes, the woman walked off a couple of steps before halting in her tracks. When she turned back around, she had a crafty smile on her face. "I ain't ridden steers in a while, but I hear the other gals talk. Sambo, he's pretty rank for a ladies' steer. Word has it he's a left-sided spinner, so you might want to hang to the right a bit."

"Thanks. I appreciate it." Lael was pleased finally to have gotten a friendly word from someone. "Say, what is your event?"

"Trick riding. Wish me luck. I'm up next."

"Good luck!"

"Same to you." The woman trotted off and fell into step with some other cowgirls. Lael saw her nod her head in Lael's direction and then lean forward, laughing. Well, she had heard that rodeo folk were kind of cliquey till they got to know you. At least, this gal had given her a few hints on how to ride Sambo.

Lael took a seat in the stands to watch the trick riding, an event she had never seen before. She watched in awe as the contestants, male and female, performed incredible gymnastic feats—vaults, shoulder stands, drags—while racing around the arena at breakneck speed. At times, she almost couldn't watch, certain that some pretty cowgirl or wiry cowboy was about to meet an untimely death by trampling. But they always kept their balance and managed to hang on. Lael realized these competitors were athletes of the highest order, every muscle well-toned and trained to react with split-second timing.

"Folks," the announcer said, "our final trick rider today is a lady well-known to rodeo fans. She's been cuttin' the rug on her horse Meadowlark for more years than the other riders combined. You don't mind me sayin' that, do ya, Maudie? Let's give a big Texas welcome to Maude Kelly and Meadowlark!"

Into the arena sprinted the bloomer-wearing cowgirl Lael had met earlier, standing upright on the back of a beautiful chestnut mare. Her feet were wedged into straps attached to the sides of her saddle. She circled the arena at full speed, then dropped to the horse's back with one foot still caught in a strap, her body hanging off Meadowlark's side. Another switch and her feet were high in the air, her shoulder supported by the seat of the saddle. One lap around the arena in that position and then she swung her feet down to the ground and vaulted back into the saddle. She exited to the cheers and applause of the crowd. Lael joined in enthusiastically, pleased that her new acquaintance was so skilled. Perhaps Maude would be willing to teach her a few tricks.

Leaving the stands, Lael caught sight of Maude, still atop Meadowlark, having a conversation with a potbellied cowpoke who had the longest handlebar mustache Lael had ever seen. She walked over to congratulate the cowgirl on her fine ride.

"I'm telling you, you got to do something about that asshole Webster!"

Lael hesitated, unnerved by Maude's harsh tone and crass language.

"Did you hear what that jerk said? . . . cutting the rug for more years than the others combined. Jesus, he made it sound like I've got one foot in the grave!" Maude's lips were set in a thin, tight line, and her eyes showed creases at the corners. In this angry state, she did look considerably older.

"For God's sake, Maude, what do you want me to do about it?" the mustachioed man replied.

"Get him fired! You're the owner of one of the largest teams at this two-bit rodeo . . . you've got some clout! Go talk to the producer and get him canned!"

"Now, Maudie, calm down. I ain't gonna get a man fired over one lousy comment. Hell, he didn't mean anything by it. He thought he was complimenting you."

"Complimenting me, my ass!" Maude swung her leg over Meadowlark's back and hopped down. She was a good six inches shorter than the cowpoke, but she went right at him, shoving her finger into his barrel-like chest. "Now you listen to me, Foster. You and I both know a trick rider gets judged on looks as much as skill. Why do you think I spend a fortune on these fancy costumes, every one of them handmade and the latest in cowgirl fashion? 'Cause judges pay as much attention to a gal's clothes, and her figure underneath her clothes, as to how she does her tricks! The last thing I want is for some jerk-off announcer to tell the whole world how god-damned ancient I am!"

Lael felt her face redden, embarrassed to be a witness to this ugly scene. She tried to slip away unnoticed, but her movement caught Maude's eye.

"What do you want, you little greenhorn?"

"N-nothing. I was just going to congratulate you on your performance. I've never seen anything like it."

Maude snorted in derision. "Get lost, kid." Pulling sharply on Meadowlark's reins, she stalked off.

Lael widened her eyes against sudden tears. She looked to the portly cowpoke for some explanation of Maude's rude behavior. But he was gazing at her with a wary expression, his droopy mustache framing a deep frown.

"Go on, get out of here," he whispered.

She turned and ran.

As the day wore on, Lael tried to dismiss the unfortunate

incident with Maude and the old cowboy, but it rankled. There had been no reason for them to be so curt with her. Why was everybody here so unfriendly?

Finally the ladies' steer riding event was called. She was one of the first ones up, and, when Webster announced her name to the crowd, there was only a spattering of applause. No one in Abilene, Texas had ever heard of Lael Buckley. Taking a deep breath, she marched into the arena, smiling and waving her battered hat. A few cheers rang out, and a lone wolf whistle from some randy male in the stands pierced the air.

As she waited for the snubber to boost her onto Sambo's back, she reviewed what Maude had told her—lean to the right to balance Sambo's tendency to twirl to the left.

"Ready?" the snubber asked.

Lael nodded. "Go!" And then she was atop Sambo, leaning as far right as she could. But something was wrong. Sambo's big head twisted to the right, and his writhing body whipped around in the same direction. Lael felt her left leg slipping loose, her backside sliding off the steer. She pulled with all her might, but it was no good—Sambo kept turning into her, not giving her a chance to get balanced. She dropped face first into the dust and came up with a mouthful of urine-soaked dirt. Coughing and spitting, she stumbled to the fence, mortified at the sound of jeering laughter from the crowd.

"No score for Lael Buckley," the announcer intoned. "Better luck next time, little lady."

Fighting back tears, Lael ducked through the fence rails and ran. Taking refuge behind the stables, she leaned against the splintery planks and took several deep breaths, willing her shaky body under control. What had gone wrong? She had never had such a miserable ride, even on the rankest of steers.

And she had followed Maude's directions to the letter, leaning to the right to compensate for a left-jumping steer. But wait! Sambo hadn't turned to the left. He had bucked clockwise from the get-go! Slowly it came to Lael that she had been had. Maude Kelly had deliberately misled her, had fed her false information, knowing it would lead to an ignominious dumping for the pretty young cowgirl. But why? What had Lael ever done to her? The older woman wasn't even competing in the steer-riding contest, so why would she have wanted so much for Lael to fail?

Embarrassment turning to anger, Lael pulled at the knot on her yellow scarf, whipping the cloth down the side of her neck. Using it to wipe the muck off her face, she pondered how to get back at the high and mighty Miss Kelly.

Just then, a figure walked around the corner of the stables, nearly bumping into Lael. It was the potbellied, mustachioed team owner. Both he and Lael were startled, and Lael mumbled a quick apology.

"Not your fault, gal. I didn't realize you was back here." The older man took in her dirty clothes and mud-streaked face. "Looks like you ate some dust. You doing OK?"

"I guess," Lael replied sullenly. "Just miffed is all. I've never gotten thrown that quick."

"Well, it ain't no wonder!"

"What do you mean?"

"You were bound to get th'owed. It's just a wonder you didn't get trampled to boot!"

Lael eyed him suspiciously. Had Maude told him of the nasty trick she had pulled? "I still don't get you, mister."

Sighing in the manner of an exasperated teacher with a thick-headed pupil, he reached out and touched Lael's bandanna with one thick, stubby finger, then quickly pulled it back. "It's your scarf, miss. Don't you know nothing about rodeo superstitions? It's bad luck to wear yella. I shoulda told you before, but, well, you kinda spooked me."

"Superstition? That's silly. That steer didn't throw me because I was wearing yellow."

"I don't know, miss. I've seen it happen more than once. Somebody gets th'owed, or hurt real bad, or racks up a bad score and, sure enough, turns out they got some little bit of yella on 'em somewhere, or maybe they left their hat on their bed. That's bad luck, too." He punctuated his statement with a brisk nod of his head that set his mustache quivering.

Lael stared in amused disbelief. Wearing yellow? Hat on the bed? Ridiculous! A small chuckle escaped her lips, and, before she knew it, she was laughing out loud. How funny this rodeo world was!

"OK, Mister . . . ?"

"Davis, Foster Davis."

"Mister Davis, I can't say I believe in all these superstitions, but when in Rome. . . ." She stuffed the bandanna into her skirt pocket, and they started walking back to the arena. "Anything else I should know about?"

"Well, let's see. Don't eat peanuts or quit roping practice on a miss. And if you win wearing a particular shirt, or hat, or pair of boots, why keep on wearing 'em . . . they's your lucky clothes."

Lael laughed again. "What if you lose? Under your theory I ought to wear a complete new outfit for tomorrow's go-round, but these are the only clothes I've got. What should I do?"

Davis pursed his lips, taking her question seriously. "Well, miss. Say, what's your name anyway?"

"Lael Buckley."

"Well, Lael, I'd say go ahead and wear the same clothes. Just make sure you leave off the bandanna."

Lael nodded, matching his serious mien. "Right. Will do. Thanks for the tip."

They walked in silence for a moment, Davis regarding her thoughtfully out of the corner of his eye. "Where you from, Lael?"

"Nebraska by way of Fort Worth."

"Good horse country, both places. You ride much?"

"Grew up on a horse is all."

"You don't say. In that case, I got a little proposition for you." Davis stopped and folded his arms across his ample chest. "I brought a relay team here to Abilene, but last week one of my riders fell and broke her leg . . . had to leave the circuit for a few months. I'm looking for someone to fill her spot. You interested?"

"You bet I'm interested!" Lael cried.

"Good. Be down here early in the morning. I'll have my wrangler get you set up for some practice runs. I'll enter you in tomorrow's race, and, if I like what I see, the job's yours."

"Thank you, Mister Davis!"

"Call me Foster, honey."

Chapter Six

Lael could hardly sleep that night, her previous anger and disappointment forgotten in the excitement of this new opportunity. Imagine! Riding the circuit as a member of a relay team! Of course, she had never ridden relay before, but how hard could it be? All you had to do was make three laps of the track, changing horses at the end of the first and second laps. And change saddles, too, of course. That might take a little practice—she had never had to change saddles on the run—but she was sure she'd catch on quickly. After all, she'd been saddling horses since the day she was strong enough to lift tack off the ground.

In the morning Lael made it to the rodeo grounds bright and early, eager to get started. She wore the same clothes as yesterday, minus the yellow bandanna. And although she would not have admitted it to anybody, she had carefully avoided placing her hat on the bed last night.

A quick look around confirmed that neither Foster Davis nor anybody else was yet stirring. With the place to herself, she wandered around the horses' stalls, checking out the stock and enjoying the familiar, pungent smells of the stables. She came to one stall and immediately recognized the palomino that had bolted from the train station yesterday.

"Well, fancy running across you again, you old rascal," she murmured in a calm voice, mindful of the horse's nervous nature. She stepped into the stall and ran her hand along its flank; its sensitive skin twitched beneath her fingers. She took another step, and suddenly her foot encountered a solid object. Surprised, Lael involuntarily gasped and jumped back. Shying sideways, the palomino knocked her roughly into the wall. The object on the floor rolled over and came to its feet, groaning and cursing.

"Dammit, you son-of-a-bitch, what is it now?"

Lael peered over the back of the horse into the stall's dark corner and was horrified to see the man from the train. She gave a sharp intake of breath. He saw her then, through eyes narrowed in anger. Pinned against the wall, there was no way to escape, although, if she could, she would have run straight back to the hotel and barred her door, so threatening did he appear. His shirt, the same one he had worn yesterday, was loose and unbuttoned, revealing a chest matted with dark hair. His neck muscles strained against a jaw clenched tight, and his thick, black hair swept down over his forehead, bits of straw sticking to it. His mouth turned down angrily, the scar at its corner white against his stubbled chin.

"What the hell's going on here?" He bit off the words, his voice eerily quiet. Lael could tell he was trying to keep the horse from spooking again, although his tone had the opposite effect on her.

She swallowed and tried to keep her voice steady. "I was supposed to meet Mister Davis down here this morning, but he hasn't come yet. I was just looking around the stables. I didn't mean to startle the horse or you. I didn't think anybody was here."

"Well, now that you know better, why don't you high-tail it on out of here before you spook the rest of the stock. That seems to be your specialty." He reached to the floor for his grimy hat and pulled it down hard on his head, slanting it over his unsettling eyes. Lael picked up a whiff of sour-smelling air emanating from him, redolent of stale sweat and day-old whisky. Disgusted, she turned to leave, but she couldn't give this drunken excuse for a cowboy the last word. "Look, you've got no cause to be so rude to me. My hat blowing off yesterday was an accident . . . could have happened to anybody. And Mister Davis invited me to be here this morning. How was I to know there'd be some hung over whisky-head sleeping it off in the stables?"

She paused, trying to think of additional epithets to throw at him. He said nothing, only stared at her sideways with eyes that flashed malevolently. She could tell she'd struck a chord with him. Finally he ducked his head just enough to hide his eyes beneath the brim of his hat. Softly, so softly she could barely hear him, he whispered: "Get out of here."

She pivoted on her heel and ran right into the protruding belly of Foster Davis.

"Whoa there, girl! Take her easy now!" He chuckled and set her away from him with beefy hands. "I see you met Rafe."

"Rafe?" Lael repeated stupidly.

"Yeah. Thought I heard you two talking, but maybe you didn't get around to making introductions yet. Lael Buckley, meet Rafe Callantine, my head wrangler."

Lael gaped at Davis, not wanting to believe what she'd just heard. This foul-smelling, uncouth cad was the man who was supposed to teach her relay riding? It was almost enough to make her back out of it.

"Lael's gonna ride relay in today's race," Davis went on. "Told her if she cuts the mustard, I'd hire her to go on the circuit with us. Get her set up with Two A.M.'s string, would you, and let her take a couple practice runs. I'll see you later. I got to get to a meeting with the rodeo committee."

Davis trundled off. Lael stared at her worn boots, not sure what to say. Callantine coughed and spat onto the straw-covered floor. He pushed past her without a word and

44

left the stables. Lael didn't know if he meant her to follow him or not. She decided to stay put. Five minutes later he came back, his shirt buttoned and tucked in, his hair slicked back under his hat. Ignoring her, he led a jet black gelding from its stall and began to saddle it up.

"I can do that," Lael said, feeling useless.

He said nothing and continued to work.

"Is this Two A.M.?" she tried again. He gave a tiny grunt which she took for yes. "Funny name. Where'd it come from?"

He hesitated in answering for so long that she thought he wasn't going to. Then he said: "How many all black horses do you know named Midnight? Got a little tired of that cliché so I named this one Two A.M. It's just as black at that time of night."

Lael gave a small laugh. For just an instant he raised his eyes and looked at her, and she saw something in those dark blue depths that moved her. Something intensely human caught inside the rough exterior.

Callantine moved to face Two A.M., squatted, and braced his shoulder against the horse's chest. Grabbing one of its legs, he slowly pulled it toward him. He repeated the procedure with the other leg. Lael knew this exercise had two purposes: to settle the saddle more comfortably on the horse and to stretch out its legs before heavy activity. One seldom saw a cowboy or cowgirl take the time to do it, however. Rafe Callantine obviously cared about the animals in his trust.

He handed the reins to her. "Warm it up," he ordered, then disappeared back into the barn. She put Two A.M. into a walk, then a trot, then back to a walk. Callantine came out again leading two more horses wearing headgear but no saddles. He walked them toward the arena. Lael followed. She found herself watching his narrow-hipped backside, his thigh

45

muscles pressing against his jeans with each step he took. She forced herself to look away, but her eyes soon wandered back to his tall figure, this time settling on his broad shoulders and his longish black hair grazing the top of his collar.

They entered the arena, and he instructed her to warm up the other horses. When she was done, she remounted Two A.M. and moved to the starting line. Rafe stood beside her, holding the second relay horse.

"You want me to time this run?" he asked.

Lael gazed ahead at the track nervously. Apparently he was not going to offer her any tips, but then he probably thought she had done this before.

"Not yet." She tossed her ponytail over her shoulder and leaned low over Two A.M.'s neck.

"Go!" he shouted.

She dug her heels in, and Two A.M. leaped off the mark. Now Lael was in familiar territory, doing what she loved most. She focused in, remembering all the little tricks she had learned racing horses back home in Nebraska. She rounded the final turn and pulled up short next to Callantine. Sliding from the saddle, she reached underneath Two A.M.'s belly, fumbling for the cinch. At first she couldn't get it, wasting precious seconds. Then it came free. She yanked on the saddle. It slid off easily enough. Grunting with the effort, she flung it on the second horse's back and reached under for the strap. She couldn't find it. Frustrated, she straightened up and slapped the animal on its rump. It danced away, and the unsecured saddle on its back slid to the ground.

Callantine gave her a dark look. "Don't ever hit a horse for something that isn't its fault."

Lael fumed at the rebuke, although she knew it was justified. She took a couple of deep breaths. "I'm sorry," she mumbled.

"This is your first time riding relay, isn't it?"

She sighed in defeat. "Yes."

"Does Foster know that?"

"No," she admitted.

"You were expecting me to teach you between now and the race this afternoon?"

Lael toed the ground and meekly raised her eyes to meet his. "Could you?"

He gave her an annoyed look. "Suppose I save us both a lot of trouble and just go tell Davis you conned him, that you don't know the first thing about relay riding."

That got her Irish up. Who was this two-bit roughneck to be lecturing her on conning people? After all, she had not affirmatively lied to Mr. Davis, just failed to mention her inexperience.

"Never mind. I don't need your help." She picked up the fallen saddle. "I'll learn it on my own."

"Yeah? Who's gonna help you in the station? That means hold the relay horses for you, by the way. You think maybe you can sweet talk Davis into that, too? Be my guest, blondie." He strolled off, his easy gait mocking her.

Her mouth set, Lael flung the heavy saddle onto the second relay horse. It shied away at the last second, and the saddle fell to the ground. She picked it up and tried again. Once more, the animal danced away. Sighing in frustration, she turned to see if Callantine had been watching her incompetent performance, but he was still walking away, hands jammed in his pockets.

"Callantine!" she called. He stopped and slowly turned around.

Taking a deep breath she swallowed her pride. "You're right. I can't do it by myself. I'd be mighty grateful if you'd . . . help me in the station."

He ducked his head, hiding his face beneath the brim of his hat. She prayed he wasn't laughing at her. He came toward her, and, when he got close, she could see his expression was serious enough although his mouth might have been turned up slightly at the corner.

"I guess we could give it one more try," he said.

She nodded, and they set to work. He showed her how to bring in the first mount a few yards short of the relay horse and where to position it. He told her to begin dismounting before coming to a full stop. He demonstrated the easiest way to flip the saddle onto the horse's back and showed her how to grab the girth as it came under the horse's belly and cinch it all in one fluid motion.

After an hour of painstaking work, she was ready for a practice run. The mid-morning sun burned down from a flat, washed-out Texas sky. Sweaty, dirty, her hands rubbed raw from lifting the saddle so many times, Lael climbed aboard Two A.M. She hunkered down and, at Callantine's signal, spurred her mount. The first switch went smoothly as did the second, although Lael felt she was a little slow out of the saddle. She wanted to take another practice run, but the wrangler said no, that would only tire the horses.

Leading the stock, they headed for the stables. Lael was beginning to think her original judgment of Rafe Callantine had been misguided. While he had not acted exactly friendly toward her, he had, at least, stopped being surly.

She glanced at him surreptitiously. A drop of sweat rolled down the side of his face and disappeared into his unshaven chin. Needing to fill the silence, she said: "How'd I do, do you think?"

"Not bad, blondie, not bad at all."

He did not smile, but it was the closest to a compliment that he'd come all day. Lael's heart skipped. She felt bold, wanted to say something flirty back at him.

"Hey, who said you could call me blondie?" she grinned, her voice teasing.

He stopped, stared at his boots. She could see his jaw muscles working. He looked up, and it was as if a shade had been drawn down over his eyes. In an icy voice he said: "Who said you could call me a whisky-head?"

Stunned, Lael could only stare back. He moved off then, the dust from his boots falling in puffs behind him.

Chapter Seven

The telegram Alice had sent was brief and to the point: Your mother ill STOP Wants to see you STOP Wire travel arrangements STOP

Louise Morris crumpled the paper and tossed it aside. She was distressed to hear her mother was in poor health, but, truth to tell, her main reaction was one of irritation. How like Big Jack simply to summon her without a thought as to whether it was convenient or not. In fact, it was not convenient, not with the Fort Worth show only two weeks away. But she could not refuse to visit her sick mother, even if that mother had been a cipher for most of her daughter's life.

In the end, she decided to go for a day or two, leaving Curtis in charge. After all, the telegram had not indicated any desire on Mrs. Morris's part to see her only son.

The Morris ranch occupied several thousand acres in West Texas. When the buggy dropped Louise at the front door of the big house, she stood for a moment and took in the familiar sights. It had been several years since her last visit, but nothing had changed. Miles and miles of rolling prairie, prime grazing land, stretched to the horizon in all directions. She could remember coming home after a day spent out on the range and spotting the house, set atop a slight knoll, from ten miles away, a wavering vision in the rising heat.

She loved this place. Loved the tall grasses and prickly sage, the trickling creeks and hidden springs, the very dirt itself. She loved the buildings—the cavernous barn with its smell of horses and old leather, the bunkhouse with its sounds of male laughter and cards slapping a table, and the big house most of all with its grand stairway hewn from the finest cedar logs. It was the inhabitants of the big house she could do without. One inhabitant in particular, to be precise.

"Louise! Welcome home!" Alice Morris came down the steps of the verandah, her arms opened wide. Louise accepted the embrace and returned it, noting how soft and ample her sister's body had become. "It's so good to see you, though I'm sorry the occasion of your visit is such a sad one." Alice linked her arm through Louise's and led her inside, out of the heat.

"How is Mother doing? Your wire left a lot to the imagination." Louise set her hat on the hall table and ran her hands through her thick, dark hair.

"Not well, I'm afraid. She's just wasting away. The doctor says there's nothing he can do."

"I suppose it shouldn't come as a surprise that sooner or later her body would follow the example set by her mind."

Alice started toward the kitchen. "Come, have something to drink. You must be thirsty after that dusty train ride."

Louise followed her into the spacious ranch house kitchen and sat at the pocked and dented oak table. Alice poured her a glass of iced tea.

"Where's Big Jack?" Although he was technically father to both women, Louise never referred to him as Pa in front of Alice. It didn't seem right somehow.

"In Austin attending to business. He'll be back this afternoon."

Louise nodded. Big Jack, she knew, spent a lot of time in the state capital, twisting arms on behalf of the Cattleman's Association. He was confidant to governors and even Presidents and was not averse to saying so.

"I know you usually accompany him on his trips, Alice. I'm sure you stayed home to watch after Mother. I appreciate that."

Alice pushed a stray strand of graying hair behind her ear. "Actually, Missus Morris has a full-time nurse caring for her now. But, of course, I wanted to be here to greet you. I only wish Curtis could have come, too."

Louise looked at her, puzzled. "Your telegram didn't mention Curtis."

"No, Missus Morris only asked to see you. But I would have liked to see Curtis." Alice sighed and moved heavily to the drainboard. Louise watched her, saddened to see the changes time had wrought on her friend and sister. Not just the extra weight and graying hair—those were only cosmetic and were bound to happen to any woman of a certain age. No, it was more that Alice had lost her spark, appeared beaten down somehow. Louise shuddered. That's what living with Big Jack would do to a person.

Just then, Alice turned and smiled at her, a shy, soft smile that brought images of Curtis to mind, and Louise felt guilty for superimposing her own feelings about Big Jack onto her sister. Alice and Big Jack had always had some understanding, some connection that was absent from her own relationship with her father. Clearly, Alice was content with her lot in life which ought to be cause for rejoicing, not pity.

"I'll go see her now," Louise said, squeezing her sister's arm as she passed by. She ascended the wide staircase, trailing her hand along the polished banister. Paintings of Big Jack's famous Thoroughbreds lined the upper hallway. Louise paused at the door to what had been her room as a girl. She opened it and peeked in. Someone had brought her bags up and placed them at the foot of the bed.

Looking for an excuse to put off the inevitable, depressing

visit with her mother, she swung the bags up onto the four-poster and started unpacking. As she placed some stockings in the top dresser drawer, her hand brushed an object that had slid to the back. She pulled it out and sank to the floor, her legs suddenly weak as a newborn colt's.

It was a song book, its pages flimsy and in some places torn from use. Most of the songs were popular numbers, songs that had been all the rage ten or fifteen years ago. Several of them had notations, in pencil, written above the music—breath marks, dynamic markings, repeats. The book fell open to the place where an envelope had been inserted between two pages. Louise opened it and removed a lock of golden-colored hair, so fine she could barely feel it between her trembling fingers. Baby hair.

Memories flooded over her. The feel of the child at her breast, its downy head so soft in the crook of her arm. The sound of the old upright, in dire need of a tuning, as Jerry banged away, rehearsing a new song. All so real, as though they had just happened yesterday and not in a different life altogether.

She had been so young, only twenty-one years old, and, although by that age she was a veteran performer, this was her first tour in vaudeville. She did her trick roping act in between Mike and Maureen, the Dueling Tap Dancers, and some not too funny stand-up comedian. The most popular act in the show, without question, was Jerry O'Sullivan, whose lyrical tenor voice charmed equally whether bouncing through a toe-tapping jingle or wrapping itself around a heart-rending ballad. Tall, blond, and dashing, he was a hit with the audience and behind the footlights as well. Every woman in the company was in love with Jerry O'Sullivan, and Louise was no exception. Jerry was not averse to a little harmless dalliance with female members of the troupe, but when it became clear that Louise Morris was not that type of girl, he married her. He could not figure out any other way to get her into his bed.

They had eloped, of course, Louise not being so foolish as to think her father would sanction the marriage. And she was right. When Big Jack found out, he was furious, threatening to disown her. He stopped sending her money, but Louise didn't care. Their needs were few, and their love was great—what need had they of Big Jack's money?

All that changed with the birth of their son. Suddenly their needs were not so few. Reduced to one income, for Louise suffered a difficult pregnancy and was forced to drop out of the show, they found they could not make ends meet. Jerry asked the show's producers for more money. They refused, pointing out that because of him they had lost one of their top acts. Jerry became increasingly angry and frustrated. He spent more and more time away from home, frittering away money they didn't have. Finally, when the baby was only a few weeks old, Louise returned to the show even though her health was still precarious. She carried on gamely, but her heart was not in it, and her act suffered as a result. Jerry, too, had lost his edge, his lovely voice often hoarse from too many late nights in too many smoke-filled bars. The producers threatened to fire them both if they didn't shape up.

When the baby was six months old, Jerry had left them—cleaned out their bank account and lit out for parts unknown. Already suffering from nervous exhaustion, this was the last straw for Louise. She collapsed backstage and was rushed to the hospital where doctors diagnosed pneumonia, pleurisy, and a host of other maladies.

They had been in Chicago at the time, which happened to be Jerry's hometown. His parents lived in a small, but clean, apartment on the south side. They took the baby, Cory by name, and cared for him during the long months of Louise's hospitalization.

Such a small child was not allowed to make hospital visits, so, when Louise was finally discharged and able to see him again, she felt as though she hardly knew him.

The O'Sullivans had cared for him well. He seemed healthy and happy, and, when her in-laws suggested she leave him with them just until she got back on her feet, she let herself be talked into it. After all, wouldn't it be better for Cory to be in a stable home with loving grandparents, instead of traipsing across the country, living out of hotel rooms and keeping all kinds of odd hours?

So she had left her son and set out to rebuild her career. It wasn't long, given her skills and showmanship, before she became America's Cowgirl. Louise often wondered what America would think of its cowgirl if it was known she had abandoned her son like so much excess baggage. She told herself it had been for his own good, but deep down she knew better. The truth of it was she was having a blast, riding on top of the world. She was romanced by movie stars and adored by the public. It was awful to say, but Cory would only be in her way.

Louise rubbed the silky lock of hair against her cheek. The movie stars were gone now, and the public, though still there, was shrinking. Cory would soon be eleven, and she could count on one hand the number of times she had seen him. Louise replaced the envelope in Jerry's old song book and started to push it to the back of the drawer again. But she hesitated, weighing it in her hands. Maybe it wasn't too late. Maybe, after this business with her mother was resolved, after the Fort Worth show, she would visit Cory and this time ask him to come with her. He might just say yes. What young boy wouldn't prefer an exciting life on the rodeo circuit to living with aged grandparents in a walk-up apartment? Of course, she wouldn't let him run wild. She would insist that he go to school, maybe hire a tutor to travel with them. Louise paced the room, becoming more and more excited as she planned out her future, hers and Cory's.

Alice's inquiring knock at the door reminded her she had not yet visited her mother's sickroom. Once again Louise felt guilty. It seemed that if she wasn't being a neglectful mother, she was being a neglectful daughter.

She found her mother propped up in bed, shriveled to a mere ghost of her former self. Steeling herself, for Louise had never been good at comforting the sick or dying, she sat on the edge of the bed, took her mother's spindly hand, and chatted with a forced gaiety. It was tough going since the older woman made no response other than an occasional blink or twitch. Louise wondered how she could possibly have been lucid enough to have asked for her presence, and she began to suspect the reason for her summons had little to do with the state of her mother's health.

Her suspicions were confirmed when, that evening, after supper, her father asked her to retire with him to his study for a private talk.

"Well, Louise, how's business?" He selected one of his many pipes and began packing it.

Louise stiffened automatically. Although Big Jack, as her primary investor, had every right to ask about business, his inquiries always put her on the defensive. "Not bad. A little slow coming out of the off-season, but it'll pick up. Fort Worth looks like it's going to be a big success."

Big Jack puffed away, his thick brows drawn together in concentration over his pipe. "That so?"

He gazed at her with shrewd eyes that Louise knew from experience were unreadable. Even though capable of erupting into fits of anger that had terrified her as a child, he was just as likely to play his cards close to his vest, concealing his motives until the hand had been played out to his satisfaction. Despite his moniker, he was not a large man, but many men of great power and influence feared and admired him.

Needing fortification, Louise crossed to the sideboard and poured herself a shot of brandy. "Yes, from all accounts it's going quite well. George has been on site for a couple of weeks, working all the marketing angles, and we've gotten a lot of the big names signed up. I'm excited about it."

"Good, good. There is one little thing I want to talk about, though." He motioned to the sofa across from his chair. Guardedly Louise poured another drink and sat. "I was in Fort Worth last week on some business or other," he went on, "and I ran into Burt Hughes. He and I go way back, you know. 'Course, you realize that as head of the rodeo committee, it was primarily Burt who was responsible for picking you to produce the Fat Stock Show this year, and it probably didn't hurt that Big Jack is your daddy."

Louise stared at the drink in her hand. She had thought her hard-won reputation for producing quality rodeos had gotten her the contract, but now she wasn't so sure. Why did Big Jack always have to rain on her parade?

"Anyway, Burt told me he'd heard some talk he wanted to pass on. Said certain members of the committee aren't too happy with some of your practices."

"Such as?"

"Such as letting the people who work for you enter the competition. They say if one of them wins, it looks bad, like the whole thing's rigged. I got to admit I see their point. It makes it mighty tough to attract top talent if word gets out the thing's a fake."

Louise slammed down her glass and came to her feet, her eyes blazing. "How dare anyone insinuate I run a crooked rodeo? Any employee of mine who enters an event pays an entry fee and takes his chances like anyone else."

"That may be true. It looks bad is all. I told Burt I'd bring it up with you, and by golly, sister, you and George better take a serious second look at it. No point in getting the committee all upset over something that doesn't matter much anyhow."

"Doesn't matter much! I guess it matters plenty to my workers. Most of them wouldn't be able to trail along with me at all if they didn't have the chance to earn a little extra by competing. I couldn't take that away from them!" Louise was mightily irritated, not only at the committee's grievance but also because Hughes had taken the matter to her father, instead of directly to her or George. But she struggled to remain calm, knowing that Big Jack would view any hysterics as weakness.

Big Jack puffed on his pipe, silently regarding her. Then he shrugged and leaned back in his voluminous chair. "Suit yourself. Just don't say you weren't warned."

"No, I can't say that, can I?" Sighing, Louise resumed her seat. "I'll wire George tomorrow and ask him to speak to the committee. I'm sure when they realize everything's on the up and up, they'll drop their objection."

Big Jack let this pass, concentrating on his pipe. The silence spun out. Louise started to feel uncomfortable. It seemed that business matters were all she and her father had in common any more. A normal family might have spent time consoling each other over the grave illness of a wife and mother, but Louise couldn't even remember the last time Big Jack had uttered his wife's name. Most likely that poor woman would slip away from the world unnoticed and unmourned by everyone but her daughter, and, Louise had to admit, even her tears would not last long.

Her thoughts drifted back to what had occurred that afternoon, finding the song book and Cory's lock of hair. Although Cory was another subject that was off limits with her father, Louise found herself wanting to share her decision with someone and, before she knew it, she blurted out: "Pa, I'm thinking of bringing Cory to live with me!"

Big Jack's thick eyebrows drew together. "What on earth for?" he asked abruptly.

"Why, because I love him and miss him. He's old enough, now, to travel with me. We should get to know each other." Louise silently cursed herself, wishing she would have kept her mouth shut. Big Jack had never accepted the fact that Cory—the "son of an itinerant Mick" as he called him—was a part of their family. In fact, Cory's name was never spoken in Big Jack's house.

"It's a bit late for that, isn't it?" Big Jack said cruelly.

Biting her lip, Louise crossed the room to stand before the huge stone fireplace. Only one picture graced its mantel, an old one of Alice with her arms around Louise and Curtis as children.

"I hope not," Louise said quietly. "He may not even want to come with me, but, if he does, I'll try my best to be a good mother for him."

"Hah!" Big Jack snorted. "A lot you know about being a good mother. You wouldn't even know the brat if he passed you on the street! Not that I blame you, you understand. No, I've always thought you did the best thing, leaving him with that Mick's parents. Let the kid be with his own kind, right? So why upset the apple cart? Why make another mistake?"

"Cory was no mistake!" Louise insisted, her temper flaring. "Jerry and I loved each other. We wanted to have a baby. My only mistake was not realizing Jerry couldn't handle the responsibility. If I had it all to do over again, I'd still marry Jerry. I'd still have had Cory. But I wouldn't have left him. I'd have figured out some way to keep my baby." Louise turned back to the mantelpiece, her voice choking.

Big Jack pounced. "Then you'd never have been America's Cowgirl," he hissed into her ear. "You'd never have started Louise Morris's All-American Rodeo. You'd have wound up in some slum, ironing shirts or cleaning privies, or worse. That kid would have brought you down, Louise. And he still could! You have a business to run, or have you forgotten that? You don't have time to be looking after some trouble-making Irish scum pot!"

Louise turned to face her apoplectic father. She had never hated him as much as she did at this moment. "He's got Morris blood in him too, Pa. He's got your blood in him. Isn't that good enough for you?"

A sudden noise at the door made them both turn and look. Alice stood there, her face white, her hands clasped together and held rigidly in front of her. How long she had been there, neither of them knew.

"Leave us, please," Big Jack growled. "This is between Louise and me."

"I've got something to say," Alice whispered.

Big Jack's eyes flickered, and for an instant Louise thought he looked almost scared.

"No, Alice," he said. "You've got nothing to say. Go now."

But Alice ignored him. Walking straight up to Louise, she grabbed her sister's hands. "Dear, there's something you should know, something I . . . we . . . should have told you a long time ago. But we didn't. We were afraid it would hurt you, that you wouldn't understand."

"Alice. . . ." Big Jack tried to steer her away, but she shrugged him off.

"No, Big Jack. It's time Louise knew. You're wrong to tell her Cory was a mistake. Wrong to tell her he shouldn't come

60

to live with her. How can you say those things after what happened with Curtis and me?"

The bottom dropped out of Louise's stomach. Whatever Alice was about to tell her, she did not want to know. And yet, she realized she'd known the truth deep in her heart all along.

Big Jack raised one hand and gently stroked Alice's cheek. It was the kindest, most loving gesture Louise had ever seen him make toward another person, and suddenly she saw that her world was not as it seemed, had never been as it had seemed. He dropped his hand and walked away, sinking into his chair in defeat.

Alice turned back to Louise. Tears shone in her eyes. "I'm sorry, dear. This should never have been kept secret for so long. But, at first, you weren't old enough to understand, and then, as the years passed, it just seemed easier not to tell you, to spare you the hurt. But now . . . because of Cory"—Alice shot a defiant glance Big Jack's way—"you need to know."

"I know," Louise whispered. "Somehow I've always known. Curtis . . . he's not my mother's child. He's yours, isn't he? Yours and . . . my father's."

Alice nodded, tears streaming down her face. "Yes. It's terrible, what we've done. The lies, the covering up . . . your poor mother."

At the mention of her mother, Louise dropped Alice's hands. "Yes, my poor mother. What about her? Is this what did it? Is this what drove her over the edge?"

Alice couldn't answer. She had broken down completely now, and was sobbing into her handkerchief. Big Jack spoke from across the room, staring sightlessly ahead. "Your mother had not been well for a long time. You were too young to remember, but she was hospitalized several times, for depression the doctors said. I couldn't understand it. What did she have to be depressed about? She had a wonderful life . . .

plenty of money, a beautiful house, a perfect child, a loving husband. God knows I tried to make her happy, but nothing I did pleased her. The doctors told me it wasn't my fault, that her condition was physiological, but I didn't believe them. I thought I could fix it, that I could make her better if she would just let me."

Big Jack dropped his head on his chest. When he raised it again, he looked at Alice who met his gaze and held it through her tears.

"I met Alice at the sanitarium. She was a young assistant in training to be a nurse. And she was everything your mother was not . . . happy, cheerful, eager to please, giving of herself in a way I'd never known with . . . Charlotte."

Louise jumped at the sound of her mother's name. It had been so long since she had heard anyone speak it.

"We fell in love. I tried not to, but I was still young, only thirty-two, and it had been so long since your mother . . . well, let's just say I wasn't too surprised when Alice told me she was expecting. I didn't know what to do. I couldn't just abandon Alice and the baby, but I couldn't leave you and your mother, either. I thought about setting up Alice in her own home and visiting when I could, but that seemed . . . tawdry somehow. And I didn't want to just be a visitor to my child . . . I wanted to be a daily part of his life. So I came up with a plan, and, after a bit of convincing, Alice agreed to it. I told Charlotte about Alice and the baby. I asked her to agree to adopt the child and raise it as her own, and to allow Alice to come live with us. I told her that if she agreed to this, in return I would never be unfaithful to her again, would never touch Alice again."

Big Jack's voice faltered, and Alice rushed to his side. Louise stood there, detesting them both but, oddly enough, envying them as well. They were so in love. How could she not have seen that until now?

Big Jack wrapped an arm around Alice's waist and continued. "Your mother . . . didn't take the news very well. She attacked me, physically attacked me. The orderlies had to restrain her. She fell into her most severe depression to date . . . she was catatonic for weeks. Slowly she came out of it, but she was changed. Her mind was . . . blank. The doctors gave me no hope that she would ever recover." He passed his hand across his forehead. Alice reached for his other hand and pressed it to her lips. Watching them, Louise suddenly felt sick. "So you brought her home with her *nurse* and a child that you passed off as hers. You got everything you wanted in the end, didn't you? And you didn't even have to keep your end of the bargain. Lucky for you, with your wife a certified loony, you didn't have to feel guilty about sleeping with the hired girl. I have to admit, though, sleeping with your *daughter* is pretty low even by your standards. How can you live with yourself?"

Alice turned her head into Big Jack's shoulder and wept. Big Jack patted her back. "I wouldn't expect you to understand. I loved Alice, but I had nothing to offer her. She couldn't be my wife . . . she couldn't even be recognized as the mother of my son. There was only one way to make her a legitimate part of the family . . . adoption. I wanted her to have the Morris name. I wanted her to know that I would always take care of her. Yes, she is legally my daughter, but, in my heart, she is and always will be my one true love. I do not believe we are sinners for sharing our affection."

"How touching." Louise's voice dripped sarcasm. "Two lovebirds making the best of a bad situation. I don't suppose it occurred to either one of you that you drove my mother crazy. That you sacrificed her on the altar of your own perverted desires!"

"That's enough! I knew you'd never understand. You

63

should never have told her, Alice."

"I'm sorry . . . I'm so sorry," sobbed Alice, clutching at Big Jack. "I never meant to cause so much unhappiness. I only thought that you two might understand each other better if you realized that we all make mistakes, that none of us is perfect."

"How dare you compare my situation to yours!" Louise cried. "At least, my son knows who his mother is. That's more than Curtis can say."

Big Jack had finally been provoked beyond the level of his endurance. Pushing Alice away, he approached his daughter, his true daughter, menacingly. "At least Curtis's mother was a constant presence in his life, even if he didn't realize it. And at least his father didn't abandon him, no matter what the circumstances of his birth. All in all, I'd say Curtis fared better than that little Mick of yours."

Undaunted, Louise faced him, her fists balled at her sides. "You're disgusting! I'm sorry now that my son has Morris blood in him. I don't know how he'll ever live it down. But I suppose I should thank you . . . you've made my decision quite easy. From now on, Cory goes with me wherever I go, but we'll never come back here. Never!"

Head held high, Louise stepped around her father and made for the door. She intended to walk out of it and never look back. Big Jack's voice stopped her dead in her tracks.

"Whether you ever return to this house is immaterial to me, my dear. But it is material to me what you do with that urchin of yours."

Slowly Louise turned to face him. He looked perfectly calm and in command now, and that scared her more than anything.

"I do not think it would be good for business if America's Cowgirl suddenly showed up with her eleven-year-old son in

64

tow. People would talk, and you do have a reputation to protect, you know."

"So there'd be talk. What of it? Rodeo people aren't saints. They judge you on how you sit in the saddle, not on what you've done in your private life."

"Ah, yes, rodeo people. Just your type. I'm sure you can count on them being understanding. But you seem to have forgotten that the people who actually hire you aren't rodeo people. They're fine, upstanding citizens, representatives of their communities who are undoubtedly impressed by the wholesome character of Louise Morris and her All-American Rodeo. Let just a whiff of scandal attach itself to your company, and I guarantee your contracts will dry up and blow away. You'll be ruined."

Louise shook her head, astonished that her normally astute father would try this tactic. "It won't wash, Pa. There is no scandal to speak of. Cory's my legitimate son, and, although people might debate my merit as a mother, no one's going to wonder why I want him with me now. There's something else, isn't there? Some other reason why you don't want me to have Cory. But I don't have a clue what it is, and, frankly, I'm sick and tired of trying to read your twisted mind. So I'm leaving now, for good. If you want to contact me in the future, go through George."

Once again, Louise turned to go.

"If you bring that boy to live with you, I'll tell Curtis. I'll tell him everything, so help me God."

Alice gasped audibly. The grandfather clock in the corner began striking the hour, its loud bongs echoing the dull thuds of Louise's heart. "What did you say?" she whispered.

"You heard me. Try to bring that boy into this family and I'll tell Curtis who his real mother is. Simple as that." Big Jack retrieved his pipe from its stand and held a match to it, his face impassive behind the flickering flame.

"You bastard! It would kill Curtis. He's not strong enough. . . ."

Big Jack chuckled. "Yes. Odd, isn't it? Not a drop of Charlotte's blood in him yet he seems to have inherited her weakness all the same. Pity."

In two long strides, Louise crossed the room to stand before her father. She raised her hand and slapped him, hard, across the face.

Very deliberately, Big Jack laid down his pipe, straightened up, and slapped her back. Calmly he resumed his seat, shook out his paper, and began reading the day's financial news.

Chapter Eight

In the two weeks since Foster Davis had hired Lael for his relay team, not much had gone right. After Abilene, they traveled to Lubbock and, from there, headed north to Amarillo. It was a grueling schedule, but the members of Davis's troupe shared a camaraderie of the road that helped to elevate their spirits. A camaraderie that did not include Lael.

Try as she might, she could not seem to break into the group, to be accepted as one of the gang. She knew some of the reasons why. For one thing, true to her promise to Roger, she had stayed in hotels at each stop while everyone else had camped in tents or trailers on the rodeo grounds. She knew this made her look snobbish, as though she didn't care to mingle with the riff-raff, but there was nothing she could do about it.

For another thing, she had made the mistake of casually mentioning that she had attended a year of college, an experience that set her apart from the rest of the cowpunchers. Despite her best efforts to explain that it had only been one year at a business school in Fort Worth, many of them viewed her advanced education with suspicion. Some even took to calling her Ivy League, or Ivy for short.

Worst of all, she had somehow managed to make an enemy out of Maude Kelly, Davis's star trick rider. Though Maude herself did not seem particularly popular with the other cowboys and cowgirls, she was indisputably one of them, and Lael sensed that her own standing would never improve as long as Maude hated her so much. The source of Maude's initial dislike of Lael was a mystery to the younger woman, although any dispassionate observer could see that the aging star viewed the pretty newcomer as a threat. But if Lael was stumped as to why Maude had been so hostile at their first meeting, she knew well enough what had fanned the flame of her animosity.

It had all started with Lael's attempt to branch out. Thanks to Rafe Callantine's expert coaching and her own racing experience, Lael had enjoyed immediate success on the relay team. And more often than not, she won her other events, broncho riding and steer riding, as well. But regardless of her success to date, Lael had realized that, if she wanted to make enough money to live on, she would have to enter as many different events as possible. For that reason, she had asked Foster Davis, the only person who treated her with any respect at all, if she could learn trick riding. He had greeted the idea enthusiastically and began instructing her himself, letting her use Meadowlark, the best trick riding horse in his stables. That is, until Maude Kelly found out.

"Get that greenhorn off my horse!" she demanded when she came upon them one day during a practice session.

"Your horse! Last time I checked that there was my brand," Davis said, pointing to Meadowlark's flank.

"You know what I mean," Maude insisted as she yanked the reins out of Lael's hands. "*I* ride Meadowlark, no one else! If a horse gets used to the feel of someone different, it messes up its timing. I don't want her using my special saddle, either."

Maude grabbed Lael's leg and unceremoniously pushed it across Meadowlark's back. "Get your butt out of there, sister!"

"Now, Maude, Lael's just beginning to make some progress," Davis wheedled. "It wouldn't be fair to make her start all over again on a different horse."

"Too bad. There's only one gal gonna ride Meadowlark, and it ain't gonna be that chippy!" And with that, Maude took herself and *her* horse off.

Davis flushed red to the roots of his sparsely-haired head, embarrassed, Lael guessed, to have been dressed down by one of his employees. They returned to the barn where he told Rafe to saddle up Cinnamon, a pretty little Appaloosa with good instincts but not much trick riding experience. Lael's lessons continued, but it was much harder with both horse and rider starting from scratch.

And then there was the problem of Rafe Callantine. Since the day he had taught her relay riding, he had not spoken more than two words to her, and those had been more in the nature of grunts than actual words. Lael wondered how he could possibly have taken such offense at being called a whisky-head, a name many men would humorously own up to. Although she fought the notion, it seemed clear that he had gotten upset because there was more than a little truth to the accusation. Yes, it appeared that Rafe Callantine was just the sort of man her father and brother had cautioned her against—a broken-down loser who had no life outside of the road and the gin palace.

But that didn't seem to matter to Lael. She still tossed and turned at night, images of his hard body and scarred face filling her head, keeping her from sleep. Why was she so obsessed with a man who couldn't have cared less about her?

By virtue of his position as head wrangler, they came into contact on a daily basis, but it was as if a wall separated them, preventing them from touching, speaking, even making eye contact. Lael had wanted to apologize for the whisky-head comment, but he was so shut off from her she couldn't figure out how to bring it up without sounding awkward.

So she moped around, unhappy and out of place, her only pleasure coming from the few seconds she spent each day in competition. She was tempted to chuck it all and go home to Fort Worth or even Nebraska. But she wasn't quite ready to acknowledge defeat. Besides, their next stop was the Fort Worth Fat Stock Show where she could stay at Roger's while competing. Maybe being with family again would lift her spirits.

One afternoon soon after they arrived in Amarillo, Lael was just finishing a trick riding practice session when she looked over and saw a tall, red-headed cowgirl wearing a blue satin blouse and leather-trimmed chaps watching from the fence rail. Since no one else had ever bothered to watch, Lael took this as a friendly sign. She strolled over to the woman and gave her a quick howdy.

The woman lifted one hand off the rail and said: "Hey." Then her eyes shifted to Foster Davis who was leading Cinnamon back to the barn. Her gaze returned to Lael, a smirk playing on her lips. "My name's Fanny."

"Nice to meet you, Fanny. I'm Lael. You here for the rodeo?"

"Sure thing. Thought I'd see how these Amarillo judges treat a northern gal."

Lael climbed the fence and hopped down on the other side. "Where in the north you from?"

"Montana."

"You're a long way from home."

"Yeah, well, I get around." Fanny stood hip shot, her arms folded across her chest. Lael looked at her closer. She didn't seem to be that much older than Lael herself, but there was a hardness about her that spoke of a life lived on the outskirts of respectability.

Lael hooked her thumbs in her pockets. "North, south, east, or west, it doesn't matter much to judges, I don't think. That ten second buzzer is the toughest judge."

"We'll see about that."

Just then, Rafe Callantine came into view, leading a couple of horses into the corral. Fanny lowered her hands to her hips and narrowed her eyes, unabashedly inspecting the broad-shouldered, narrow-hipped wrangler. Something inside Lael tightened.

"Look at that, would ya," Fanny murmured. "Been nice talking to ya, honey. Mama's got work to do now. See ya later."

With that, Fanny sidled over to Rafe, her hips swinging provocatively. She said something to him that Lael couldn't hear. He dropped the hoof he was cleaning and straightened up. His perpetually lowered hat brim kept Lael from seeing his eyes, but his mouth looked grim. He turned and walked toward the barn in long strides. Fanny hurried to keep up with him, chattering in a bright, girlish-sounding voice.

That was all Lael could stand to watch. This Fanny woman, wherever she came from, was the type who gave all cowgirls a bad name. At least Rafe seemed impervious to her come-on. Lael went about her business and forgot all about it.

But that evening, as she sat by herself in the hotel lobby composing a letter, in walked Fanny hanging on the arm of one of Davis's cowboys. Fanny caught her eye and smiled broadly. She turned to her companion and whispered in his ear. He laughed and slapped her lightly on her bottom, then went into the adjoining bar. Fanny sidled over to Lael.

"Hey there, cutie. Waiting for somebody?" She raised one eyebrow in a knowing leer.

"What?" Lael was flustered. "No. I'm by myself."

"Really? That's not what I hear. Listen, when he gets here, you two come have a drink with me and Roy. We oughta get to know each other better." Fanny winked conspiratorially.

"When who gets here?" Lael asked, confused.

Fanny cocked her head, her red curls framing her pretty, diamond-shaped face. "Smart cookie. You're being discreet, ain't ya? Well, you don't need to play games with me, honey. I know all about it."

Lael spread her hands helplessly. "All about what?"

"Davis, of course. Hell, that's the first thing I heard when I showed up here today. Maude Kelly, now she ain't no friend of mine, mind you, but she took me aside this morning and said . . . 'Fanny, I probably don't need to be telling *you* this, seeing as it takes one to know one, but there's a new girl on board been putting the squeeze on Foster Davis. Got him wrapped around her sassy little finger.' And she was talking about you, sweetheart. Now, if I know Maude, I ain't the only person she's been telling, so I wouldn't worry too much about keeping it under wraps. Oh, by the way, you were right about the judges here . . . they're a pretty straight-laced bunch. But I don't give no never mind . . . I've found me a pretty good deal!" Fanny nodded toward the bar where Roy had disappeared. She winked again and flounced off, the fringe on her skirt swirling about her legs.

Lael sat dumb struck, the color rushing to her face. How could anyone think that she and Davis . . . ? Her heart pounding so loudly she was sure everyone in the lobby could hear it, she rushed upstairs and sprawled across her bed, shaking uncontrollably.

That damned Maude Kelly! How dare she spread rumors like that? No wonder no one had befriended her—they all thought she was Davis's chippy, that she was trading sexual favors for special treatment from the boss! That explained why no one had helped her, encouraged her. Why no one would look her in the eye.

My God, what must Rafe think? Lael groaned and rolled over on the bed, hiding her tortured eyes beneath her arms. Surely he wouldn't believe it. But why shouldn't he? He knew nothing about her life, her background. For all he knew, she was the worst sort of tart.

Lael sprang from the bed, grabbing the footrail as she fought sudden dizziness. She had to do something about this. She couldn't just let it go. Pulling her old boots on with a satisfying *thwap* and twisting her hat into a rakish angle on her head, she stared at her reflection in the mirror. Her cheeks blazed; her eyes had darkened to the color of winter moss. For a moment, she faltered, but then regained her fervor. If she didn't confront this now, she never would.

It was not hard to find Maude's tent, pitched in a field on the rodeo grounds. "Maude! Maude Kelly!" Lael called, hands on hips. "Come out here. I want to talk with you."

A moment passed before the tent flap parted, and Maude emerged, wearing silk pajama bottoms and a man's oversized flannel shirt. Her hair was wet and combed back from her face. She had dark circles under her eyes.

"I don't appreciate being bothered like this. You got something to say to me, come back tomorrow." She started to step back into her tent.

"No. Let's settle this now. Tomorrow you'll be too busy explaining to everybody in this camp how wrong you were about me."

Without make-up, Maude looked like a washed-out kewpie doll. She had no eyebrows, and her lips were thin and colorless. She glanced behind Lael at the two or three people who had stopped to watch the scene unfold. Bringing her gaze back to the younger girl, she smiled contemptuously.

"Cut the crap, kid. I don't owe no apologies to no whore."

Lael snapped. She reared back and swung as hard as she could. Maude ducked, and the blow caught her on the ear, splitting it open. For an instant they stood there, Lael heaving with anger, Maude clutching her bleeding ear. Then the older woman screamed and launched herself at Lael, taking them both down in the dust. They fought and scratched and bit, rolling around like two cats in heat. The crowd, which numbered in the dozens by now, egged them on, most shouting encouragement to Maude, although a few cries of—"Atta girl, Ivy!"—could be heard.

Maude, on top now, landed a solid punch to Lael's eye, blacking out the younger woman's vision in a swarm of stars. Fighting to stay conscious, Lael fended off more blows. She grabbed a handful of Maude's wet hair and yanked. Maude yelled and tumbled to the side. Lael brought a knee up hard into Maude's solar plexus. The air *whooshed* out of the older woman, and she lay motionless, struggling for breath. Lael rolled to her feet and crouched, ready to continue the fight if need be, but it was over. Maude did not get up.

Swaying, one eye swelling shut, her shirt bloodied, and her hands bruised and raw, Lael studied the suddenly silent crowd. "I'm nobody's whore!" she cried, looking each member in the eye. "If there's anybody don't believe that, step on out."

Nobody said a word, but to a man and woman they met her gaze, and Lael could see new respect in their faces. Reaching for Maude's hand to help her up, she stumbled. A pair of strong arms caught her. Her face brushed against something soft. She inhaled an incredibly comforting smell—a combination of freshly laundered cotton, sweet hay and supple leather, and, underlying all that, a distinctly masculine scent of whisky and sun-toughened flesh. She was not at all surprised when Rafe Callantine's voice murmured in her ear.

"Leave her. They'll take care of her. Come with me."

She regained her balance, and he led her away, holding her firmly by the elbow. He took her into the barn and sat her on a crate in the tack room, then left for a moment. When he came back, he carried a wet cloth and a bottle of iodine. Squatting in front of her, he began sponging off her cuts, working carefully around her swollen eye. With her good eye, she studied his face. His brows were drawn together in concentration, but he didn't seem angry or put out. His lips were full against the dark shadow of his chin, and the tiny scar throbbed almost imperceptibly with each beat of his heart. Lael closed her good eye and felt her head start to pitch forward.

"Easy now," Rafe said, bracing her shoulders. "Do you want to lie down?"

She shook her head and took some deep breaths until it cleared a little. "I've never done anything like that before," she said.

He was silent. Pouring some iodine on the cloth, he hesitated before warning her: "This will hurt a little." Then he touched the cloth to her face gently. She winced and bit her lip against the sting. She thought she heard him whisper—"I'm sorry, Lael."—but the dizziness had come back and there was a whirring in her ears. One by one, he picked up her battered hands and rubbed the abrasions with the iodine. His ministrations done, he restoppered the bottle and gazed at her, assessing his handiwork, elbows resting on his knees, hands hanging down between his thighs.

"I'm a mess, aren't I?" Lael mumbled.

"Never looked better." His mouth turned up at the corner, and Lael tried to smile in response, but it hurt her bruised lips too much.

"Rafe," she began, the words jumbling together in her woozy brain, "I've never . . . I don't like to fight. But Maude . . . she was saying . . . I had to. . . ."

He touched her cheek with his callused palm. Lael stopped talking, and they looked at each other with the kind of directness and understanding that usually only passes between couples of twenty years or more. Lael felt a curious lightness that had nothing to do with being light-headed. It was as if a heavy burden had been lifted from her shoulders.

"You should put some ice on that eye," he said. "Ask for some when you get back to the hotel."

She nodded, unable to speak.

"I'll take you back now, if you think you're ready to go."

She didn't want to leave, but he stood and held out his hand, so she took it. He helped her onto Cinnamon and walked her back to the hotel. Climbing the stairs to her room, she went immediately to the window where she was just in time to see him disappear down the street, swallowed up by the night.

Chapter Nine

"Lael, wait up! Darn it, girl, you can't keep running away from me!"

Lael turned in her tracks to see Fanny hustling to catch up, her dimpled cheeks pouting prettily. "Ever since Amarillo you've been scarcer than a June bug in January. I'm trying to apologize, dammit, and you won't let me."

Lael paused, flushing pink at the accusation. It was true that she had been avoiding the flashy cowgirl. Now that her own reputation had been salvaged she had no desire to see it sullied again by keeping company with a self-professed chippy. Nevertheless, her innate sense of good manners told her it would be rude to spurn Fanny's apology.

"It wasn't your fault, Fanny. It was Maude spreading the rumors, not you."

"Well, I shoulda known better than to believe anything that dried-up old prune said. I'm glad you chased her on outta here!"

Maude Kelly had left the circuit following the fight with Lael—to recuperate, she said, although the only real injury she had suffered had been to her pride. Unfortunately, she was not the only member of Davis's entourage to leave. The next day, Lael had gone to the barn to thank Rafe for doctoring her the previous night, and could find neither hide nor hair of the wrangler. Later, Davis told her Rafe had been called away on some unnamed family emergency and wasn't sure when, or if, he would return. Lael's heart sank like a bucket of bullets. Had he really been called away or had he left because of her?

What did it matter? The man was gone, and she might as well get used to the fact. They were in Fort Worth now, preparing for the Fat Stock Show, one of the premier rodeos in the Southwest, and she had plenty to do without mooning over some enigmatic cowboy, especially one who was decidedly absent.

Fanny tilted her head in the direction of the rodeo headquarters building. "I'm on my way to check tomorrow's draw. You heading there, too?"

Lael hesitated, uncertain about being seen with the red-headed cowgirl. But Fanny seemed kind, and Lael knew all too well how it felt to be friendless. Smiling, she fell in step. "I am. Rumor has it I drew Calypso in the broncho riding. Ever ridden him?"

" 'Fraid not, but I'll ask around for you. Say, did you meet Louise Morris yet? Not a bad-looking dame, considering all the mileage on her. Why, I can remember hearing stories about her when I was just yea high." Fanny held her palm hip high. "America's Cowgirl they called her then."

"I haven't seen her yet. I hear she's going to compete in several of the events, though. Do you think any of the rest of us will have a chance going up against her?"

"Oh, sure. She's past her prime. About the only thing she still does better than anybody else is trick roping. Did you know she and Tom Mix were like that?" Fanny held up two crossed fingers. "They say they were that close to getting married, but then he went off to Hollywood and left Louise behind." She sighed dramatically. "Can you imagine . . . jilting America's Cowgirl? What a cad!"

Lael tried to suppress a giggle at Fanny's new-found sense of propriety, but it leaked out anyway. The laughter was contagious, and, by the time they reached the headquarters building, both women were guffawing loudly, holding their aching sides. They lingered on the front step, wiping tears from their eyes and gasping for air.

Suddenly, the big, glass-paneled doors swung open, knocking lightly into Lael. Curtis Morris stepped outside, peering around the door to see whom he had bumped. At sight of Lael, he removed his Stetson and apologized profusely. Still fighting for breath, Lael raised a hand to signal she was fine and proceeded to enter the building.

"Ladies," Curtis called them back, "are you checking your draws for tomorrow's roughstock events?"

They assured him they were. He smiled shyly, his large brown eyes never leaving Lael's face. "Well, if you aren't familiar with any of 'em, you just tell me. I know all the stock right well, and I'd be glad to give you some tips. Any time, just . . . I'm Curtis Morris, by the way. Just ask me, any time." Hat in hand, Curtis took a nervous step backwards and stumbled off the step. He recovered, flashed the women an embarrassed grin, and turned to leave.

But Fanny's ears had perked up at the mention of his name. "Say, cowboy, you wouldn't happen to be related to Louise Morris, now, would you?"

"Sure enough. I'm her brother." Curtis spoke to Fanny, but quickly cut his eyes to Lael to catch her reaction.

She gave him a friendly smile, unaware of the effect it was having on him.

Fanny, missing nothing, frowned slightly. She sidled forward, placing herself between Curtis and Lael. "Well, then, I'll bet you know just every little thing that goes on around here. What say I drop by your tent later on and get the skinny on . . . the stock, for starters." She gazed up into Curtis's eyes from beneath long lashes. This was a no-fail technique, guaranteed to turn men into putty. And Curtis did, indeed, appear hooked, just not by her. He swallowed hard and looked over her head toward Lael.

"Yes, ma'am," he said. "I'd be happy to have you and Miss. . . ."

"Buckley. You can call me Lael."

Curtis's eyes shone. "Please come by my tent this evening. I'm right behind the stables."

Fanny pursed her lips. "You sure you're issuing that invitation to the both of us?"

Curtis wrenched his gaze away from Lael. "Of course. I'm sorry, ma'am, I didn't catch your name."

"Maybe that's 'cause I didn't throw it," Fanny said sarcastically. "Fanny Lavelle. Pleased to meet you."

Curtis shook her hand, and then held out his own to Lael. She shook it sturdily, noting how smooth it seemed for someone who spent his life roping and riding. He released her grip slowly.

"Well, then, see you tonight Miss Lavelle . . . Miss Buckley."

"What's with all this *miss* business?" Fanny said, tossing her head. "It's Fanny and Lael, OK?"

"Right. Sorry." Curtis jammed his hat on his head, gave them a two-fingered salute, and started off.

"Curtis," Lael called to him. "Thanks for the invite, but I can't come tonight. I'm staying with my brother here in Fort Worth, and he's planning a special dinner for me this evening. Thanks anyway."

Curtis's face fell a good yard. Fanny immediately put on a sweet expression. "Too bad, Lael. Well, cowboy, guess you'll have an audience of one tonight. See you then!" Smiling, Fanny propelled Lael through the doors. She sank down on one of the wooden benches lining the hallway.

"I gotta quit hanging out with you, sister. I ain't used to playing second fiddle."

"What do you mean?" Lael laughed.

"Don't tell me you didn't notice. That man has a hard-on for you from here to Dallas!" Fanny picked up a stray copy of *Hoofs and Horns* and began fanning herself.

"Oh, he does not," Lael blushed.

"Oh, he does, too," Fanny minced back. "It's as plain as the nose on that fresh young face of yours. Listen, if you want him, he's yours. I won't even try to go after him, 'cause it'd be no good. But if you ain't interested, tell me now. I ain't too proud to pick up your droppings."

"This is ridiculous," Lael said, shaking her head. "Curtis Morris isn't mine to give away. And, anyway, what about you and Roy? I thought you two were still together."

Fanny shrugged. "That was then, this is now. In case you hadn't noticed, Curtis Morris is the best catch in town, maybe in all of rodeo. He's the brother of Louise Morris, for God's sake. They're rolling in dough! And besides, he's kind of a looker once you get past that goofy grin."

Lael stared at Fanny, appalled. "You don't feel a thing for that poor boy. All you care about is what he can do for you. You make me sick."

Mad at herself for having been taken in by Fanny's friendly come-on, Lael spun on her heel and made for the door.

"You got a lot to learn, kid," Fanny's world-weary voice followed her. "Maybe I feel something for him, maybe I don't. It don't really matter. I learned a long time ago looking for *true love* don't get you very far." She paused and fixed Lael with a look. "I reckon you're just finding that out about a certain Mister Rafe Callantine."

Lael's hand froze on the door handle. Her back to Fanny,

she let the pain cross her face for a split second before pushing out into the heat of the day.

The parade down Fort Worth's main street took place the next morning. Lael proudly rode Cinnamon, pleased that her mount sported a fancy, silver-studded bridle even if she could not match its finery. She had had to spend her first weeks' winnings on bloomers and special trick riding shoes. A new hat and boots would have to wait.

She spotted Roger and his family in the crowd and kneed Cinnamon over to the side of the street. Benjy sat gaily atop Roger's shoulders, a child-size cowboy hat obscuring most of his head. Molly bounced up and down excitedly, waving a tiny American flag.

"Aunt Lael, Aunt Lael," the little girl cried, "where's all the bulls and bucking bronchos?"

Lael laughed. "Why, honey, they're resting up back at the rodeo grounds. Saving their energy for the show. You'll be there to see me, won't you?"

Molly turned questioning eyes toward her mother.

"Of course," Amy answered, finally reconciled to her sister-in-law's unorthodox profession. "We'll be Aunt Lael's own special cheering section!"

Lael tipped her hat at them and rejoined the parade. As she had hoped, being with family again had rejuvenated her, made her feel as though she belonged somewhere. True, now that she had vanquished Maude, her rodeo colleagues were beginning to warm up to her, but she still felt like an outsider, not yet one of the gang. Rafe's departure had only added to her sense of displacement, although why that should be so baffled her.

"Why the long face?"

Lael jumped, startled out of her reverie. Curtis Morris, resplendent in black and white batwing angora chaps and ten-gallon hat came up beside her riding a beautiful blaze-marked stallion.

"No reason. Just thinking about something, I guess." Lael gathered herself and smiled broadly, lifting her face to the sky. "There truly is no reason to be long-faced today, is there? The sun must be shining all across Texas!"

Enraptured, Curtis could only gaze at the lovely girl beside him—at her golden hair that caught the sun's rays and threw them back, at her white teeth glowing in her generous mouth, at her pink cheeks that he knew would feel so soft to the touch.

"Yes, ma'am, it surely is a nice day." Curtis knit his brow, certain that was the stupidest remark he had ever made in his life. He cast about for something more intelligent to say. "Did you have any questions about the stock you drew, Miss Buckley?"

"Lael," she reminded him.

"Lael." He gave her a shy smile, and she noticed how it made his eyes crinkle in the corners.

"Yes, as a matter of fact. What can you tell me about Calypso?"

"That's a good draw for you. He'll give you a lot of action, so he scores high with the judges, but he isn't too tricky. Lots of crow-hoppin', but nothing real mean."

"OK, thanks." Then curiosity got the better of her. "Did Fanny look you up last night to get some pointers?"

Curtis blushed and dropped his eyes. "Yes, ma'am. I think I'm the one who got educated, though."

Lael suppressed a grin. "Fanny does come on a bit strong, although I can't help feeling there's a decent person under all that glitz and glamour."

"Take it from me, there's a lot of woman under all that

glitz and glamour, but none of it is what I'd call decent!" Curtis's blush deepened as he realized he had gone too far in describing last night's encounter with the red-headed cow-girl.

Lael started to giggle in spite of herself, the image of head-strong Fanny overwhelming this polite, well-mannered young man too much for her. Curtis shot her a quick glance to assure himself he wasn't being made fun of, then joined in her laughter.

"I don't mean to mislead you, Miss Buckley."

"Lael."

"Sorry . . . Lael. Miss Lavelle did have some shenanigans in mind, but, well, I didn't, if you get my drift."

"Don't worry, Curtis. You don't have to defend your honor to me."

"I just don't want you to get the wrong impression," he said earnestly.

Once again, Lael laughed. "You certainly are an original. Most men are dying to come off as lady-killers."

Chagrined, Curtis looked away, wishing he could start this whole conversation over. Luckily his sister rescued him from further embarrassment. Sitting tall atop the high-stepping Cancan, Louise pulled up next to the pair, a concerned look on her face.

"Curtis, meet me at headquarters after the parade. We have a problem." Louise spoke low, but her words carried to Lael.

"OK. Louise, have you met Miss Buckley yet?" Curtis inclined his head in Lael's direction.

Louise forced a smile, the lines around her eyes and mouth betraying fatigue and worry. "No. I saw your name on the contestant list, though, and it stuck with me, probably because it's so unusual. Lael, isn't it?"

"That's right," Lael grinned. "It's short for something, but I have to know a person real well before I'll say what."

Louise chuckled, momentarily erasing the worry lines. It came as no surprise to Lael that this woman had attracted the likes of princes and movie stars.

"It's a real honor to be performing in your rodeo, Miss Morris."

"Thank you, Lael. We appreciate new young talent like yourself. Curtis, don't forget now." The rodeo producer nodded her head at them and spurred Cancan to the front of the column, putting on her best America's Cowgirl smile.

"Is anything wrong?" Lael asked.

"I don't know," Curtis said, following his sister with his eyes. "Lou hasn't been the same since she came back from a visit home a couple of weeks ago. Our mother's been ill. I guess that's it."

"I'm sorry," Lael murmured.

Curtis shrugged. "Let's talk about you. What brings Lael Buckley to the Fort Worth Fat Stock Show?"

As they followed the parade route through the dusty streets of her adopted home town, Lael told him of growing up in Nebraska, her first encounter with rodeo, and her move to Fort Worth. She told him how her parents disapproved of her new-found career, but that she hoped her success would persuade them to change their minds. She had him in stitches with her description of Mr. Snively and the way she had finagled a job with the prissy accounting instructor. Before they knew it, they had reached the end of the route. All around them, the group was disbanding, heading back to the rodeo grounds.

Curtis reined in the stallion. "It's been a pleasure talking with you, Miss . . . Lael. I'd ride with you back to the stables, but I best be looking up Louise now. I'm counting on seeing you again soon, though." He looked at her expectantly, almost like a child on Christmas morning waiting to open his presents.

A bit unnerved, Lael reached forward to stroke Cinnamon's neck. "You know where to find me," she said noncommittally.

He touched his hat, and rode off. As she watched his finely clad figure recede, images of Rafe Callantine in his faded jeans and battered leather chaps danced before her eyes. Sadly she turned Cinnamon and walked away, wondering what it would take to make her forget.

Chapter Ten

Curtis met Louise and her partner, George Early, in their tiny office at rodeo headquarters. His sister perched on the edge of a scarred wooden desk, her foot jiggling nervously. "What's up?" he asked, tossing his hat on the desk.

Louise and George exchanged stricken looks. "We've been canned," the cowgirl announced quietly.

"What?"

"Fired. The rodeo committee told us to pull up stakes and make for the hills."

"I don't understand," Curtis said, baffled. "How can they kick us out the day before the rodeo opens?"

"It's their right," Early said, sinking down in the room's only chair. "The committee can cancel our contract at any time."

"But why would they?"

"They say they don't like my practice of allowing my employees to enter the competitive events," said Louise angrily. "According to them, some of the top stars have complained that I'm running a crooked rodeo and threatened to walk out. Between you and me, I'll be a city slicker if that's the real problem."

"What do you think it is, then?"

"I don't know exactly, but it's got Big Jack written all over it." Louise got up to pace the room.

"That makes no sense," Curtis argued. "Why would Pa sabotage a business he has an interest in?"

"Because he's a rotten, vindictive old bastard!" she shouted, pounding her fist on the wall.

Curtis blanched at her outburst. "I know he's difficult sometimes . . . ," he began, but Louise interrupted, her voice bitter.

"You don't know anything, Curtis, not a damn' thing." She seemed to catch herself before going on. "The committee's already hired a new producer to take over . . . Ty McCall. They've given us until midnight to move out."

"Isn't there anything we can do, Lou?" Curtis looked at his sister with a stunned expression.

"No," Louise said flatly. "The fix is in."

Ty McCall was a first-rate cowpoke and an all-around good old boy, but he was in way over his head, trying to produce the Fort Worth Fat Stock Show. To staff a show as large as Fort Worth, he had had to supplement his small outfit with several new hires, some of whom barely knew the difference between a snubber and a hazer. His greenhorn announcer performed miserably, and his contract acts—the trick ropers, knife throwers, and whipcrackers—were second-rate at best.

Worst of all, the entire rodeo turned into a scheduling disaster. Forced to pull out in the middle of the night, Louise and George felt no compunction about taking their meticulously planned schedule with them. Ty McCall was left with no option but to improvise a schedule each day. Confusion reigned everywhere—from the contestants who weren't sure when their events would be called, to the stock contractor who didn't know whether to send out bronchos or bulls, to the audience whose programs rarely reflected reality. The rodeo committee was roundly criticized for dumping Louise Morris's All-American Roundup, but, in the end, the committee's goal was achieved—none of the stars, with the exception of Louise Morris herself, walked out.

On the final day of the rodeo, Lael waited behind the chutes for the cowgirls' broncho riding event to begin. Reflecting on the past chaotic week, she had to admit that, by and large, it had been good to her. She had won two go-rounds in the steer riding and would take home some money for relay riding as well. Her trick riding was improving, and she hoped to place second or third in that event. Not bad, considering she was up against some of the biggest names in female professional rodeo. Her performance this week would get her talked about in rodeo circles. She was on her way.

Tempering all this good news was her disappointment that Louise Morris's company had gotten kicked out. It had all happened so fast that, by the time she heard the news, the Morris outfit had left town. Lael regretted missing the opportunity to get to know the famous cowgirl better, and her brother, too, who had been so nice to her. There was some consolation in the knowledge that the rodeo world was a small one. Surely she would run into the Morrises again.

Glancing down the fence line, Lael watched as Fanny Lavelle slowly lowered herself onto the back of a mustard-colored broncho. Since their run-in over Curtis Morris, the two women had been cool toward each other. Despite her general live and let live outlook, Lael disapproved of Fanny's loose conduct, concerned that it cast all cowgirls in a bad light. There was something about Fanny, though, that didn't fit the chippy stereotype—an earnestness that belied her carefully crafted cynicism—but Lael was too busy to puzzle over it.

Fanny's broncho rattled the rails of the chute, tossing its big head and rolling the whites of its eyes.

"Looks like you got yourself a wild one there," said the

snubber, assisting the red-headed cowgirl. "You want I should hobble the stirrups?"

Fanny shook her head. "Can't afford to lose the points."

Just then, the broncho pitched to the side, painfully pinning the cowgirl's leg against the rough planks. Bracing himself, the snubber planted his boots on the animal's backside and pushed it away from the wall. "You ain't careful, you're gonna lose your life on this rank piece of shit," he grunted.

For just a second, Lael saw a look of fear and uncertainty flash across Fanny's face. Lael knew that feeling, although for her it always vanished the moment the gate banged open. But Fanny, her wide eyes now fixed on the bronchos flattened ears, said in a nervous voice: "I changed my mind. Hobble 'em."

"You sure?" the snubber asked.

She swallowed and nodded vigorously.

Lael looked away, trying to restrain herself from marching over there and telling Fanny what a fool she was. Riding with hobbled stirrups—stirrups tied together beneath the horse's belly—was like bargaining with the devil. While it made it easier to stick in the saddle, if one did get bucked off the likelihood of getting a foot stuck in the stirrups was magnified ten times. By choosing to ride hobbled, Fanny was increasing her chances of staying on the horse, but at a dangerous cost. Riding "slick"—without hobbles—required more skill and was, therefore, worth more points. And if a slick rider left her seat, odds are she would be thrown free.

Working quickly, the snubber fitted a piece of rawhide through both stirrups and underneath the jittery horse, strapping it to the cinch to hold it tightly in place. Fanny worked her boots into the snugly tied stirrups, scrunched her seat down into the saddle, and grabbed the braided halter rope. As the gate slammed open and the broncho sprang into the arena, whiplashing Fanny from side to side, Lael heard the befuddled announcer introduce the rider as Lael Buckley of Fort Worth, Texas. Not for the first time this week, Lael rolled her eyes at the incompetence of the new production company.

Meanwhile, Fanny's broncho was doing its best to earn a reputation as a widow maker. It pitched and rolled violently, sunfishing into the air with wicked thrusts of its powerful hind legs. Lael could tell immediately that Fanny had no chance of staying on, and sure enough, with one particularly nasty buck, the cowgirl lost her seat. But instead of sailing clear, her foot caught in the hobbled stirrup, and for a few endless seconds she was dragged behind the enraged animal, flipping like a rag doll until, with an audible snap, her foot broke free from the stirrup.

Lael watched in dismay as Fanny lay in the dirt, not moving, her lower leg twisted at an unnatural angle to her body. As the announcer blathered on stupidly—"Don't worry, folks, this kind of thing happens all the time in broncho riding, and I personally know this little lady is a tough cookie. Let's hear it for Lael Buckley!"—several cowboys rushed to Fanny's side and placed her gently on a stretcher. Lael would have followed them to the medical room, but she was up next, and she knew she must honor rodeo's show-must-go-on tradition.

She rode slick, of course, getting in as many good licks with her spurs as she could. Her movements were almost instinctive by now, and, although Fanny's accident had dallied with her concentration, she rode the broncho to the buzzer and slid smoothly onto the pick-up man's horse. Without waiting to hear her score, Lael raced off to find Fanny, not certain what she could do to help but knowing that, if it were she lying broken and injured, she would want a familiar face to comfort her.

Peering through the door of the makeshift doctor's office, she saw Fanny lying on a cot, moaning in pain, her face white and her red hair darkened with sweat. A grizzled old man who looked like he'd be more at home doctoring livestock than people stood over her, preparing a hypodermic needle. "This'll numb the pain there, doll, so's I can splint your leg. Then we'll get you to the hospital to get it set."

"Just hurry, Doc!" Fanny groaned.

Lael noticed several cowboys standing uselessly against the wall, including Roy, the man with whom Fanny had most recently shacked up. Not a one of them stepped forward to hold the stricken cowgirl's hand or wipe the sweat from her brow. As the doctor started removing the boot from her broken leg, Lael knelt by the cot and grasped Fanny's trembling hand.

The injured cowgirl turned to her with wide, dilated eyes. "Lael? That you? Oh, God, I've really done it now. Jesus, Doc, when's that shot gonna kick in?"

"Just lie still now, doll, this is gonna hurt a little," the doctor advised. Carefully he aligned the broken bones in Fanny's lower leg. She screamed in agony, squeezing Lael's hand until Lael started to worry about broken bones of her own. At last, the doctor finished. "That's a mighty bad fracture there, little lady. They'll be able to tell you for certain over to the hospital, but that there leg may never be the same."

Lael shot him an angry look. "Whatever happened to bedside manners? I'm sure Miss Lavelle will be just fine. Don't you worry now, Fanny. I'll go with you to the hospital. We'll make sure you get the best bone doctor in town."

Fanny attempted a woozy smile, finally feeling the effects of the shot. Lael stood and caught the eye of Roy who immediately glanced away.

"Why don't you come with me?" Lael said to him. "I'm sure it'd please Fanny to have you there."

Roy cleared his throat and stuck his hands in his back pockets, still refusing to meet her gaze. "I'd like to ma'am, but I'm up pretty soon in bronc' riding. Can't afford to miss that, seein' as I'm in the running for all-around. Fanny'd understand."

Purposefully she took Roy's arm and led him out into the hallway. "Listen, I know you and Fanny were kind of . . . together for the last month or so. Are you going to be able to take care of her when she gets out of the hospital?"

Roy looked at her, shocked. "Me? Take care of her? I can't do that! I'm riding the circuit for the next three months, maybe longer'n that if I head down toward Arizona this fall. I can't drag no gal with a broken leg around with me. Hell, I can barely afford to feed myself and my horse much less some . . . woman!"

"I see," Lael said icily. "So it's just fine to keep company with a lady as long as she's no trouble, but the minute there might be some responsibility involved, it's cut and run."

"That ain't no lady in there," Roy said matter-of-factly. "You and I both know what Fanny's game is, and she knows it, too. Sure, I've been paying her way and in return she . . . kept me happy. Well, the deal's off. She ain't gonna be keeping her end of the bargain no more, so, the way I see it, I'm off the hook." Emboldened by his frankness, Roy offered Lael a leering smile and reached out to fondle her arm. "The position's open if *you're* interested in applying."

Lael smacked his hand away, her eyes narrowed in disgust. "I'd rather die!" she declared.

Roy chuckled, unfazed by her rejection. "I wasn't really serious there, Ivy, ma'am. Everybody knows you're too high and mighty to hang out with a simple cowpoke like me." He eyed her up and down appreciatively. "It sure is a god-damned shame, though." Shaking his head, Roy strolled off, leaving Lael fuming in his wake.

Just then, Roger rushed up, the scared look on his face turning to relief when he saw Lael standing whole by the door. "What happened? I heard you got thrown. They said you were hurt pretty badly."

"It wasn't me. It was my friend Fanny. The announcer mixed up our names. She's got a broken leg." Lael surprised herself with her spontaneous description of Fanny Lavelle as her friend.

"Thank God," Roger breathed. "I don't know how I'd have explained a broken leg to Pa."

"Well, I'm glad it wasn't me, too," admitted Lael, glancing back into the doctor's office as they prepared to move Fanny back onto the stretcher. "But it's a raw deal for poor Fanny. She's got no one to take care of her, no money, no way to support herself now. I don't think she has anywhere to go when she gets out of the hospital."

"Welcome to rodeo," said Roger sardonically.

"I know. But it's too bad. I wish there was something I could do to help her."

"She must have some family somewhere. Maybe you could contact them for her."

"If she does, they're all in Montana. She needs a family right here, right now, just like I have." Lael paused, a thought coming to her. "You know, Rog," she said, cocking her pretty blonde head, "if I'd gotten hurt somewhere far away, wouldn't you appreciate it if some nice family took me in until I was back on my feet?"

"Yes-s-s," Roger drawled warily. "What are you getting at?"

"Well . . . would you and Amy be willing to take Fanny in,

just for a few days? I know there isn't much space, but she could have my room, and I could move in with Molly. What do you say?"

Roger wilted under Lael's supplicating gaze. He had no desire to play nursemaid to one of Lael's rodeo friends, especially not one who looked, by the shade of her hair, to have been around the block a time or two. But he was essentially a kind man, and, besides, he'd been on the opposite side of an argument with Lael often enough to know what the likely outcome would be. Sighing, he acquiesced. "If Amy says it's OK. But only for a few days."

"Thanks, Rog," Lael beamed. "You're the best!"

Roger raised his eyes to the heavens. "Let's hope my wife thinks so."

Amy Buckley was not, in fact, pleased to have "that rodeo trash" under her roof but, besieged by her sister-in-law's pleading, agreed to it temporarily. She made Lael promise to find Fanny other arrangements as soon as possible which Lael undertook to do, writing to the Montana address Fanny gave her.

One afternoon, two days after Fanny had moved into the Buckley home, Lael entered the bedroom, carrying a tray with some soup and crackers. The doctors at the hospital had been more optimistic than the rodeo doctor, assuring their patient that her leg would heal properly, although it might never be as strong as before. Nevertheless, the leg was swollen and sore, and Fanny was in quite a bit of discomfort. She pushed up in the bed as Lael closed the door behind her.

"Here you are waiting on me again. I ain't never been so pampered!"

"You'd do the same for me," Lael smiled, setting the tray on the bedside table.

"Would I? I ain't so sure. I mean, you and me ain't exactly been bosom buddies. I know what you think of me . . . you told me flat out I make you sick."

Lael flushed, disturbed to hear her hasty words thrown back at her. "That was too harsh of me, Fanny. I hope you'll forgive me. The truth is, I don't know what to think of you. I don't know why you do what you do."

"You mean trade sex for a place to park my boots?" Fanny snorted, wincing as the sudden movement jostled her leg. She patted the side of the bed. "Sit down here, sister, and I'll tell you why."

Lael sank down, not sure she wanted to listen but unwilling to discourage her patient from opening up.

Fanny continued, a little tremor in her voice. "I ain't like you, Lael. Never was. I ain't all fresh and clean and hopeful. I was dirty from the day I was born, at least that's what Daddy told me. Said me and my brother was white trash just like Momma, who ran away and left us. Said the only thing I was good for was . . ."—Fanny swallowed hard but did not look up, mesmerized by her shaking hands—"was for a poke in the dark. And he, well, he did that to me more times than. . . ."

"Fanny," Lael interrupted, grabbing the wretched girl's hands. "Stop, please. I don't want to hear any more."

Fanny looked up apologetically. "Yeah, you're right. It don't do no good to remember. Don't do no good to feel sorry for yourself."

"You have every right in the world to feel sorry for yourself. My God, the man ought to be thrown in jail!" Lael exclaimed angrily.

"That's where he is, last I heard," Fanny chuckled mirthlessly. "You ain't likely to get a response from that address I gave you. Far as I know, he ain't lived there in years."

"What about your brother?"

"He died in the war."

"Oh, Fanny, I'm so sorry." Lael's eyes filled with tears.

Fanny shrugged, her well-worn mantle of hardness settled back on her.

"So you must have left home at an early age," Lael prompted.

"Fourteen. Ran away with the first man I could find who turned out to be the drunkenest cowpuncher ever rode the range. He dumped me somewhere in Idaho, so I found me another man and then another. You get the picture. Somewhere along the way I figured out that rodeos were a prime place for finding unattached men . . . men without roots, like me. I could do a little riding and roping, enough to not get myself killed anyway, so I joined the circuit. Easy men, easy money when I could bribe the judges with a little . . . you know."

"But why?" Lael asked. "Why bribe the judges? You're a good rider. You've got a lot of style. Why not take your chances on getting high scores legitimately?"

"Don't make me laugh," said Fanny scornfully. "I'm not really any good, and you know it. Oh, I've picked up a thing or two, enough to keep from embarrassing myself, but I'm not good enough to win any money. You want to know the truth of it, honey, rodeo don't treat women like it does men. For a cowgirl to win enough money to keep riding the circuit, she's either got to be one of the stars, the *crème de la crème* so to speak, or she's got to hook up with a man. That's why so many of 'em are married to cowboys. They can pool their earnings and share road expenses that way."

Lael knit her brow, instinctively wanting to deny the truth of Fanny's words, but unable to do so. She had, indeed, noticed that most of her female colleagues were married to rodeo cowboys, although many of those unions seemed less than harmonious. It had not occurred to her that some of them may have been marriages of convenience only.

"Fanny," Lael said, getting up to pace the room, "why does it have to be a man and a woman sharing expenses? Why couldn't two women travel together, sharing expenses and pooling their income?"

"They could, I guess, long as they didn't mind what people said about 'em."

"Well, I don't mind what people say. I used to, but no more. How about it? Should we be partners?" Lael paused at the foot of the bed, her eyes alight with the possibilities.

"It'd never work," Fanny scoffed.

"Why not?" Lael demanded.

"A million reasons, not the least of which is that you'd be making all the money. How long would it be before you'd get tired of supporting little old me? At least with a man I got something to offer that he needs. But unless you really got me fooled, I don't think you'd need me for anything like that."

"Fanny, you're awful!" Lael reddened, laughing in spite of herself. "I do need you. I need a traveling companion. If you and I traveled together, I wouldn't have to stay in hotels . . . I could stay in a tent on the rodeo grounds like everyone else. We could help each other with all the little chores . . . laundry, cooking, that type of thing."

"Oh, honey," Fanny sighed, "I know you mean well, but don't fool yourself. You don't need me. Remember, I said there were two types of women who could make it in rodeo . . . married women and the stars? Well, sugar pie, that's what you are . . . a star. Maybe your star's still rising, maybe not everybody's seen it yet, but there ain't nobody on the Texas circuit who don't know it. You're headed for the big time, Lael. You don't need me for one damn' thing." Fanny laid her head back on the pillows, exhausted from the conversation.

Lael stood quietly, letting Fanny's words sink in. Then she came around the bed and took her friend's hands again. "The company took up a collection for you. It isn't much, but it ought to get you through the summer. Of course, you can stay here until you have somewhere else to go."

"Which won't be any too soon for your sister-in-law, will it?" Drained, Fanny closed her eyes, feeling more tired than she ever had in her life. "Don't worry. I know somebody who'll take me in. And if he doesn't, well. . . ." Fanny gave Lael a half-hearted smile. "It won't be the first time Fanny Lavelle's been on her own."

Chapter Eleven

New York City. The Big Apple. Gotham on the Hudson. The Metropolis of Mankind. No matter what you called it, it was bound to be busier, noisier, ruder, and more exciting than anywhere else Lael Buckley had ever been. She couldn't wait.

As the special train chartered by Tex Austin to bring his staff and contestants to New York for the first ever Madison Square Garden rodeo pulled into Pennsylvania Station, a hum of anticipation, as real as the smell of dung that wafted up from the stock cars, permeated the train's luxurious passenger compartments. Although many of these cowboys and cowgirls had toured the Eastern seaboard in Wild West shows or small-time rodeos, today's arrival presaged a significant moment for the rodeo world, a fact that was lost on nobody. If the upcoming event at the Garden, that mecca of American sport, was successful, rodeo would enter the big leagues as it never had before, attracting media attention, fans, corporate sponsorships, and big money.

It would not be easy. New York had a checkered history when it came to the support of rodeo. Only six years ago, in 1916, another famous promoter, Guy Weadick, had brought his Stampede to the Sheepshead Bay Speedway. Lack of publicity, a streetcar strike, and an outbreak of polio had kept the crowds away in droves, and many of the contestants had gone home empty-handed, the producer too broke to pay them. Not to be deterred, Tex Austin was counting on a healthier, more prosperous post-war populace, enamored by the glamorous cowboy of Hollywood movies, to fill the arena for ten days of rock 'em, sock 'em action.

All of this ran through Lael's mind as the train slowly wound its way through the dark tunnels beneath the streets of the city. When Austin had signed her to the show, he had been very clear about what he expected of her. As one of rodeo's better-known, most successful cowgirls—he stopped short of calling her a star—she must be available for all promotional appearances—always attired in her finest rodeo garb—must accede to all interview requests, and must make every effort to be seen by the public. Lael had agreed to these conditions with no qualms. After all, she wanted the Madison Square Garden rodeo to succeed as much as anyone.

For there was now no question in her mind, if there ever had been, that rodeo was to be her career, her life. During the last two years she had achieved phenomenal success, not only in small-town events, but at places like Cheyenne, Calgary, and Pendleton as well. Her earnings to date amounted to over six thousand dollars and could have been even more had her parents allowed her to join the 101 Wild West Show during the off-season. But in return for their approval of her chosen profession, they insisted that she return to Fort Worth to earn her associate's degree at the business college so she "would have something to fall back on" when her rodeo career was over. Although Lael could not envision such a time, she had agreed, happy to have the peace of mind that making peace with her parents gave her.

So she was coming to New York a rising young star, well known in the world of rodeo but not yet having crossed the threshold into national prominence. She smiled as she thought of the train ride she had taken to her first rodeo as a professional cowgirl in Abilene, Texas. She had been nervous and frightened until, glancing out the window, she had seen the young girl racing the train and had remembered all the reasons why she was on this journey—the thrill of adventure, the love of competition, the freedom of the road. And then she had disembarked and her hat had blown off and her life had changed in a way she had not thought possible.

The rodeo world was a small one, and she had criss-crossed it extensively for the past two years, but she had never again run into, or heard tell of, Rafe Callantine. It seemed as though he had dropped out of that world completely, leaving no trace that he had ever been part of it. Lael had tried to accept it and move on, had even gone out with a young man from Fort Worth for a time. But there were still moments when some small something—a whiff of whisky, a rakishly cocked hat, a pair of rough, work-worn hands—would bring it all back, and a heavy sadness would settle on her.

The train came to a halt. Lael rose abruptly, determined to keep her thoughts of Rafe at bay. She turned to reach for her valise from the overhead compartment. Suddenly, the train lurched backward, and Lael lost her balance, falling into a pair of strong, leather-clad arms. She caught sight of dark hair and square shoulders, and her heart lurched along with the train, fooling her for just an instant into thinking the impossible. But then the stranger spoke, and once again her hopes were dashed, just as they had been countless times before when she had seen some figure reminiscent of Foster Davis's former wrangler.

"Careful there, miss," her rescuer said, standing her upright. Lael looked up into the smooth, handsome face of Curtis Morris. "Why, it's Miss Buckley, isn't it? My goodness, it's nice to see you again!"

"And you, too, Curtis. Thanks for catching me."

Curtis tipped his hat, grinning awkwardly.

"How is it we're only now running into each other?" Lael went on. "I thought I knew everyone on this train."

"Louise and I boarded in Saint Louis yesterday. Lou isn't feeling too great, so we stuck to our compartment. If I'd known you were on board, though, you can bet I'd have looked you up! I've heard a lot about you in the last couple of years, Miss Buckley . . . there's nothing I'd like better than to hear your story straight from the horse's mouth. Or, well . . . you know what I mean."

Lael laughed, amused by his earnestness.

"Curtis, give me a hand with this satchel." Louise Morris duck-walked up the narrow aisle, a heavy suitcase held in front of her.

Lael barely restrained a gasp of surprise, so unexpected was the older woman's appearance. Curtis's comment that his sister wasn't feeling well had suggested a mild malady, but this woman looked like she was suffering something far more serious. Her skin was dry and sallow, dark circles surrounded her red-rimmed eyes, and her silk blouse hung from sharp-edged shoulder blades.

Curtis reached for the suitcase and tucked one hand protectively under his sister's elbow. "Lou," he spoke as if to a child, "you remember Lael Buckley, don't you?"

Lael could see the older woman searching her memory, coming up blank. Nevertheless, she smiled gamely. "Of course. It's been a while."

"Two years. We met at the Fort Worth Fat Stock Show my rookie season." Too late, Lael realized her error in bringing up the occasion of their last meeting—that disastrous week when Louise's company had gotten the boot. The older woman's smile faded, her eyes went blank, and her thoughts turned inward.

Lael struggled to recover. "Curtis told me you were a bit

under the weather. I certainly hope you feel better by opening day . . . the New York crowds would surely hate to miss seeing America's Cowgirl!"

Louise's head started to shake with a slight tremor.

Tucking her arm firmly under his, Curtis nodded to Lael. "Thank you, Miss Buckley, she'll be fine. If you'll excuse us, we'd best be going now."

Lael stood aside to let them pass. When they reached the end of the car and were about to exit the sliding glass door, Curtis turned around and, looking over all the people milling in the aisle, gave Lael the softest, most hopeful smile she had ever seen.

Louise sat at the vanity in her hotel room, staring at her reflection in the mirror. It seemed as though the person that stared back was not someone she really knew. When had the skin beneath her eyes started to sag? When had those wrinkles at the corners of her mouth appeared? She pulled at the tie of her robe and let it drop below her shoulders. How long had her collar bone stuck out like that? Taking a deep breath, she reached for her powder puff. Her hand shook.

Exasperated, she whirled around in her seat, no longer able to look at this ruined version of herself. It wasn't like she had had a choice, after all; every one of those wrinkles had been earned. She had worked outside in the sun and wind and dust since childhood, and there had always been the burden of dealing with her demented mother and overbearing father. Now there was the added strain of keeping the secret from Curtis. It was no wonder she needed a little pick-me-up now and then. Not a thing wrong with that.

Made bold by self-justification, she moved urgently to her trunk and fished around in a drawer. Nothing. She tried another and another, frantically dumping their contents on the floor. "That little shit!" she cried, rocking back on her heels. Although she couldn't prove it, she was certain Curtis had once again disposed of her secret stash. Dropping her head in her hands, she rubbed her forehead vigorously, trying to wipe away this urge for a drink, just one lousy drink. It was no good, and she knew it. It had been some time since she had been able to talk herself out of giving in.

Then a thought came to her. Curtis could not possibly have searched her private reticule, and, if she was not mistaken, there was a little something cached away there. Ripping open the bag, she found the precious bottle, poured two fingers, and tossed it back in one gulp. A delicious, calm warmth seeped through her nerve-jangled body. Her head fell back as she luxuriated in the feeling of regained control. Pouring another drink, she crossed to the window and looked down on Broadway, the cars weaving this way and that, like busy little black ants. It was a long way down. What if she just opened the window and stepped out on the ledge and. . . .

Don't be ridiculous! Have you forgotten that your one goal in life is to outlive Big Jack so that one day you and Cory can be together? That was truly all she lived for now. In the aftermath of the Fort Worth fiasco, Louise Morris's All-American Roundup had collapsed. Then her mother had died, and when she and Curtis had returned to the ranch for the funeral, seeing him and Alice together, so alike in ways she had never noticed before, was almost unbearable. Big Jack had blamed her for Fort Worth, and there had been a big row. She had left in anger, intending to go to Chicago to visit Cory. But, afraid that her son would spurn the love of a mother whom he barely knew and no longer able to offer him the excitement of touring with her now-defunct rodeo company, she had made it only as far as St. Louis. There, she had taken a small apartment and lived off her meager savings, discovering that her one true, devoted friend was the bottle.

That's where Curtis had found her, bringing with him the news that the famous producer, Tex Austin, was putting together a Madison Square Garden rodeo, and he wanted Louise Morris, America's Cowgirl, to be one of his headliners. Louise had protested that she hadn't picked up a rope or stepped into a saddle for over a year, but Curtis had brushed off her objections. Austin wanted her no matter what, he said, even if all she did was lead the grand entry. She had let herself be talked into it, although as she stood here this evening, enjoying a rare moment of clarity, she could not for the life of her understand why. The Madison Square Garden rodeo mattered not one whit. Reclaiming the title of America's Cowgirl was the last thing she wanted. All she wanted now was to outlast Big Jack.

Raising her full glass to the New York skyline, Louise smiled and whispered: "I'll do it yet, you mean old bastard. Just wait and see."

Chapter Twelve

The taxi pulled up to the brownstone on East 55th and discharged its three occupants. Flashbulbs popped, and shouting reporters crowded around elegantly clad Mabel Strickland as her husband, Hugh, guided her to the door. Lael trailed behind, shouldering her way through the mob. The threesome made it to the front door and were admitted by a tuxedoed butler who relieved them of their wraps and asked if they cared to freshen up before joining the party. The ladies accepted his offer while Hugh agreed to meet them upstairs.

Once inside the exquisitely finished lounge, with its polished marble sinks, gleaming brass fixtures, and delicately filigreed mirrors, Mabel turned to Lael with a wry smile. "Sorry about that zoo out there, honey. Hope you didn't get run over in the stampede."

"Not at all. I'm just glad I was able to bask in a little of your reflected glory," Lael teased.

"Go on with ya," scoffed Mabel, patting a dark curl back in place.

Lael adjusted the bodice of her velvet evening gown, the first and only such gown she had ever owned. It was colored a deep emerald green and brought out her eyes most becomingly. Lael was pleased Tex Austin had included her on the guest list for this affair, a dinner for rodeo participants given by Mrs. William Hamilton, chairwoman of the Argonne Association. In order to gain publicity, Austin had arranged for some of the profits from the contest to go to this organization of Manhattan socialites who raised funds for French war orphans.

"Don't be modest, Mabel," Lael said. "Face it, most New Yorkers wouldn't know Lael Buckley from Annie Oakley. But they know who you are . . . the winner of the McAlpin Trophy . . . the champion all-around cowgirl at Cheyenne Frontier Days."

"I s'pose you're right. I'm just a little nervous, I guess. I ain't never been to a fancy shindig like this before. What if I do something awful, like use the wrong fork or choke on an olive pit?"

"Listen to you!" Lael laughed. "This from a woman who rides bucking bronchos to a standstill? Come on, sweetie, let's knock 'em dead!"

Linking arms, the two cowgirls, feeling like Cinderellas at the ball, climbed the wide, red-carpeted stairway to the Hamiltons' elegant sitting room. Lael relinquished Mabel to Hugh, a champion broncho rider and steer roper in his own right, and joined a group that included Tex Austin, arena director Frank Hafley, and the evening's hostess, Mrs. Hamilton, a chic, slender woman, sporting the latest bobbed hairstyle. A waiter took their drink orders, and Lael, following her hostess' lead, asked for a glass of champagne. Prohibition did not appear to be in effect in Upper East Side salons.

Austin was explaining to Mrs. Hamilton how they had adapted their show for New York audiences. "You see, ma'am, out West a rodeo might last all day long what with all the contract acts and exhibitions in addition to the competitive events."

"Contract acts?" Mrs. Hamilton asked, leaning forward to let Austin light her cigarette in its long holder.

"Yes, ma'am, like knife throwing or fancy roping. Acts just for the audience's entertainment. But we figured New Yorkers might be looking for a little faster-paced show, so we pared down the number of events, particularly ones like relay racing that don't work so well in an indoor arena."

"I see," said Mrs. Hamilton, although Lael got the distinct impression this woman wouldn't know a relay race from a potato sack race. Mrs. Hamilton puffed in Lael's direction. "And is this charming young lady one of your contestants, Mister Austin?"

"Yes, ma'am, this is Lael Buckley, one of rodeo's newest sensations."

"Such a petite thing," Mrs. Hamilton said, giving Lael's fingers a light squeeze. "It's rather difficult to picture you flailing around on one of those mammoth beasts."

"I try to keep the flailing to a minimum," smiled Lael.

"But look at you. That beautiful golden hair and creamy complexion. Why, you're just a little porcelain doll, my dear."

Lael laughed nervously, unaccustomed to such praise. All in all, she'd rather be called a tough-as-nails rodeo jock.

"I can't argue with your conclusion, ma'am, but take it on my authority, Miss Buckley's not as fragile as she appears." The group turned to admit Curtis Morris, resplendent in a Western-cut tuxedo and lizard-skin boots. "Rodeo folk are a tough lot . . . they have to be."

"Of course. I only meant how charming it is to see such a lovely young woman as a representative of your sport. Why, you could have a career in pictures, my dear. I can just see you starring with that man, what's his name . . . Tom Mix? Now if you'll excuse me, I'll see how the kitchen is doing."

"She's right, you know," Curtis said, drawing Lael to a private corner of the room. "You could be in pictures."

"I don't think so. Not my style." Lael sipped her champagne and regarded Curtis warily. She remembered that two years ago he had seemed somewhat smitten with her, and she wondered if time had dulled his interest. Surprising herself, she realized she hoped not. Of all the cowboys she had met, including Rafe Callantine, *especially* Rafe Callantine, Curtis was the smoothest, most well-spoken, most gentlemanly of all. Why shouldn't she want him to like her?

"You sound just like my sister," said Curtis, shaking his head in dismay. "Always bad-mouthing Hollywood. For my money, it's the greatest thing to ever happen to rodeo. Do you think there'd be a McAlpin Trophy or a Madison Square Garden . . . do you think we'd be standing in some Manhattan socialite's drawing room without Hollywood? 'Course not. Fellas like Tom Mix and Broncho Billy and gals like Texas Guinan have made all of us seem glamorous."

"That's just it! Hollywood paints a pretty picture, but it's so unrealistic. Rodeo isn't glamorous. It's hot, dirty, sweaty, back-breaking work! The public can't appreciate the difficulty of what we do when all it sees is Texas Guinan in her brand new ten-gallon hat and spotless jodhpurs prancing around on some poor horse whose front end she probably can't recognize!" Lael's cheeks flushed as she made her point. Tantalized, Curtis moved in closer, bracing his hand on the wall behind her.

"You don't strike me as the naïve sort, Miss Buckley"—Lael raised a warning finger—"sorry . . . Lael. Don't you know people want it to be all white hats and shiny stars? For the hero to always beat the villain and get the gal to boot? Happy endings sell. Clean cowboys sell. So what if Texas Guinan can't ride worth a damn? That's where someone like you comes in. Though frankly, you're far too pretty to be anyone's stunt double."

By this time, Curtis's face was so close to hers, she could smell the expensive bourbon he was drinking. It was a sweet, heavy, masculine smell that was not at all offensive.

"So you really think more people will come to see our show just because they like movie cowboys?" Lael challenged.

"Absolutely. Tonight's proof of that."

"Hmm. I'm not so sure. One fancy dinner does not a successful rodeo make. If we sell out ten days' worth of shows, then I'll concede your point."

"Why, Miss Buckley, I thought you were from Nebraska, not the show-me state!"

Laughing together, Lael grew increasingly comfortable in the tall young man's company. Then Curtis caught sight of something over Lael's shoulder. His brows drew together in a frown. Lael turned and saw Louise Morris standing in the doorway, gorgeous, despite her sallow complexion and thin frame, in a high-necked, beaded black gown.

"Your sister is here," Lael said unnecessarily.

"So I see. Would you excuse me?" Touching Lael lightly on the elbow, Curtis moved smoothly across the room, managing to reach Louise before anyone else.

"What are you doing here?" he asked unceremoniously.

"I was invited to a dinner party, and I came. Is that so awful?"

"But you told me you weren't feeling well enough to come."

"I recovered," Louise said, blinking slowly as she scanned the room through heavily made-up eyes. Curtis had no doubt what had spawned her speedy recovery.

"Lou, this isn't a good idea. Why don't you let me take you back to the hotel?" Curtis tried to shepherd her backwards into the hallway, but Louise shook him off.

"For God's sake, Curtis, stop acting like my nursemaid. I'm perfectly all right." Louise snagged a glass of champagne

Spotting

from a passing tray. "Now scoot. You're cramping my style."

Curtis stood back helplessly as Louise glided over to greet Mabel and Hugh Strickland. He knew exactly what would happen if he didn't somehow get his sister away from here. At the moment, the alcohol coursing through Louise's veins was propping her up—making her feel glib and energized. But a few more drinks, and it would all come crashing down. He couldn't let that happen. Not here, at a New York society dinner where there were doubtless reporters lurking behind the potted palms.

Spotting Tex Austin across the room, Curtis decided to enlist the rodeo producer's aid. Just then, a white-gloved butler appeared and invited the guests to follow him into the dining room, where dinner was about to be served. Curtis managed to whisper his problem in Austin's ear, but, by then, it was too late. Louise was entering the dining room on the arm of their host, William Hamilton. Tex shrugged his broad shoulders and clapped Curtis on the back. He had no idea how bad this was.

Meanwhile, Lael found herself seated between Hugh Strickland and a pudgy man with frayed cuffs, whom she couldn't place. He was certainly no cowboy, yet with his shabby appearance he could not possibly be one of the society guests. The mystery was solved when he introduced himself as Peter McCaskill with the *New York Herald*.

"A reporter?" Lael asked.

"Yes. Does that make you nervous?"

"Should it?"

"I hope so. People trying to hide things make good copy."

"Well, you'll be sorely disappointed with me as a dinner partner, then. I have absolutely nothing to hide." Lael picked up her spoon and began sipping her soup delicately.

McCaskill trained a curious eye on her. "As the paper's society reporter, I thought I'd met most of New York's finest. But I don't believe we've been introduced."

Lael dabbed her mouth with her linen napkin and gave the reporter a feigned look of injury. "Don't tell me you've forgotten, sir!"

McCaskill half turned in his seat and took in the beautiful young woman next to him—thick blonde hair pulled back with a jeweled barrette from which tiny wisps had escaped to play about her face, huge eyes that were somewhere between gray and green and were like no color he'd ever seen, full, pink lips that turned down slightly at the corners in what he took to be an expression of dismay. The heat rose in him as he abandoned his carefully acquired reporter's neutrality and gave in to a feeling that was a combination of attraction and embarrassment. "It does not seem remotely possible that I could have forgotten you, miss. Please enlighten me, I beg you."

Lael's frown turned to a dazzling grin, and her eyes sparkled merrily. Stunned by the force of her smile, McCaskill fell back against his chair, his heart pounding.

"Gotcha!" said Lael with a wink, an affectation he normally found contrived and annoying but which in her seemed genuine and endearing.

"I . . . I beg your pardon?" he stuttered.

Lael laughed and leaned in conspiratorially.

He caught a whiff of delicate perfume and thought his racing heart would leap right out of his chest.

"Don't let this get around," she said in a stage whisper, "but I'm not one of New York's finest. I may not even be one of Nebraska's finest, though I'm not real sure what it takes to win that honor."

"Nebraska?" he repeated, as though he had never heard the word. "I'm afraid I'm lost."

Lael held out her hand. "Lael Buckley, native of Nebraska, late of Fort Worth, Texas. I'm here with the rodeo, and I was pulling your leg earlier. We've never met before."

McCaskill shook her hand limply and gave her a look of relief. "Thank God. I was beginning to think my powers of observation had deserted me completely. But you can hardly blame me. You certainly don't look the rodeo type."

"What exactly does the rodeo type look like?"

"Well, I pictured someone bigger, tougher, more hardened than you appear to be, Miss Buckley."

Lael sighed inwardly, wondering if this masculine image of cowgirls was universally held by New Yorkers. Biting back a smart retort, she leaned her head to one side and batted her eyes prettily. "I'm just tough enough to get the job done and no tougher. And truth to tell, bigger isn't necessarily better in rodeo. A smaller person often has the advantage in certain events."

"Really? This is quite interesting. Do you mind if I take notes?" McCaskill said, pulling a steno pad from his breast pocket.

Across the table, the sound of a woman's high-pitched laughter, shrill and out of control, caught the room's attention. Lael looked up to see Louise Morris, her arm draped cozily around the shoulders of the man seated next to her, raise a tumbler of brown liquid to her lips. Still chuckling as she drank, some drops dribbled down her chin and spilled on the front of her dress. Oblivious to the sudden quiet around the table, Louise set her glass down, knocking it against her china plate as she did so, and leaned over to whisper some confidence in her somewhat chagrined dinner partner's ear.

As Louise's outburst subsided, the hum of dinner conversation returned. Lael caught Curtis's eye and offered him a sympathetic look. He dropped his eyes and stared at his plate, debating whether trying to remove Louise from the room would improve or worsen the situation.

"Isn't that Louise Morris?" asked Peter McCaskill, casually spearing a piece of lettuce.

"Yes," Lael replied carefully, noting the pad and pencil sitting next to his coffee cup. He had written her name down, the first name spelled L-a-l-e with a question mark after it. "Incidentally, my name is spelled L-a-e-l."

He corrected his notation and then glanced over at Louise again who was instructing the waiter to bring her another bourbon. His reporter's instincts aroused, he turned to Lael and offered her a chummy smile. "America's Cowgirl appears to be a bit pickled, wouldn't you say?"

Lael set her fork down and lowered her lashes. When she looked up again, a hint of a tear brimmed in her large, emerald eyes. "Mister McCaskill," she said fervently, "Louise Morris has done more for the sport of rodeo than any one person I can think of. Almost single-handedly, she took us from the era of the Wild West show into the realm of true competition. She proved to people that rodeo is as much about athleticism as it is entertainment. She pioneered many of the production techniques that you'll see on display at the Garden. She made it possible for women like me to have a career in rodeo, and for that I will be forever grateful. I do hope you will have it in your heart to ignore any personal failings of Miss Morris and to make note only of her many positive contributions to rodeo."

Thoroughly taken in by Lael's earnest petition, McCaskill reached out to cover her firm young hand with his own plump fingers. "Beautifully said, Miss Buckley. If you don't mind my saying so, not only do you not look like a cowgirl, you don't speak like one, either. I haven't heard one y'all or reckon so out of you yet. Are all Nebraska girls so refined?"

Pleased to have redirected his attention, Lael refrained from pulling her hand from underneath his hot, sweaty palm. "Some are, I'm sure. Most wouldn't give two hoots about such *refinement* as you call it. It's not considered to be much of an asset where I come from."

"Tell me about it. In fact, Miss Buckley, tell me all about yourself."

For the next half hour Lael talked, not entirely comfortable confiding her life story to a newspaper reporter, but aware that every minute she kept McCaskill focused on her was a minute he would not have to think about poor Louise Morris. He filled two pages with notes before dessert arrived. She had just finished describing how she performed a Russian drag, one of her more difficult tricks, when Louise's shrill laugh once again cut through the dinner conversation. Every pair of eyes in the room turned to the former champion cowgirl as her laugh reached a crescendo and then was abruptly cut off as her face plunged directly into her raspberry chocolate truffle cake.

The sun was not yet shining through her hotel room window when Lael was awakened by a soft but persistent knocking at the door. Stealing a sleepy glance at the alarm clock by her bed, she was surprised to see it was already nine o'clock in the morning. Then she remembered that, blocked by skyscrapers up and down Broadway, the sunshine wouldn't penetrate her room until close to noon. Swinging her feet out of bed, she pushed one arm into her old flannel wrapper and called: "Who is it?"

"Curtis Morris," came the reply.

Lael paused halfway to the door. She couldn't see Curtis Morris looking like this! "I'm just out of bed. Could you give me a few minutes?"

"I'm sorry to bother you so early, but I've got something to show you."

His voice sounded urgent. Lael threw a glance at herself in the dresser mirror, picked up her hairbrush, and then, realizing it was hopeless, put it down again. Tightening the belt of her wrapper, she wished she had been able to afford the beautiful silk peignoir she had seen at the shop where she had bought the evening gown she wore last night. Shaking her head at her own vanity, she opened the door to admit Curtis who, as usual, looked fresh and dapper. Dancing into the room, he tossed a newspaper onto her dressing table and grabbed her waist with both hands.

"Thank you, thank you, thank you! Let me say it again . . . thank you! I could kiss you . . . and I think I will!"

Horrified at the notion, given that she hadn't even had time to brush her teeth, Lael leaned away and held up a hand to fend him off. "You're welcome. What did I do?"

Grinning from ear to ear, Curtis released her and picked up the paper he had brought. "Look at that!" he exclaimed, pointing to a story on the front page of the second section. LADYLIKE BRONCHO BUSTER CHARMS NEW YORK SOCIETY, Lael read, and below that in smaller type: Meet 'Ivy League,' Rodeo's Cultivated Cowgirl. Atop the headline was a picture of Lael in her evening gown, snapped as she descended the Hamiltons' elegant staircase.

"Oh, my," Lael breathed, noting without surprise Peter McCaskill's byline on the story.

"Oh, my, indeed! I don't know how you did it . . . well, yes I do, come to think of it. What man wouldn't be so engrossed in you at a dinner party that he could totally ignore everything going on around him? But still, you didn't have to do it . . . didn't have to open yourself up to him like you did. But you knew you were giving him a great hook for his story, a better hook than writing about Louise, so you did it. And these comments about Louise!" Curtis quoted from the paper:

> "Miss Buckley had nothing but praise for another of the evening's attendees, Louise Morris, fondly known as America's Cowgirl. 'Miss Morris is one of rodeo's pioneers,' said the refined young woman. 'She has proven that rodeo performers are athletes as much as entertainers.' "

"Perfect, absolutely perfect! Austin's so impressed he's talking about you and Louise leading the grand entry together."

"I'm glad it worked out," Lael smiled. "How is Louise this morning?"

Curtis's face dropped. Shrugging, he threw the paper onto the unmade bed and looked out the window, his hands jammed at his waist. "I haven't seen her yet this morning, but it won't be pretty." He paused, then went on quietly. "I don't know what happened, I mean, what happened to turn her into this pathetic . . . I might as well say it . . . she's a drunk. Sometimes I feel like I'm the only thing standing between her and the gutter. And I don't know why. Sure she took a hit when we got kicked out of Fort Worth, but she's been through worse things than that and bounced back. It's like she just gave up."

Touched by his concern, Lael came up behind him and put a hand on his rigid back. "Don't blame yourself, Curtis. Sometimes people don't behave the way we want them to, no matter now hard we wish it." *People like Rafe Callantine,* she thought unhappily.

He turned to look at her—face scrubbed clean of make-up, hair all askew, wrapped in an old, threadbare robe.

Over her head, he saw her rumpled bed, probably still warm from where she had lain. Without thinking, he bent his head and gently touched his lips to hers. Jarred by the sudden familiarity so soon on the heels of her thoughts of Rafe, Lael pulled away abruptly.

Embarrassed and angry at himself for rushing things, Curtis looked at her ruefully. "Think of that as a thank you kiss."

Lael managed a polite smile, and Curtis took his leave, promising her a night out on the town whenever she was in the mood. Closing the door behind him, Lael crawled back into bed and picked up the cast-off newspaper. The picture of her was quite flattering. She wished she knew where to find Rafe so she could send it to him.

"Damn!" she cried, throwing the paper across the room and curling into a ball. She would not think about him. She would not care about him. She would not!

Chapter Thirteen

Madison Square Garden was good to Lael. Although she lost the trick riding championship to Mabel Strickland, she took the broncho riding title and its four hundred dollar prize. Curtis's prediction that the show would sell out came to pass; by the end of the run, they were turning people away. Tex Austin took every opportunity to showcase his bright young star, the Cultivated Cowgirl, although Lael drew the line at his suggestion that she wear evening attire while parading in the grand entry.

True to his word, Curtis treated her to dinner at Delmonico's, but by mutual consent the evening ended early. Curtis felt obliged to check up on Louise, and Lael was tired after a full day of competition, or at least that was the excuse she gave. It was not that she didn't enjoy the handsome Texan's company. But she was still unnerved by the kiss he had stolen and the way he had looked at her in her tattered old robe—as though he could well imagine what was underneath the flimsy garment.

Later, back in her hotel room, she chastised herself for being such a cold fish. Here she was in the most exciting city in the world and she was spending every night playing solitaire in her room. So the next day, she asked Curtis if he would mind escorting her again that evening.

"Mind? It would be my pleasure!" he replied, grinning ear to ear. For the rest of their run, the obliging cowboy squired her about the city, to speakeasies and supper clubs, on carriage rides through Central Park, on strolls down Fifth Avenue. Often they were accompanied by Mabel and Hugh or some other rodeo couple, and Lael got a taste of what it felt like to be part of a twosome. It wasn't all bad. In fact, it was right nice and convenient as hell. Curtis made all the arrangements and insisted on paying all of their tabs, although Lael threw in some money whenever she could get away with it. She liked the feeling of having a protector in the big city, and she liked being able to giggle with the other girls about their men. It was all laughs and high spirits and gay times, until the end of the evening when they would return to the hotel and the married couples would disappear together into their rooms, sometimes barely concealing their anticipation. Lael and Curtis would be left standing at her door, awkward in their sudden solitude, Curtis clearly aching to be allowed into the inner sanctum. She let him kiss her, of course—she *wanted* him to kiss her—but that was all she wanted, and, to his credit, he didn't push for more.

Ten glorious days and then it was over. An exhausted troupe of rodeo folk, their fancy duds and shiny spurs packed away, boarded a train heading west. The Morrises were bound for St. Louis where Curtis intended to talk Louise into giving up her apartment and moving back to the ranch in Texas. Lael was headed for Fort Worth, at least until she decided how to spend the off-season. She had several offers from the Wild West shows, but for some reason had put off making a decision. Curtis made her promise to write him with her whereabouts for the winter. She did so reluctantly, not sure why it bothered her to be making promises.

Her dilemma was resolved when she reached Roger's house and found a letter from Fanny waiting. The red-headed cowgirl had kept in touch sporadically over the last two years. After recovering from her broken leg in Arizona, she had bounced around the Southwest, finding the odd rodeo job, but otherwise being rather secretive about how she earned her keep. The postmark on this letter was from Los Angeles.

Greetings, Ivy dearest. How do you like my imitation of a fancy lady? This gal, fancy or not, has landed in the land of milk and honey, and, honey, is it sweet! This is a cowgirl's paradise, and I don't mean because it is crawling with handsome cowboys (though it certainly is!). No, it's because of Hollywood. The studios are churning out a Western picture every five days (!) and that calls for lots of horses and riders. All you got to do is go down to Universal City in the morning and wait around to see how many extras they're going to need—it's usually however many show up—and then spend the day racing around the back lot. Five dollars a day plus lunch—the easiest money I ever made! One day, they chose me to be a stunt double for Lois Wilson and I got ten dollars!

Lael, you'd love it here! Not only do you get paid for riding a horse all day, but lots of times on the week-ends all the rodeo folks will get together for a little riding and roping. It's the most fun I ever had outside of a bedroom! I've got me a nice little apartment but I ain't used to living by myself. Why don't you come out here for the winter? You could earn a hell of a lot more than in any of them Wild West shows!

Lael tapped Fanny's letter against her chin, considering. Truthfully, she had not been looking forward to touring with a show all winter long. Having spent the last several months on the road, it would be nice to stay put for a while. And what better place to winter than sunny Southern California? Not that she was all that interested in being in the movies, but if what Fanny said was true—that you got paid to ride around on a horse all day—well, there were worse ways to make a living.

Thus it was that two weeks later, Lael Buckley arrived in the City of Angels, accompanied by her trick-riding horse, Dancer, two saddles, five trunks (three of which contained tack and other rodeo gear), and a lemon pound cake that Amy had insisted she carry halfway across the country to Fanny. That astonished young woman, when she saw Lael's load stacked on the train station platform, dropped her jaw in amazement.

"Maybe I forgot to mention it's a small apartment," Fanny said, eyeing Dancer in alarm.

Lael shrugged. "My days of traveling light are over. Here, take this." She shoved the pound cake at Fanny. "You have no idea what lengths I've gone to trying to keep this thing from getting smashed. It's a present from Amy."

Fanny held the cake like it was a brick of gold. "No kidding? I didn't think she liked me."

"Sure she does. Especially since you're responsible for getting me out of her hair for the winter!" Lael grinned.

A porter approached gingerly. "Need help with that luggage, miss?"

"You bet!" Lael pointed to the trunks. "These two go with us, the other stuff can go with Dancer in the trailer. Where is the trailer anyway, Fanny?"

"What trailer?"

"What trailer! The trailer I wrote you I'd need to take Dancer to the stables. You did arrange to stable him, didn't you?" Lael looked at her friend expectantly.

123

"Honey, I'm prepared to stable you and you alone. I don't know nothing about no horse!"

"But I wrote you, I'm sure I did." Lael sighed, shrugging out of her jacket in the heat of the noonday sun. "Lord, is it always so hot here in December?"

"Three hundred and fifty days of sun a year!" Fanny beamed, proud of her adopted home town. "Listen, don't worry about Dancer. I know a good stable in town that rents out to all the movie studios. We'll go give them a call and have them send out a trailer. Look lively there, buster, can't you see us ladies need to get out of the sun before we start to freckle!"

Laughing, Fanny threw an arm around Lael as she directed the overburdened porter to follow them. Within the hour, they had boarded Dancer at Hunt's Valley Stables and headed back up Sunset to the Beaudry Arms, the small, gray-framed apartment house that would be Lael's home for the next few months.

Dropping her trunks in the middle of the postage-stamp-size living room, Lael cast her eyes about the tiny apartment. She could see the entire thing without moving from one spot. To her left was a sink, portable hot plate, and miniature ice box—the kitchen. Down a short hallway to her right was a bedroom with twin beds and the bathroom. Aside from the beds, the only other furniture was a table and two chairs, a threadbare sofa, and a bookcase upon which Fanny had placed her few mementos—a silver buckle she had won years ago at a county fair, a china angel with a chipped halo, and a huge ceramic ashtray in the shape of a horseshoe. The room's only redeeming feature was a balcony off of the living room that was shaded by two large palm trees.

Fanny crossed her arms over her chest. "It ain't very big," she said apologetically. "I thought maybe we could move into one with two bedrooms after we've saved a little money."

"No, this is great, Fan. No kidding, I like it." Stepping out onto the balcony, Lael leaned over and fingered a broad palm leaf. Just then, a gentle breeze brought the warm, sultry smell of the ocean to her nostrils. She closed her eyes and inhaled deeply. So far, Los Angeles had it all over Texas, where a gust of wind brought nothing but grit in the face. "I really like it!"

Later, after Lael had settled herself in the apartment, the two friends walked to the corner drugstore. They sat at the counter and ordered ice cream sodas. The drugstore seemed unusually busy for midday, with several groups of handsome young men and women occupying the booths or wandering the aisles.

"Probably didn't make the call for extras today," Fanny explained, "so they don't have nothing better to do than hang out here, hoping some big shot will walk in and discover them. Look around, though . . . see anybody that looks like they could set a horse?"

Lael sized up the crowd. To a person, they were sleek and chic, the men with slicked back hair and stylish, V-necked sweaters, the women sporting short haircuts and pretty shoes with straps across the top. In her heavy brogans and plain Jane ponytail, Lael felt decidedly out of place. "Not a one," she admitted.

"Too bad for them. They'd be working today, if they could. Seems like the studios can't never hire enough riding extras. You'll see how it is tomorrow when we go down to Universal." Fanny smiled around a spoonful of ice cream in her mouth.

Lael pushed her soda away and spun around on the stool, propping her elbows on the counter. "You know, Fan, I may try to find something else to do. I just don't seem to have a hankering to be in pictures."

"What?" Fanny sputtered, spraying flecks of ice cream on her chin. "Are you nuts, kid? You ain't interested in making five dollars a day just to ride a horse? Not to mention that with your looks it's only a matter of time till they make you a star!"

Lael waved her off. "Star, my foot. You've been reading too many movie magazines. The money sounds good. I can't argue with that. But today, when I was at the stables, Mister Hunt told me he'd pay me the same to work for him. I think I'd like that better, just being able to work with the horses and not worrying about any of this moving picture stuff. Plus, he's willing to board Dancer for free and give me as much time as I want to practice my trick riding."

"That's a darn' good deal," Fanny admitted. "Not that you ain't deserving, honey, but how did you talk him into it?"

Lael reddened a bit. "I didn't have to talk him into anything. It was all his idea. He recognized me. Said he saw my picture in *Hoofs and Horns*, and it would be an honor to have such a fine rodeo champion working for him."

"Uhn-huh, I see. You sure he only wants you to take care of the horses?" said Fanny archly.

"I don't get you," Lael said.

Fanny shot her a grow-up look. "Are you really that innocent or is it an act? Come on, Lael, you know what most men are after whenever they see a pretty girl."

Lael's color deepened. "Fanny, Mister Hunt must be fifty, if he's a day."

"Even worse," Fanny said sagely. "At that age, they think they got something to prove."

"I'm not even going to dignify that with a response. He seemed like a nice man, and I'm happy to have the job." Lael paid for the sodas and hopped off her stool, leaving Fanny to follow.

They strolled down the street for a while, Lael noting the number of large, expensive cars that drove by. Not too many flivvers like you saw on the streets in Fort Worth. And nary a buggy in sight.

"I saw your picture the other day, too," Fanny said, kicking a rock down the sidewalk. "It was in the newspaper after you won the broncho riding at the Garden. There was a whole story about it. It said Louise Morris was there to lead the grand entry."

"That's right," Lael said, deciding to keep the business of Louise's drunkenness to herself.

"Was her brother there, too?" asked Fanny casually, giving the rock another kick.

Lael stole a quick glance; she recalled that Fanny had seemed sweet on Curtis back in Fort Worth. Of course, Fanny could be counted on to feel friendly toward any person of the male persuasion. Nevertheless, Lael decided to downplay her budding relationship with Curtis, just in case Fanny still cared.

"He was there, all right. He kind of looks after Louise, you know."

Fanny gave the rock one final kick and plopped down on a cement retaining wall fronting a huge mansion surrounded by an ornate iron fence. "Is he as good-looking as ever?" she asked, avoiding Lael's eyes.

Pursing her lips, Lael stared through the iron bars at the ostentatious abode. A fountain played in front of a circular drive containing several luxurious cars. "This must be some movie star's home . . . no ordinary person could ever afford it. Let me guess. Is it Mary Pickford's or Rudolph Valentino's?"

"You're changing the subject," accused Fanny. "Why don't you want to talk about Curtis?"

"I don't mind talking about him. It's just that there's not

much to say. Sure, he's still good-looking, if you like the pretty type."

"And you don't, is that it? Now that I think of it, it does seem like you went in for the more rugged kind of guy. Ever hear from Rafe Callantine?"

Lael pulled herself up sharply, amazed at the ache in her heart at just the mention of his name. "Why would I?" she muttered, angry at her reaction and her inability to control it, even after all this time.

"No reason." Fanny was sorry that she had touched on such a sore subject but, nevertheless, was secretly pleased that the pretty cowgirl's interests lay somewhere other than in Curtis Morris's direction. Although she knew it was an impossible, hopeless dream, Fanny still pined for the long, tall Texan. He had struck her as the embodiment of what a Western man should be—well-mannered, gracious, rich, and a good hand with the horses. Definitely not the type, however, that would be attracted to Fanny Lavelle.

Sighing, she draped an arm over Lael's shoulders. "We're a sorry pair, ain't we, honey? Always wanting what we can't have."

"No, that's not the problem," said Lael, encircling Fanny's waist as they continued down the street. "The problem is figuring out what we want."

Chapter Fourteen

"Someone here to see ya, Lael."

Looking over the back of the horse she was grooming, Lael was surprised to see Curtis Morris standing behind Mr. Hunt, doffing his hat courteously.

"Afternoon, Miss Buckley . . . I mean, Lael." He grinned at their ongoing joke.

"For heaven's sake, Curtis, what are you doing here? How did you know where I worked?" Lael found herself full of conflicting feelings at this sudden appearance. Part of her was downright glad to see the good-looking, lanky cowboy. The other part was worried that his presence spelled trouble.

"You wrote me you were coming to L.A. I stopped in Fort Worth on my way to the ranch and looked up your brother. He told me where you were working. I figured this time of day, that's where I'd find you."

"You saw Roger?" Lael was impressed at the effort Curtis had expended to track her down.

"Sure did. Met the whole family. They're great people, but that isn't surprising, seeing as they're Buckleys." Curtis gave her one of his soft, shy smiles, and Lael couldn't help but smile back.

Mr. Hunt cleared his throat. "I'll see you two later. Nice to meet you, son." With a nod at Curtis, he exited the barn.

Alone at last, Curtis came around the front of the horse and pinned Lael against the rough stall. "God, have I missed you," he whispered, and then kissed her, gently at first and then more urgently as he felt her begin to respond. His ardor did excite her, but it scared her, too, and, when they finally came up for breath, she put her hands on his chest to fend him off.

"Curtis, don't. I don't know what I think about all this . . . you following me all the way to California and everything."

"What do you mean, honey? After New York, I thought you knew how I felt about you." He picked her hand off his chest and touched it to his lips.

"I guess not," Lael said weakly.

"Well then, let me show you." Pressing on her shoulders, he bent his head to her again. She let him kiss her, although this time she felt no answering heat. Sensing her indifference, he backed off. He turned to stroke the gleaming horse, his expression confused and defensive.

"You're not the only reason I'm here, you know. I always meant to try my hand at the motion picture business, and now seemed like a good time to do it." He cut his eyes at her sulkily. " 'Course, it didn't hurt any that you were here, too."

Lael walked up to him and took his hand. He was so tall that even though he stood with his head hanging, she still looked up into his large brown eyes.

"I'm glad you're here," she said. "I really am. We had a lot of fun in New York, and we can here, too. But I'm not quite sure yet how I feel about us being a couple. I don't think I'm ready for that yet. Can you live with that, for now, anyway?"

Hope reborn kindled in Curtis's eyes. "I can live with that."

Lael flashed him a heart-stopping grin. "Good. Help me finish up here, and we'll trot on over to the Waterhole. I'm meeting Fanny at five."

Fanny was ecstatic over the arrival of Curtis. But she was

also suspicious of his motives, so she gave Lael a thorough grilling. Unwilling to admit, to Fanny or to herself, that Curtis had moved to Los Angeles because of her, Lael explained that he wanted to get into the movies and had looked her up only because he thought she could provide an *entrée* for him. Satisfied with this less than candid explanation, Fanny announced that she had set her cap for the handsome Mr. Morris and that she would do whatever was necessary, including reforming her ways and becoming "a good girl like you, Lael" in order to catch him.

Chagrined at the hole she had dug, Lael cast about for a way out. She could not risk telling Fanny the truth—that Curtis was most likely in love with her—for fear of alienating her best friend. Nor could she confide in Curtis, lest he set Fanny straight in a less than tactful manner. Based on their last meeting, when the brazen red-head had jumped all over him, Curtis was already leery of Fanny, and Lael wanted him to like her friend. As long as he didn't like her too much.

That was where it got confusing. Between trying to keep Fanny from getting disappointed and trying to figure out whether she wanted Curtis for herself, Lael was truly befuddled. It would have been better, she realized, to have dealt truthfully with everybody from the get go, but she couldn't turn back the clock now.

In the meantime, the three of them made an interesting trio, spending almost every evening together. Curtis took a room in a boarding house just around the corner from the Beaudry Arms, close enough to pop over at the drop of a hat. It annoyed him that Lael insisted on Fanny accompanying them whenever they went out, but, wary of pushing too hard, he held his tongue. Meanwhile, Fanny viewed Lael as the third wheel. But, in her new persona as the well-bred, gracious lady, she refrained from suggesting to Curtis that they cut to the chase. A lady, she believed, waited for the man to take the lead in matters of the heart, no matter how slowly he went about it. It did not escape Fanny's attention that Curtis seemed to dote on her roommate. But as long as Lael did not return the sentiment, she figured she had a chance. Especially since, as it turned out, she often had him all to herself.

Lael had told the truth about Curtis's desire to be in the movies, and Fanny was more than happy to show him the ropes. She introduced him to all the studio people of her acquaintance, and before long, with his superior riding ability, he was assured of daily work before the cameras. A routine developed where every morning he and Fanny met for a cup of coffee and a donut and headed out to Universal or Fox or one of the independents—whichever studio had put out the call for riding extras. Male riders were in more demand than females, but it was not unheard of for a casting director short on cowboys to hire a cowgirl to fill in. With her hair tucked under her hat and wearing a bulky shirt, no one could tell the difference.

These working hours they spent together, without Lael, were oddly liberating for Curtis. Free of the need constantly to impress her with his wit or hold back his feelings or worry about saying the wrong thing, he could simply be himself. And whatever he said or did seemed to please Fanny. As they became more comfortable together, he even sought her advice about Louise's drinking problem. No doubt about it, Curtis looked forward to their daily companionship, although not in the same way he anticipated seeing Lael.

For her part, Lael was happy to escape to the stables each morning where she could care for the horses, practice her riding, and forget for a few hours the complexities of her social life.

One day, about a month after Curtis's arrival, the stables

got a call from Fox. The studio needed to rent several horses for a large chase scene it was shooting that day. Mr. Hunt asked Lael to oversee taking the horses on location. The pretty wrangler eagerly agreed—although she herself had no desire to be in pictures, she had heard enough tales from her friends to make her curious about the filming process. This would be her chance to see how it was done. Not only that, but this particular shoot was for a Tom Mix Western so, with any luck, she would get to see the master at work.

The sun was barely up when Lael arrived with her string of horses on location in the hills about fifteen miles outside of town. It was a gray, foggy morning with an unusual chill in the air, hardly ideal weather for filming a movie, it seemed to Lael. Following Mr. Hunt's instructions, she scouted out the movie's director and told him she had brought the requested horses.

"Good, good," replied the director, a slight man sporting a pencil-thin mustache. Barely glancing at her, he returned to a perusal of his clipboard.

Lael waited politely a minute or two before it became clear he had forgotten about her. "Where do you want me to take the horses, sir?" she ventured.

He turned to her with a distracted look on his face. "The horses. Ah, yes, we called for extra horses, didn't we? Well, you see, my dear, I have absolutely no idea where they ought to go. Fortunately, here comes the man who does. Tom, this little lady would like to know what to do with the horses."

Twirling around, Lael came face to face with an imposing, dark-haired man dressed in splendid cowboy garb. His looks were somewhere between rugged and commanding, his face dominated by a long, slightly hooked nose. A strong brow and exceedingly dark eyes suggested a wild, perhaps exotic heritage.

"Tom Mix, miss," he introduced himself, which Lael thought was quite charming given that there was probably no better known individual in the entire Western world. "You must be from Hunt's stables."

"Y-yes," Lael stammered, conscious that she was staring. "Where would you like me to take the horses?"

"Follow me, I'll show you." He turned and marched off, all business. Lael sprinted to catch up.

"You're not the usual wrangler Hunt sends out," Mix noted, his black eyes looking her up and down. "Not that I'm complaining any," he added with a half smile.

Lael kept silent, not sure the movie star expected a response. Just then, a handsome young man with sandy hair and brilliant blue eyes caught sight of them and hurried over. "Tom," he began, ignoring Lael, "I think I've figured out a way for us to go ahead and shoot in spite of this blasted fog. We'll line up all the cars on hand right at the base of the knoll. In front of the cars we'll set up a wall of reflectors. When it's time to roll film, we'll switch on all the headlights. Hopefully, the reflectors will make it seem bright as full daylight. What do you think?"

"I think you're brilliant," Mix clapped him on the back, then added, "if it works. Dan, meet George Hunt's new wrangler, Miss . . ."

"Buckley, Lael Buckley." Lael would have extended her hand, but they were all walking at such a fast pace, shaking hands would have seemed awkward. She settled for a smile. Dan barely glanced at her, but Mix caught the gesture and returned it, showing a row of small, white teeth.

"This is my cameraman, Dan Clark. What he lacks in manners, he makes up for in talent behind the lens."

Clark pursed his lips and nodded curtly at Lael. "Forgive me, Miss Buckley, if I seem a mite preoccupied. But we have an entire day of shooting scheduled, and time's a-wasting." With a pointed look at Mix, he headed off in the opposite direction, calling out to members of the crew as he went.

Chuckling, the famous star came to a halt in front of a roped-in pen that contained maybe a dozen horses. A large group of cowboys stood about, hands jammed in pockets while they stamped their feet against the unaccustomed cold. When they saw Mix, they quieted down and ceased milling around.

"Put your horses here," Mix instructed Lael. "We'll probably be ready to start shooting in about half an hour. When that happens, all you riders"—he turned to include the whole group—"go to the top of the knoll over there. On cue, you'll race down at top speed, chasing me and Tony. I'll turn in the saddle and take a couple of shots. I want two of you to take falls. Any questions?"

"There's one problem, Mister Mix." One of the cowboys stepped forward carrying the ubiquitous clipboard. "The studio didn't send us enough extras. We put out a call for twenty riders, but only fifteen showed up. Reckon they figured with the cold and fog today we wouldn't be shooting. Can we go ahead with just fifteen?"

"Not if we don't have to," said Mix, annoyed. "See if you can rustle up anybody on the set who can ride. The more pursuers we got, the better."

Lael turned to get her horses.

"I bet that gal there can ride," Mix's voice followed her.

Lael brought her hand to her chest as if to say—"Who, me?"

"Don't worry, we use gals all the time, don't we Fred? Just tie up that hair and get yourself a man's coat somewhere. Thatta girl!" Mix stalked off, his mind already on the next problem.

Lael opened her mouth to protest, but Mix was long gone.

The cowboy extras resumed their stamping and muttering while Fred, the crew chief, ambled over to her. "Didn't figure on getting to be in the movies today, did ya? Well, it ain't bad pay . . . five dollars, plus we'll feed ya lunch. Here, fill out this form."

"I can't be in the movies," Lael argued, still stunned by the turn of events.

"Why not? You can ride, can't ya?"

"Well, sure, but . . . my job's to take care of the horses."

"Sweetheart, all your horses are gonna be riding in the scene we're about to shoot. The best way to keep an eye on 'em is to be in the scene yourself. Here, sign this."

Reluctantly Lael took the form and signed. "Is Mister Mix always so involved with everything?" she asked curiously. "I mean, I thought the director would be the one telling everyone what to do. Don't the stars just sit in their trailers until the cameras roll?"

"Not Tom Mix," Fred stated proudly. "A Tom Mix picture is exactly that . . . his creation from start to finish. Sure, he hires a director, but everybody knows who's in charge. Now let me see if I can rustle up something to hide that pretty figure of yours."

An hour later, Lael and nineteen cowboys sat their mounts at the top of a long, sloping, sage-dotted hill. Fred had managed to find four additional riders among the crew, although none of them looked happy to be there. Daniel Clark's lighting strategy had been tested and found adequate, so they were ready to roll.

"OK, folks," Fred reviewed their directions. "When you hear . . . Action! . . . Tom's gonna start off down the hill on Tony. Wait for my signal, then follow him. Stay together, but don't bunch up too much. Rex and John are gonna take their falls when they get even with the bandanna tied on that sage-brush yonder. Everybody got that?"

All nodded although the conscripted extras appeared nervous and confused. Another fifteen minutes passed as they waited. Lael was beginning to get the impression movie making involved a whole lot of sitting around doing nothing. Then the word came that the cameras were rolling, followed by the director's megaphone-amplified voice shouting: "Action!"

As planned, Mix spurred his horse down the hill, the posse in hot pursuit. But one of the stuntmen—Lael wasn't sure if it was Rex or John—took his fall too soon, before he was in proper camera range. Mix insisted on another take. By the time camera angles had been reset and the riders had trooped back atop the hill, another thirty minutes had passed. On the second take, the stunts came off perfectly, but one of the brand new extras, who had started the day as a lighting technician, came out of his stirrups and bounced around on top of his horse like a rag doll. Mix thought it would be distracting on film so they headed back up for take number three, this time minus the hapless technician.

And so it went through takes three, four, and five, the perfectionist movie star never quite satisfied with his all-important chase scene. The fog burned off, lunchtime came and went, and Lael found herself getting increasingly frustrated, although most of the veteran players seemed completely unfazed. Finally, toward the end of the afternoon, they managed what seemed to Lael to be a perfect take. But as she reined in at the bottom of the hill and looked back up the slope, her spirits sank. One of the stunt men was still on the ground where he had fallen, clutching his shoulder in pain.

"Rex is hurt!" she called to Fred, and raced up the knoll to check on the injured man. Dismounting quickly, she placed a hand on his good shoulder. "You OK, there?"

"Broke my damn' collar bone again," Rex moaned, struggling to his feet. "I oughta know by now to fall on the other side."

Fred trotted up, appearing more annoyed than concerned.

"He broke his collar bone," Lael informed him, brushing aside a wisp of hair that had come loose from underneath the dirty Stetson she wore.

"Tough luck, bud. I sure hope we got that take in the can."

Lael glared at him and was about to comment on his notable lack of empathy when Tom Mix rode up, looking grim. "What happened here?"

"Rex thinks he broke his collar bone. We better get him into town to see a doctor," said Fred apologetically.

The movie star angrily slapped his reins against his gloved palm. "Damn! That would have been the perfect take, but it turns out one of the cameras malfunctioned. Clark thinks we missed the stunt falls completely. We'll have to shoot it again."

"Can we do it with only one stunt man?" asked Fred, knowing the answer he would get.

"Of course not. Bob Stratton," Mix named his character in the film, "is supposed to be a crack shot. How would it look if he only brings down one man? Christ, Fred, you've got twenty riding extras. How hard can it be to find one who can do a fall?"

"With this group, damn' near impossible," muttered the crew chief as Mix rode off. "How 'bout it, Rex? Who have we got besides you and John who can take a fall?" Fred picked up Rex's crushed hat and began escorting the injured man down the hill. Lael fell in behind, leading the horses.

"Shorty maybe could do it. But he's pretty slow . . . it'll take him a coupla takes to get it right."

"We don't have time for that. The light's fading fast."

"I can do it."

The two men stopped in their tracks and turned around to look at the pretty, petite cowgirl. With her hair tucked up and her bulky clothes there was nothing about her that looked particularly feminine—unless you noticed her wide, green eyes and full, pink lips. "In one take," she added, those luscious lips parting in a sly smile.

"You ever done stunt work before?" Fred asked skeptically.

"I've removed myself from a horse in just about every way imaginable, intentional or otherwise." Lael neatly side-stepped the question.

"That so? Well, I ain't in no position to be particular. But you got only one chance, sister. If you don't get it right in one take, I'm finding me somebody who can."

"Fair enough," Lael said, and, leaping into the saddle, she charged back up the hill. As she waited for the others to join her, she wondered what had possessed her to volunteer for this job. She told herself it was because she was tired of all the waiting around—since she knew she could do the stunt perfectly, she might as well just do it, and get them all out of here before night fell. But, if she were totally honest, there was more to it than that. She had not seen a rider here today who could come close to her level of ability. Why not show them what a true professional could do?

Once again, the cowboys gathered at the crest of the knoll, Mix in the forefront. She had no idea if he knew who was replacing the injured Rex. If he did, he did not seem to care. The familiar cues were given, and Lael took off, hunkering down over her horse's neck. Timing it perfectly, she kicked loose a stirrup and plunged over the side of her mount, hitting the ground hard but rolling with the impact. She came to a rest face down, arms and legs sprawled until she heard the word—"Cut!"—from down below.

Coming to her feet, she brushed herself off, no worse for wear. She might have a few bruises tomorrow, but nothing serious. She knew she had performed well. If everybody else had done their part, they could all go home.

From down below, a lone rider detached himself from the crowd of people and cameras and bolted up the hill. Reining in his magnificent Tony, Tom Mix grinned down at the winsome cowgirl. "That's a print!"

Chapter Fifteen

The flivver pulled up to the curb in front of the Beaudry Arms, chugging for a second or two before it died. Curtis had purchased the old car so he and the girls could get about town more easily, but lately he and Fanny had even been driving it to work, saving themselves a ride on the crowded trolley car. Today, they were returning from Universal City and the set of KINDLED COURAGE.

Coming around the front of the car, Curtis, as always, opened Fanny's door for her, a gentlemanly gesture she found completely disarming. If only all those gestures of his were an indication that he felt something for her besides friendship. . . .

"Come up for a beer?" Fanny asked, planting a perky smile on her face.

"Sure, why not?"

Fanny led the way up the stairs. "Lael must not be home yet," she said, tossing her coat on the sofa and doing a quick check of the apartment. Removing a precious bottle of bootleg beer from the icebox, she held its mouth against the kitchen counter and hit it hard with the heel of her hand, popping the lid neatly. Repeating the procedure, she then handed a bottle to Curtis and clicked her own against it. "Here's lookin' at ya," she winked, and took a long swallow.

Suppressing a smile, Curtis drank, too, surprised at the small tug of affection he often felt now whenever Fanny did something so . . . well, so Fanny-like. He knew quite well she was trying to behave for his benefit, probably at Lael's urging, so when she forgot for a moment and reverted to her old, bawdy ways, it was almost refreshing.

Suddenly the door burst open, and Lael entered, looking like the Cheshire cat. Curtis turned to greet her, his eyes brightening. With a sinking heart, Fanny realized that the way he looked now, alive and hopeful, confirmed what she already knew—that his heart belonged to the genteel little cowgirl standing before her.

"Guess what!" Lael exclaimed. "We're all going to a party at Tom Mix's place tonight!"

"What'd you have to do to get that invitation?" Fanny drained her beer and tossed it into the trash with a loud clank.

"Nothing. I was just standing there . . . we were on location in Mixville today . . . and he walks up and tells me he and his wife are having a party to celebrate the completion of CATCH MY SMOKE, and would I like to come. Well, sure, I said, and is it OK if I bring my friends? The more the merrier, he says, and then walks off."

"What, and didn't even give you the address of his humble abode?"

Too excited to notice the irony in her roommate's voice, Lael prattled on. "Oh, don't be silly Fan, everyone knows where Tom Mix lives. Fifty-Eight Forty-Five Carlton Way. It'll be fun. Everybody who's anybody in Hollywood will be there."

"Since when do you care about Hollywood big shots?" teased Curtis.

"I don't really. You know that. But Tom's been so nice to me . . . why, you know the only pictures I'll do are Tom Mix pictures. I guess I'm just excited that he likes me enough to invite me to a party." Lael suddenly felt foolish. She had, after all, carefully fostered her reputation for staying aloof from all the Hollywood hoopla.

Laughing, Curtis swept Lael into his arms and began two-stepping around the tiny living room. "Well, I for one will be more than happy to escort two such lovely ladies to Mister Mix's party. I might even have to fight him, if he wants more than one dance with the beautiful Miss Buckley. How would that look in the morning papers . . . Texas Cowboy K.O.'s Mix in Lover's Quarrel!"

"Oh, Curtis," Lael giggled, "you crack me up!"

Fanny watched the smiling couple dance around the apartment before helping herself to another beer. Taking a long swallow, she silently toasted Louise Morris. Sometimes comfort really was as close as the nearest bottle of booze.

"Holy cow," Fanny whispered as they parked some distance down Carlton Way. "This is a popular place to be tonight."

As they left Curtis's modest little flivver, and followed a line of Packards and Bentleys to the front walk of Tom Mix's Hollywood home, Lael began to worry that she had not dressed appropriately, even though she was wearing a new silk blouse she had embroidered herself and her best skirt. What did one wear to a wrap party, anyway? Judging by some guests alighting from a car ahead of them, tuxes and evening gowns.

Lael glanced at Fanny who also wore her best Western duds. Picking up on her roommate's train of thought, the red-headed cowgirl patted Lael's shoulder. "Hell, this is a Tom Mix party," she drawled. "They ain't all gonna be wearing monkey suits." Well after her third beer, Fanny had all but forgotten her recent efforts at elocutionary improvement.

Linking arms, the threesome ascended the broad front steps of the roomy bungalow. Once inside, the theme turned decidedly Western. Every wall of the house was hung with trophy heads, racks of elk antlers and steer horns, Mexican hats and serapes, and antique guns. There were an elaborate tooled, silver studded saddle, hats, Indian headdresses, and a well-stocked gun closet in the den, and Navajo rugs everywhere on the floor.

"Look over there." Curtis nodded into the den. "That's William Fox and Carl Laemmle. Two studio heads in the same room . . . now that's power."

As he spoke, the powerful man himself, decked out in a white, Western-cut tuxedo with rhinestone-studded lapels, approached. "Howdy, Lael," he called. "Glad you could make it. What do you think of my place?"

"It's really something. Did you bag all this game yourself?" Lael eyed the huge buffalo head staring down at her. Mix just laughed. Blushing at her obvious *faux pas,* Lael quickly introduced Fanny and Curtis.

Shaking hands firmly, Mix cocked his head at the younger man. "Morris, eh? From Texas, are you?"

"Yes, sir. West Texas." Curtis declined to elaborate. He did not dare bring up the movie star's long ago liaison with Louise.

Mix continued to stare at him as though on the verge of a fleeting memory. "I knew a Morris family in those parts. Big rodeo folks as I recall."

"Well, sir. . . . ," Curtis began but was interrupted by a small, dark-haired woman who sidled up to Mix and planted a kiss on his cheek.

"Mama needs a drinkie-poo, sweetie," she cooed in his ear.

Smiling, Mix wrapped an arm around the woman's shoulders. "You all know my wife, Vicky," he stated. And, indeed, they did know Victoria Forde, once a young starlet who had risen to fame as Tom Mix's co-star both on and off the screen.

Barely acknowledging her guests, Vicky grabbed her husband's arm and pulled him in the direction of the bar.

"Even the rich and famous gotta fetch drinkie-poos for Mama," cracked Fanny. "Speaking of which . . . ," and she drifted off to find herself a libation.

Guests continued to stream in. Much to Lael's relief there were just as many people like herself, cowboys and cowgirls from the studio, as there were muckety-mucks. The two groups tended to segregate, with all the fancily clad moguls and their wives gravitating to the den, while the more raucous cowboy-types took over the main room. Liquor flowed freely as more and more people poured into the house. Lael thought it was certainly a strange wrap party, since a lot of these people surely hadn't been in the picture or worked on it, but everyone seemed to be having a good time.

Later in the evening, needing a break from the noise and smoke, Lael commandeered Curtis out to the front porch. A shimmery glow emanated from the windows.

"The rich live differently, don't they?" she commented, settling into a wooden rocking chair and stretching out her legs.

"You can say that again." Curtis sat at her feet on the steps, staring reflectively out at the street. "And it's all such a crap shoot. I mean, who's to say you or I won't be the next Tom Mix or Victoria Forde? All it takes is one lucky break."

"Well, it won't be me, that's for sure." Lael smiled. "I can fall off a horse good enough, but I could never act in front of the cameras . . . I'd freeze up like an ice cube!"

Curtis turned to look at her. "Who are you kidding, Lael? You'd be a natural. You've got a face the cameras would love, not to mention every red-blooded male in America."

"No. If anybody's going to make it in films, it's you. You're just as talented as Tom or Hoot Gibson or Bill Hart. And handsomer to boot."

A huge grin creasing his boyish face, Curtis climbed up and drew Lael close to him. "You really think so?" he asked, encircling her with his arms.

"Um-hmm," she murmured, snuggling into his embrace. She had not really intended to entice him with her compliment, but now that she had, she found his nearness pleasurable.

Needing no further encouragement, Curtis kissed her. His mouth tasted of smoke and fine whisky. She kissed him back, enjoying the feel of a strong, solid man in her arms. Curtis tried pinning her with his body as his kisses deepened. For just a second, Lael pulled back, feeling light-headed.

"Come back here," he growled. They kissed again, and, in her dizziness, she somehow imagined him to be someone else—that other cowboy whose image she had banished from her daytime thoughts but who still came to her in dreams. Lit from within, she pressed against the man beside her, thinking she wanted him, and then again she pulled away, her lips ready to call out another man's name. She looked at the face before her and realized with sickening certainty that her love was not here. Fighting a blackness so deep she thought she would faint, she pushed away violently, struggling out of the embrace.

"Lael, what's wrong?" Curtis cried.

"Go away," she whispered, turning her back to him. "Just go away."

"Are you all right?" He put his hand on her shoulder.

She shied away from him. "No. I'm not all right. But I will be if you just leave me alone."

Curtis dropped his head and let out a miserable sigh. Suddenly, all the built-up anger and frustration burst out. "God dammit, Lael, what the hell are you doing? One minute you're so hot for me I'm like to burn up, and the next you're treating me like shit you scraped off your boot heel. You told me to be patient, and God knows I have been, but my patience is wearing mighty damn' thin!"

He was right, of course. She had treated him awfully. She had unashamedly led him on, played a cruel game of cat and mouse with him ever since he had been in Los Angeles, and the only proper thing would be to apologize. But she was still so shaken by the way she had literally conjured up Rafe Callantine that she couldn't summon the words. Uttering a soft cry, she stumbled away, disappearing down the front walk.

Curtis gave himself a minute to gain control and then went back inside in search of a drink. He found Fanny next to the bar.

She greeted him with a tipsy smile. "Hey there, where you been?"

Curtis chuckled, the effect of the the whisky he hefted almost blocking out his run-in with Lael. Fanny brought her fingers to her heart and then touched them to Curtis's chest. It was a simple gesture, but eloquent. Curtis was amazed to find his throat closing up, his emotions too near the surface. Here, at least, was a woman who appreciated him, who didn't play games, who was exactly what she appeared to be. Setting his drink down firmly, Curtis grabbed Fanny's hand and led her away.

"Where we going?" she asked in surprise.

"Some place quieter."

"What about Lael?"

"What about her?" he grumbled, dragging her out the front door.

Wordlessly, Fanny slid into the front seat of the flivver. If there was one thing she knew, it was when to keep her mouth shut.

Lael composed herself and then returned to the party, intending to call a cab to take her home. Instead, she ran into a few acquaintances from Fox who offered to give her a ride. Needing to clear her head, she asked them to drop her off a few blocks from the Beaudry Arms.

The night was surprisingly warm considering the chilliness of the afternoon. Los Angeles was a beautiful place, in some ways a magical place, but it was not her place. She needed to get back on track. She had not been thinking about her rodeo career. She had gotten so wrapped up in her work at the stables and so many other things that she had hardly ridden Dancer at all. And here it was only a month until the rodeo season started.

She needed to straighten things out with Curtis and Fanny, too. She had behaved abominably toward Curtis tonight. Somehow, in her passion, she had gotten confused. It wasn't Rafe she loved, it was Curtis. Curtis, who was so kind and thoughtful, who cared for her, who was there for her. She had no choice but to apologize immediately and ask him to forgive her. And, harder still, to break the truth to Fanny.

Lael turned the key in the lock and opened the door to her apartment, snapping on the light as she entered. Her stunned eyes fell on Fanny and Curtis, locked together on the sofa, their clothes strewn about the room. With a gasp that was half sob, Lael backed out the door, and ran.

Chapter Sixteen

Steam poured from underneath the hood of the dust-covered automobile as it rattled to a stop at the side of the road. "Not again!" groaned Lael, slumping wearily in the driver's seat. This was the third time, since leaving Winnemucca yesterday morning, that the car had broken down. The radiator leaked badly. It could be fixed once she got to town. *If* she ever got to town.

Lael reached behind her and hauled out a five gallon jug of water, wincing at the pang in her sprained left wrist. It was a minor injury, caused when her hand became entangled in the halter rope of the broncho she had ridden at Winnemucca. It had not kept her from winning there, and would likely not interfere with her upcoming performance at Pendleton. Thankfully her right wrist, the one she used to shift gears, had not been injured.

As she waited for the radiator to cool, Lael gazed out at the wheat fields of eastern Oregon spreading in every direction from this deserted stretch of highway. The late afternoon sun burned down, scorching the back of her neck, and Lael suddenly felt as if she were a million miles from civilization, caught in an endless expanse of prairie desert. But that was ridiculous. Pendleton was only about thirty miles away.

Recapping the radiator after filling it full, she stowed the water jug and did a quick check on Dancer. The trained horse seemed to be enduring the journey in his comfortable trailer better than she was herself. Hopping back behind the wheel, she regained the road, eager to reach Pendleton before nightfall.

Her purchase of this automobile and trailer had been a daring move, but, all in all, one she did not regret. Most rodeo folks still traveled from town to town on trains, but now that she had Dancer to haul around, Lael preferred the convenience of her own car. A few couples—including Hugh and Mabel Strickland—had jumped on the automobile bandwagon, but Lael was the only single cowgirl driving the circuit. Her family was predictably not happy that she was out on the road alone, and camping on the rodeo grounds now, too, but she had long ago stopped trying to please them. She now earned her own keep and called her own shots.

Nellie Buckley, in particular, had been disappointed at Lael's decision to leave Los Angeles. The Nebraska farmwife had thrilled to her daughter's stories of Hollywood's glamorous stars and secretly hoped Lael would become a permanent part of that world. When Lael had pulled up stakes and returned to the circuit, Nellie had expressed her surprise and displeasure. Her daughter had shrugged her off, noting that she had never intended to stay in Hollywood beyond the winter off-season.

Which was true as far as it went. Lael did not bother to explain that, if things had worked out with Curtis Morris, she might still be making movies in L.A., or she might be living on a ranch in West Texas, or maybe traveling the circuit with a husband and partner in tow. But things had not worked out—in a big way.

Almost a year had passed since Lael had caught her two best friends in a compromising position, and even now a flush rose to her cheeks and a twinge of shock and betrayal caught in her chest. That night, she had slept at Mr. Hunt's stables. The next day, she took the first train out of town. She did not want to face Curtis and Fanny, did not want to listen to their feeble apologies and excuses. She had trusted Curtis when he had said he wanted her, had trusted that Fanny understood she and Curtis had a "thing" for each other despite her own denials. They had let her down.

Months later, when she could look at things a little more dispassionately, her conscience was tweaked by the notion that she had been as much deceiver as deceived. There had been much in her own behavior that she was not proud of. But it was too late for second thoughts. She had burned her bridges and moved on.

Lost in her reverie, Lael failed to notice the sharp rock lying in the middle of the road until she ran right over it. Cursing mildly, she prayed it had not punctured a tire, but within seconds the car began pulling to the right.

"Damn!" Lael pounded the wheel in frustration, grimacing as pain shot through her left wrist. "This is not fair!" she screamed to anyone who might be listening. But there was no one listening—only Dancer and a magpie feeding off some carrion in the road ahead.

Once again, Lael rummaged under the back seat for the jack and wheel wrench, and then went to the rear of the car to get the spare tire. After blocking the wheels with rocks scrounged from the shoulder of the road, she positioned her tools and was ready to get to work. But she found she did not have the strength to raise the car using only one hand on the jack. She would have to push down with both hands, a painful proposition considering her injured left wrist. Taking a deep breath, Lael braced her feet and pushed. A searing pain coursed through her arm. She cried aloud and released her grip on the jack. How could she do this, injured as she was? But she had no choice, unless she saddled up Dancer and rode into town. A ride of that distance would not be good for her little trick-riding pony, not the day before the elimination try-outs.

Lael bent to her task once more. Just then, she heard the unmistakable sound of a car coming down the highway. Leaving the jack, she stood in the middle of the road, waving broadly at the approaching vehicle. The driver started honking his horn, and Lael recognized the Stricklands' brand new Dodge touring car and trailer.

"Thank God you came by!" Lael peered toward the passenger side as Hugh pulled alongside. "I'm having a devil of a time changing this tire."

"What's the matter?" asked Mabel.

"It's this darn' wrist," Lael complained, holding up her bandaged arm. "I can't push down hard enough on the jack."

"Now you just let Hugh take care of that for you."

The quiet and courtly Hugh did just that, pulling to the side of the road behind Lael's trailer and going efficiently to work. As he labored, the two women sat on the Dodge's running board on the shady side, sipping from a thermos of lemonade that Mabel had brought along.

"Doll, you oughta get yourself a man," Mabel said. "They ain't good for much, but they do come in handy at times."

"Under normal circumstances, I'd consider those fighting words, but, at the moment, I'm hard pressed to disagree with you."

"I used to think I could do everything on my own, and push come to shove I guess I still could. But it's nice having someone to help with all the chores and share all the headaches. Besides, I like the company." Mabel gazed contentedly in Hugh's direction, and Lael felt a familiar surge of envy. Not for the first time, she wondered if she were destined to go through life alone.

"I'm not trying to prove anything. I just haven't found the right guy yet."

"I know, honey." Mabel laid a solicitous hand on Lael's

shoulder. "It looked like you and Curtis Morris was gonna hit if off there in New York. What happened?"

"It just didn't work out." Lael drank the last of her lemonade as Hugh finished packing away the road tools.

"Mabel and me'll follow you on into town. That spare has a few patches in it, and I ain't too sure but what it might go flat on you."

Lael thanked him and climbed back behind the wheel. With help immediately at hand, she relaxed and let her thoughts turn to the week-end ahead. The Pendleton Roundup was one of her favorite places to compete. For one thing, it was huge. Over a hundred thousand people likely would attend the three day event, and the arena was the largest west of the Mississippi, seating forty thousand spectators. For someone like Lael who fed on the crowd's noise and enthusiasm, those kinds of numbers got the blood racing.

Lael also liked the way the Roundup committee included the local Indian population, not only in the pageantry of the rodeo parades, but in the competitive events as well. She loved the colorful costumes and rhythmic beating of the drums, and there was no doubt the Indians excelled at riding and racing. Why, Jackson Sundown, the legendary Nez Percé Indian, was one of the best rough riders ever to fan a broncho.

But what Lael liked best about Pendleton was the way female competitors were treated there. Although the rodeo world, unlike other parts of society, generally treated women well, awarding them equal prize money with the men and equal respect as athletes, Pendleton was notorious for letting the cowgirls fly—literally. It was currently the only rodeo to allow cowgirls competing in the relay race to leap from the back of one horse to another without touching the ground. Lael had *flown* for the first time last year, and couldn't wait to do it again.

The next day, Lael breezed through the try-outs, sticking on Hot Foot, a randy little cayuse, like a burr to corduroy. Her sprained wrist, the one she grasped the halter rope with, pained her some but not enough to matter. If need be, she could get the rodeo doc to shoot it up with pain-killer for the actual competition.

As she finished her ride, she noticed three of her good friends from the circuit—Mabel, Fox Hastings, and Lorena Trickey—watching her from the bleachers. All three were champion cowgirls and, with the addition of Lael, comprised the cream of the women's professional rodeo crop. Lael walked over to greet them.

"Hey, doll," Mabel patted the seat next to her, "we was just talking about you."

"Oh, oh. What did I do now?"

"It's not what you did. It's what you're not allowed to do," said Fox wryly.

Lael cocked her head at the three indignant-looking women. "I'm free, white, and over twenty-one. What am I not allowed to do?"

"Compete for the all-around title," announced Lorena.

Lael raised her eyebrows in surprise. "The cowboy's all-around title? How on earth could I compete for that?"

"That's the point," Fox explained. "The way things are set up now, you can't. No woman can. The only contests for women are broncho riding, relay racing, and Roman racing. If we could compete against the men in the bull riding, steer roping, and bulldogging, our scores could be entered in the all-around title competition, just like the men's are."

"That's right," Mabel said. "It ain't fair that they shut us out of all those events. Even Hugh thinks so. Shoot, I can throw a steer in twenty-five seconds flat . . . that's pert near a world's record and a darn' sight better than most cowboys can do!"

"It's been sticking in my craw a long time," Fox added. "We thought this would be a good place to get things changed. Pendleton's always been pretty fair to women."

"That's true." Lael wondered why it had not occurred to her to challenge the status quo. She would love to be able to vie for the all-around title. "What should we do?"

"We gotta go to the rodeo committee and ask 'em to include us," Lorena said.

"Well, we better hurry . . . competition starts tomorrow."

"Let's go right now," suggested Mabel. All in agreement, the four cowgirls strode purposefully downtown, their fringed skirts slapping their knees as they walked. At the door to the American National Bank building, rodeo committee headquarters, Fox held back.

"Wait a minute. We got to have a plan. Who's gonna do the talking?"

In unison, three pairs of eyes turned to look at Lael.

"Hold on," Lael protested. "Why me? I'm just along for the ride."

"Because you talk better than the rest of us," said Mabel. "Because you got a way about you that makes people think they're doing themselves a favor at the same time they're doing exactly what you want 'em to. I saw how you snowballed that New York reporter. Well, we need a little bit of that . . . how do you call it . . . finesse, right now."

Fox and Lorena nodded their agreement, and Lael saw that she had been chosen whether she liked it or not. "I think I've been set up," she complained, but a smile tugged at the corners of her mouth.

"Well, it couldn't happen to a nicer girl. Now come on, Miss Ivy League, show us your stuff." Wrapping her arm around Lael's waist, Mabel led the plucky group of cowgirls up the stairs to committee headquarters on the second floor.

Most of the committee members were on hand, and the women had no trouble rounding them up for an impromptu meeting. Lael presented their case politely but unapologetically, pointing out that from its inception in 1910 the Roundup had had a history of highlighting its female contestants. What they were asking for now, Lael said, was completely consistent with that philosophy.

Slack-jawed, the committee members stared at her in disbelief. Finally the Roundup Association president gathered himself.

"Surely you gals can't be serious about this," he said, blinking furiously. "We'd have a full-scale revolt on our hands, if we let you do what you're asking."

"Says who?" Mabel broke in. "My husband, for one, thinks it's a darn' good idea, and I bet there's a lot of cowboys would agree with him. Do you think the men would be worried about losing to a woman? Hell, they'd be rarin' to compete against us."

"I doubt that," the president grumbled. "Come here, let me show you something."

Leading them over to a glass-enclosed case, he reached inside and reverently removed a large trophy. "I don't need to tell you ladies this is the Roosevelt Trophy."

The women gaped at the beautiful award, admiring the silver lariat falling from the saddle of a silver horse supported by a silver and gold globe. Lael had never seen anything so shiny.

"Look at this," the Roundup president went on, pointing to where the lariat coiled around the globe to form letters. "Unless I'm plumb cock-eyed, that says World's Champion Cowboy. Ain't nothing there about no cowgirl."

"So what?" challenged Mabel. "Heck, if I won that thing, I wouldn't care if it said World's Champion Horse's Ass!"

"That ain't the point," the president said, giving Mabel a

nasty look. "The point is, the winner of the Roosevelt Trophy always has been and always will be a cow*boy*." Noticing the women's angry and disappointed expressions, he modulated his tone. "Now, I don't mean to give you gals offense, but you can't just waltz in here the day before the rodeo starts and expect us to tinker with things. Hell, the schedule's been set for months now."

Lael had to agree with him. They had been foolish to think they could change things so quickly. What they needed to do was retreat gracefully and then build support for an adjustment in next year's program. Lael thanked the committee for listening and herded her friends out the door.

When they reached the street, Mabel turned to her, livid. "Why'd you back down like that? Why, I woulda told that old fart right where he could go!"

"Calm down, Mabel," Lorena said. That wouldn't have done any good. Lael did the right thing. We don't want to make 'em too mad at us, or they'll just keep turning us down."

"We just have to get organized next time. Maybe circulate a petition in support of the idea, and get the men to sign it, too," Lael said.

"That'll be the day," Fox put in. "Hell, I could barely get Mike to sign our marriage license. He'll never sign no petition."

The women shared a bittersweet laugh at the foibles of the male of the species and then split up. Each had plenty to do before tomorrow's opening day.

Lael needed to familiarize Dancer with the Pendleton arena, so she headed back to camp to change into the jodhpurs she wore for trick riding. Stepping into her darkened tent, she gasped in surprise at the tall figure sitting on her cot.

The man came to his feet. "It's just me, Lael."

"My God, Curtis, you scared me to death!" Lael took a deep breath. Her hands shook, whether from shock or nervousness, she didn't know.

"I'm sorry. I should have waited outside, I guess."

Lael looked at him more closely. He had not changed a bit, maybe put on a pound or two around the middle, but he was still the tall, handsome Curtis she remembered. If he smiled that soft, shy smile at her, she might forgive him everything. But he wasn't smiling. In fact, he appeared downcast.

"It's been a while," she started lamely.

"I could tell you the exact number of days, if you're interested."

Lael tossed her hat on her footlocker and gestured to the cot. "Have a seat. What brings you to Oregon?"

Curtis remained on his feet, twisting his hat restlessly. "You do."

She waited, but he appeared to have run out of words. "Come on, Curtis. You'll have to do better than that. The last time I laid eyes on you, you were wrapped around my best friend and roommate. It's a long way from there to here."

"You don't understand, Lael. That night with Fanny was an accident. We'd both had too much to drink, and, well, after what happened out on the porch, I wasn't thinking too clearly. What Fanny and I did didn't mean a damn' thing, but you high-tailed it out of town so fast you didn't give me a chance to explain."

"Maybe it meant nothing to you. What about Fanny? She was nuts about you, or were you too pig-headed to notice?"

Curtis hung his head. He knew quite well how Fanny felt about him. That night, after Lael had left, Fanny had poured out her heart to him, begging him to let her make him happy, telling him that Lael didn't love him, would never love him, and was cruel to toy with him. Somewhere deep inside,

158

Curtis recognized the truth of Fanny's words, but he had rejected them nonetheless.

"I can't help how Fanny feels," he murmured. "All I know is, it's you I want. I must have written you a dozen letters, trying to tell you that, but you never answered. Maybe that's an answer in itself, but I need to hear it from your own lips. What about it, Lael? Do I have a chance with you or not?"

His large brown eyes were so full of hurt and need and desire that Lael did not have the heart to turn him down. Besides, even after all this time, she still was not sure how she felt about Curtis Morris. The one thing she was sure of was that she could not be dishonest with him any more.

"The truth is, I don't know. That night, after I left the party, I had decided to tell you I loved you. Then, when I saw you and Fanny . . . well, I just ran from it. I've been avoiding thinking about it . . . about you . . . ever since."

"You were going to tell me you loved me?" He pounced on her words, his confidence restored. "If you would have then, you can again. Lael, I've thought about you every day since that night. All I want is to be with you, to take care of you. Please don't run away from me again."

Confused and somewhat dazed by the turn of events, Lael turned her back to Curtis and wrapped her arms around herself protectively. "I feel like my brains just got shook up by a side-winding outlaw. You'll have to give me some time to get things sorted out."

Turning her around to face him, Curtis gave her the smile she had waited to see. "I'll give you time, Lael, but I'm not going away without an answer. I'm tired of waiting . . . I want you now." Folding her to him, he kissed her deeply and then was gone.

Chapter Seventeen

Lael took her time putting up Dancer after their practice session. The events of the morning—first, the rodeo committee's cavalier rejection of her proposal to let women vie for the all-around title, and then Curtis's showing up, pushing for a decision—had left her drained. She took comfort in the mindless, repetitive motion of brushing her pretty little pony, staying at it for over an hour until its coat gleamed like copper.

At last she left the stables, pausing outside to appreciate the view on this gorgeous Indian summer day. Sloping down to the river, the white teepees of the Umatilla Indians sat in a grove of cottonwood trees, their green and gold leaves fluttering in the gentle breeze. Beyond, lay low hills and rangeland rising to meet an autumn-blue sky.

All seemed calm and peaceful until her attention was drawn to a large crowd gathering around a nearby livestock corral. Curious, Lael wandered over. As she got nearer, she could see the crowd was listening to a skinny little man wearing angora chaps and strutting back and forth, waving a fistful of cash in the air.

"That's the deal! Who'll take me up on it? Who's man enough to ride Sharkey, a ton and a half of the freshest beef you'll ever see? Threw thirty-six riders in three days down in Salinas. Not one of them jaspers could stay on longer'n three seconds. But I can tell this is a bunch of real men, buckaroos through and through. Come on, who'll give it a go? One hundred dollars to the man who stays on ten seconds, five dollars to give it a try!"

Lael spotted Mabel and Hugh Strickland standing on the fringes of the crowd. "What's this all about?" she asked, as the little man continued to exhort the assemblage.

"That's Happy Jack Hawn," Mabel said, a look of disapproval on her face. "He's trying to gin up a little business with that renegade bull of his."

"Any man who takes that bet is nothing but a damn' idiot," added Hugh, his normally placid features drawn together in a frown. "That Sharkey's got a reputation as a real ball-buster. Pardon my language. Ride him the day before the rodeo starts and you risk getting knocked out of the entire show."

Nevertheless, one of the younger cowboys succumbed to Happy Jack's taunts, handing over his five dollars with a devil-may-care smile.

Everyone hung themselves over the fence to watch the action. In the middle of the corral, his head covered by a gunny sack, stood the formidable-looking Sharkey. A jet black, Belgrade bull, its huge hump stood a good fifteen hands off the ground. With a three foot girth, it would be a challenge for even the longest-legged of men to grip the animal's mid-section.

"What are the rules?" asked the cocksure young cowboy.

"Ain't no rules. Hang on to whatever you can, son, with one hand or two, makes no difference." Happy Jack jerked off the blind, and with one wild gyration Sharkey tossed the rider into the air like a beanbag. The young cowboy picked himself up quickly and ran for the fence, all the brashness bucked right out of him.

Laughing and shouting, several of his colleagues also rose to the challenge, no one faring any better than their hapless friend. Enjoying the show from their perch on the fence, Lael and Mabel laughed along with the rest. Leaning close, Lael muttered: "It's pretty obvious what these guys are thinking with, and it ain't their brains."

Mabel giggled and elbowed her friend in the side. Unfortunately, the cowboy next to Lael overheard her comment and turned a furious face to her. Lael recognized Skeeter McGraw, a man reputed to have a nasty and violent temper. "Who're you bad-mouthing?" he sneered. "I've got more balls than you'll ever have, lady."

"No doubt," Lael fired back. "But as for brains, well, that's another matter."

McGraw's thick features turned a mottled red. "Hey, ain't you one of the gals who was angling to get in the all-around contest?"

Surprised that he would have already heard of her pitch to the rodeo committee, Lael was thrown off balance. "Yes. What of it?"

"Well, I ain't never heard of no all-around champion who warn't a damn' good bull rider. Why don't you show all us dick-for-brains men how a *real* champion rides that there bull?"

"Shut up, McGraw," said Hugh Strickland sternly. "I don't cotton to that kind of talk around a lady."

"That's OK, Hugh," Lael cut in coolly. "Mister McGraw was merely being descriptive. I took no offense."

McGraw appeared momentarily perplexed. He was not certain, but he thought he had been insulted. He turned to his buddy, an equally dull-looking fellow missing his two front teeth. "Hey, Junior, this lady," he drew out the word sarcastically, "thinks she can ride that bull better'n a man."

"I did not say that," declared Lael, her temper flaring.

"Come on, Lael, let's leave. I don't like the company around here." Hugh Strickland, his arm already encircling

162

Mabel protectively, took a firm hold on Lael's elbow.

Loathe to walk away from such an ignorant brute, nevertheless she let Hugh lead her off, knowing it was the smart thing to do.

McGraw's raspy voice followed her. "Guess I learned that bitch a lesson. Maybe now she knows her place."

Twirling around, Lael pulled free from Hugh's grasp and marched right up to McGraw, wanting with all her might to wipe the disgusting smile off his ugly face. "And just where exactly do you think my place is?" she spat.

Leering broadly, McGraw rocked his hips back and forth in an unmistakably suggestive move. "Why, you oughta come with me, swee' pea. I got a nice place for ya."

Fists balled, Hugh started forward, ready to defend Lael's honor. But she stepped in front of him, blocking his way. "Don't worry about me, Hugh. I can handle this goon. I'd rather get trampled by that bull than come anywhere close to you, McGraw."

"It'd just tickle me pink to see a bitch like you get trampled, too," McGraw rasped.

Her blood boiling, Lael stomped over to Happy Jack Hawn who was about to collect five dollars from another victim. "Give me that," she cried, yanking the bill from the cowboy's fingers and stuffing it into Happy Jack's hand, "and start counting out a hundred dollars."

The crowd was stunned into silence. Happy Jack swallowed hard, his Adam's apple bobbing up and down nervously. "Here now, miss, take this back. Sharkey ain't fit for no ladies to ride."

"That ain't just any lady," came a voice from the crowd. "That's Lael Buckley. Reckon she's got as good a chance as any of us."

Murmurs of assent rose from the assembled cowboys,

most of whom, unlike Skeeter McGraw, had great respect for Lael's abilities.

"Mabel," Lael called, "lend me your boots." The rubber-soled trick riding shoes Lael wore would never do if she expected to stay in Sharkey's bull rigging.

Mabel bent to remove her boots, her spurs jingling eerily in the sudden silence.

Hugh came up beside his wife and spoke softly into her ear. "Honey, this ain't right. This could turn out real bad. Try and talk her out of it."

Mabel paused. Looking up into her concerned husband's face, she whispered: "No, I won't talk her out of it. Let 'er buck." It was the war cry of the Roundup, but Hugh knew, at this moment, it meant something even more to his cowgirl wife and her courageous friend.

Serenaded by shouts of encouragement that all but drowned out the jeers of Skeeter McGraw and his sidekick, Lael approached Sharkey, concentrating hard on the task at hand. She had ridden bulls before, although never in competition, and knew that it was a far different experience from broncho riding. It was much tougher to grip a bull's broad back, and its slippery hide made the saddle slide all over the place. Not only that, but a bull's movements were almost impossible to anticipate. She would have to be prepared instantly to counter every one of the animal's wily maneuvers.

Squaring herself in the saddle, Lael gripped the horn with one hand and the strap behind the cantle with the other. At her signal, Happy Jack jerked the blind. Up she went as though a pound of dynamite had exploded beneath her. She was thrown off balance. Sharkey immediately detected his advantage and flew into a series of teeth-shattering, spine-crushing twists, weaves, corkscrews, and sidethrows. Somehow, she stayed on, although she felt as though every joint in her body was turning inside out and her brains were slamming against the top of her skull. For some reason, she could no longer grasp the cantle strap with her left hand. She groped wildly for some other handhold, but her arm flapped in the air uselessly. With a tremendous burst of energy, Sharkey let loose a mighty buck, and Lael came out of the saddle.

But something was wrong. Instead of landing free of the enraged bull, Lael was being dragged, a spur on Mabel's boot hung up in the cinch. Instinctively, she grabbed her head as flying hoofs scissored into her flailing body. With the last of her strength, she twisted her leg hard to the side, forcing her foot right out of the entangled boot. As blackness overtook her, the last thing she could remember was feeling like a jigsaw puzzle with its pieces scattered helter-skelter in the dirt.

The gossamer image floated in front of Lael's eyes, its edges blurred and indefinite. She blinked, and the image came into focus. Leaning forward, a white-uniformed nurse laid a cool wrist against Lael's forehead.

"Welcome back," the nurse said. "We weren't sure when you planned on rejoining us."

Lael tried to swallow, but her mouth and throat were too dry.

"Here, try a sip of water." The nurse held a straw to Lael's parched lips. "You've been out for two days. The doctor was starting to get worried. I'll go tell him you're back in the land of the living."

"Wait!" Lael closed her eyes against the sudden pain that started in her chest and radiated all the way to the top of her head. Breathing shallowly, she let the pain recede before trying to speak again. "What happened?"

"The way I hear it, some renegade bull gave you a real run

for your money. Don't you remember any of it?"

Closing her eyes again, Lael tried to think. She had been practicing with Dancer, and then there had been a big crowd and some ugly, nasty man had called her names. She could see a huge, hulking bull standing blinded in the middle of a corral, but all the rest was gone. Perhaps blessedly so.

"Well, don't worry about it. You've had quite a shock. It'll probably come back to you, bit by bit." The nurse took Lael's right wrist and measured her pulse.

"How bad am I hurt?" Lael whispered.

"Oh, I've seen a lot worse, especially during rodeo week," came the cheery response. "Your left arm's broken, your right knee's wrenched, you've got three cracked ribs, a concussion, and enough bruises and scrapes that, if I were you, I wouldn't go parading around in my skivvies for a while."

"My head feels like it's going to explode." Lael tried to raise her good arm, but the effort was too much.

"I shouldn't wonder. They say that bull landed you a good one right between the eyes. We took a few stitches, and you've got a dandy pair of shiners, but, all in all, I'd say you were lucky. I'll go get you something to take for that headache." At the door, the nurse turned back. "There's a young man been waiting to see you ever since they brought you here. Should I send him in?"

For an instant, Lael's hopes soared until she remembered that Curtis Morris had shown up at her tent right before the incident with Sharkey. Chastising herself for imagining it might be Rafe Callantine, she nodded her assent to the nurse, reminding herself that Curtis was the one who cared enough to be here when she needed someone.

Entering the room quietly, the lanky cowboy's eyes widened at the sight of her. He clamped a smile on his handsome face.

166

"It's that bad, is it?" Lael said, attempting a grin.

Perching on the side of her bed, he took her good hand in his. "You're always beautiful to me, no matter what."

"Oh, Curtis," Lael sighed, "you're the sweetest person I know." A tiny tear trickled down her bruised cheek.

"Hey, what's that for?" he asked, gently wiping it away.

"Just . . . because. Because I've been very stupid."

"Getting on that bull may not have been the smartest thing you ever did, but you'll recover. I just saw the doc in the hall. He says you can leave in another day or two."

"I'll miss the entire Roundup," Lael sulked. "And anyway, I wasn't just talking about that damn' bull."

Curtis hesitated. "What else have you been stupid about?"

"You," Lael admitted. "I'm sorry about the way I treated you, Curtis. It was wrong of me to be so off and on with you. I was just . . . confused. But I'm not confused any more."

The tears fell freely now. Curtis took out his clean kerchief and patted her cheeks. "So what have you decided, honey? What do you want me to do?"

Lael twined her fingers in his and looked lovingly at the strong, capable man beside her. This man would never let her down, would never abandon her. Weeping again, but with a sense of relief, Lael said: "I want you to take care of me."

Curtis raised her hand to his lips and kissed it tenderly. Smiling his special smile, he told her: "I thought you'd never ask."

Chapter Eighteen

"Hey, Red, over here! I ain't got all day, ya know."

Blowing a strand of sweaty hair out of her eyes, Fanny set down the coffee pot and rushed over to table number five, pad and pencil in hand. "What'll it be?"

"Gimme the special and how's about a little of this sweet stuff on the side?" said Deputy Sheriff Willard Bromley, reaching out to pinch Fanny's backside.

"Hands off, Willard," said Fanny tiredly, swatting away Bromley's grimy paw.

"Aw, now, don't play hard to get, Red. It just ain't in your nature." The corpulent lawman grinned yellowly across the table at his slovenly companions, none of whom, judging by their collective stench, had bathed or changed their reeking clothes in the recent past.

Ignoring Bromley's remark, Fanny finished taking their orders, brushing off the deputy's wandering hands once more before retreating to safety behind the counter. Back when she first started working this lousy job, she used to give Bromley as good as she got, calling him every choice name she could think of. But then Del found out and ordered her to be nice to the fat jerk, being as he was a friend of his and all. She didn't much like the situation, but it wasn't worth fighting over—not with Del's temper.

At two o'clock, Fanny finished her shift and exited the small café into the glare of the desert sun. She adjusted her hat to block its searing rays, knowing she looked odd in her waitress uniform and a Big Four Stetson—one of the few remaining possessions from her cowgirl days—but not able to muster the energy to care. Moving slowly down the dusty street, she promised herself a long soak in the tub when she got home, even if it took an hour to heat the water.

A tall, dark-haired cowboy coming toward her on the street briefly sent her heart racing until she realized it was not Curtis Morris. Why, after all this time, did the thought of Curtis affect her so? Hadn't she lived through enough rejection to know when it was time to pick her pride up off the floor and move on? That was why, after all, she had moved to Tucson, although she had not really wanted to leave Hollywood and her career in the movies. But her pride could not take being snubbed every day by Curtis, who blamed her for what had happened between them and for Lael's departure. He had made it clear they could no longer be even friends. Heartbroken, she had run to Del, the man who had taken her in once before when she had needed time to convalesce.

Del had been happy to see Fanny and treated her well, at first. A cowboy by trade, he was gone for long stretches of time, hiring out wherever help was needed, but Fanny had not minded. When he came back home, their reunions convinced her his absence had been well worth it. Somewhere along the line, Del had started calling her his wife. Fanny had gone along with him, pleased that anyone would want her that much that worrying about ceremonies and legalities had seemed petty and ungrateful. Yes, her first year with Del had almost made her happy, had almost closed the hole in her heart.

But then everything had changed. Del's horse had fallen on him, crushing his pelvis and breaking his leg in three places. He had been laid up for six months, and, when he finally could get around again, he walked with a crippling limp.

His cowboying days over, he had taken to hanging around pool halls and roadhouses—anywhere down-and-outers like himself congregated.

With no money coming in, Fanny had taken the waitressing job, a move that Del perceived as a threat to his manhood. That was the first time he had hit her, back-handing her hard enough to bloody her lips and nose. Scared, Fanny had offered to quit her job but, perversely, he had re-fused to let her. Since then, she had walked a tightrope, never sure whether what she did would please or anger him. More than once, she had packed her bags to leave, only to realize that she had nowhere to run.

Fanny let herself into their ramshackle cottage and began heating water for her bath. While she waited, she pulled out an old copy of *Hoofs and Horns* and turned to a well-worn page. On it was a picture of Louise Morris standing proudly next to her horse, Cancan. In the background, talking to an-other wrangler, stood Curtis, his handsome profile to the camera. She wondered what Curtis was doing right that second, and then decided she didn't want to know because, whatever it was, it had nothing to do with pining for her.

The bath finally ready, she lowered herself into the rusty old tub, sighing in relief. Varicolored bruises, some yellow with age, others freshly blue and purple, covered her entire mid-section. Del had learned not to hit her where it showed after people at the café had started to ask questions. Not sur-prisingly, his pal Willard Bromley, Deputy Sheriff Willard Bromley, had never raised an eyebrow, no matter how beaten up she looked.

Relaxing into the steamy water, Fanny let her mind fly away from this broken-down shack in the middle of the desert to a place where ocean breezes blew the sweet scent of orange blossoms toward the lush, palm-lined hills. Unbidden visions of Curtis scrolled through her brain—the handsome Texan galloping across the back lot on a fine black stallion, handing her into his cheap little flivver with a jaunty smile, strolling down Sunset Boulevard with his cowboy's rolling gait. Suddenly Fanny could picture him on their last night together, his eyes strangely hooded, yet gleaming with urgency. She could feel his hands touching her, his lips crushing hers with the intensity of someone searching for release.

The bathroom door slammed open.

"What the hell? It's the fuckin' middle of the day." Del staggered in, reeking of booze and tobacco.

"I know damn' well what time it is," said Fanny, annoyed. "Is there some law says I can't take a bath in the middle of the day?"

Del watched appreciatively as she stood, water sliding from her well-proportioned, if multicolored, body. "Reckon not. But there oughter be a law says you gotta wait for me. Sit back down there, darlin'. I'm gonna climb in with ya. I could use a good soak." Hopping on his good leg, he yanked off a cracked and dirty boot.

"Truer words were never spoken," said Fanny dryly. She stepped out of the tub and wrapped herself in a towel. "Go ahead and soak. I'll have dinner ready when you get out."

"Nah, that's not what I had in mind, sugar. Let's you and me have a little fun. Don't have to be in the tub, if you don't wanna." Del leaned against the sink and removed his other boot.

Fanny knew he was drunk. The question remained, was he mellow drunk or mean drunk? Ordinarily she would not consider denying him when he was in the mood for sex. That was a sure-fire way to start a fight. But today she just could not bring herself to give in, not with thoughts of Curtis so fresh in her mind. Something inside her would die if she had to submit to this smelly, uncouth piece of vermin.

"Maybe later, Del. I got work to do." She mustered a small smile and tried to push past him. He reached out and grabbed her arm.

"I guess you didn't hear me. Man comes home, finds his wife waiting for him all nekkid, he expects a little something. Can't blame me, can ya?" He pulled her to him roughly. The towel slipped from her body as he rubbed against her bare skin.

Don't fight it, her brain screamed, but she had to. She could not give in, not this time. "I ain't your wife," she snarled. "You don't own me. Now turn me loose, you miserable peckerwood."

Del's bloodshot eyes narrowed in anger. "You lousy whore. Can't stand to do it with a cripple, is that it? God-damned ungrateful bitch!"

Dragging her across the hall, he threw her on the bed. Pinning her down with one arm, he fumbled with his pants.

"No, no, no!" Fanny sobbed, struggling against his hold. She struck out, her fingernails slashing red lines down his neck.

"Shit!" His hand involuntarily covered his wound.

Momentarily free, Fanny scrambled off the bed and ran for the door. He caught her from behind, slamming her to the floor.

"God-damned fucking bitch!" he screamed, grabbing her by the hair and pulling her to her feet.

Fanny knew she was beat. It was now only a question of survival. "I'm sorry, I'm sorry," she whimpered. "I didn't mean it."

But his anger had metastasized into a disease-filled knot of hate. With animal-like ferocity, he set upon his prey, punching, hitting, and kicking until she lay broken and bloody before him. As she sank into unconsciousness, the thought came to her that she would not be sorry if tomorrow never came.

Chapter Nineteen

After two years of marriage to Curtis Morris, Lael was still not certain she was happy to come home to her husband. Oftentimes, she felt relieved to return to their cottage in the San Fernando Valley, but she suspected that had more to do with being eager to leave behind, for a little while, the grind of riding the circuit than it did with anticipating a joyous marital reunion.

Shaking off such a disconcerting notion, Lael decided she was simply tired, bone tired, from six months of nearly constant rodeoing. Returning from the Pendleton Roundup, traditionally the final big rodeo of the season, she was looking forward to an extended rest.

The 1926 season had been good to Lael. With earnings around $8,000, she was unquestionably in the top tier of professional rodeo performers, male or female. She was considered the cowgirl to beat in relay racing and had recently added Roman racing—a difficult event where the contestant rode two horses, standing with one foot on each mount—to her repertoire. And although more and more venues were treating trick riding as an exhibition act, she was still likely to win where it was a contested event.

Inevitably there had been disappointments along the road. The Pendleton Roundup Association, for instance, still refused to let women compete for the all-around title. And every year, it seemed, more women dropped out and fewer entered the ranks of professional cowgirls, for reasons that were not entirely clear to Lael. But it was still, without doubt, the life she loved, and she counted herself lucky to be living it.

Lael pulled around to the back of the house and climbed out stiffly. After fifteen hours behind the steering wheel, she could feel every mile of rutted highway throughout her entire body. Especially her right knee which she still favored after her accident at Pendleton two years ago.

So much for having a husband to share the burdens, she mused before pushing the thought away. This was territory she and Curtis had already fought over, and she was not about to challenge their uneasy truce. She realized she had no more right to expect him to leave the job he loved for her sake, than *vice versa*. But it still rankled.

Lael unloaded Dancer and took her time walking the little pony around the yard, working out the kinks in both of them. One of the reasons she loved their home here in the valley was that it was big enough to keep horses. One of these days, when she had time, she intended to start a business raising Thoroughbreds.

A car door slammed out front. With a gentle slap to the rump, Lael turned Dancer loose in the small corral and went around the house to greet Curtis. "Hey there, stranger. I see you survived."

Curtis was returning from two weeks back at the ranch in Texas. Big Jack had finally died, and his only son had been summoned to attend to family matters. "Just barely," said Curtis with a wan smile. "I missed you something awful."

"I missed you, too," Lael said simply. There was no use re-hashing her reasons for not accompanying him to Texas. A good wife would have dropped everything to join her husband at his father's funeral, she supposed. But it would have meant missing the Roundup, and she just could not bring herself to do that. They had argued and finally parted with hard feelings on both sides. Now they faced each other warily, wondering how to patch things up.

Lael made the first move. She walked to Curtis and placed her arms around his neck and her head on his broad, strong chest. Dropping his bags, he enfolded her in a long, silent embrace, slowly stroking the golden ponytail that fell in a tangled sheaf down her back.

Stepping back, Lael looked up into his dark eyes. For the first time, she noticed tiny crow's feet edging out from the corners. "How bad was it?" she asked guiltily.

"Bad. I have a lot to tell you," he said, giving her a curiously guarded look. "But first, tell me about the Roundup. Did my favorite cowgirl pull a sweep?"

Lael laughed. "Not quite, but it was close."

Arms wrapped around each other, they retreated into their little cottage as Lael recounted her successes at Pendleton. Curtis could not wait too long before pulling her into the bedroom, and they made love as the sun slipped below the Santa Monica Mountains to the west. Later, as they lay close together with a cool breeze blowing the curtains, Lael asked him again about his trip to Texas.

Curtis sighed heavily. "Well, for one thing, Louise is in pretty bad shape. You know, she hated Big Jack so much I thought she might actually be glad when he died, might snap out of her funk. But she's too far gone. She stayed drunk the whole time. Hardly even came out of her room. It's almost like she's become her mother."

"What on earth could make a strong woman like Louise fall apart like that?" mused Lael, absently stroking Curtis's chest.

He stayed quiet a long time. Swinging his legs out of bed, he rested his elbows on his knees and rubbed his head as though it hurt. "I know one reason for it," he announced, and then sighed again. "Lael, this is hard for me to tell you. I was thinking all the way back on the train how to put it, but there isn't a good way."

Lael scooted over and put a hand on his back. "Whatever it is, it can't be that bad."

Another pause, then: "I'm not who you think I am, honey. I'm not who *I* think I am."

"I don't understand."

"Neither do I. How can one man ruin so many peoples' lives?" Pulling on his pants, Curtis crossed to the window, leaning his forearm on the sill and gazing down the valley. When he turned to look at her, she saw dread in his eyes.

"Lael, please don't hate me for this . . . I'm . . . I'm not my mother's son. What I mean is . . . my father's wife did not give birth to me. My real mother is the woman I thought was my adopted sister."

"Alice?" Lael whispered in amazement.

Curtis nodded miserably. "After the funeral, she took me aside and told me everything. When I was born, Big Jack brought her home so she could be near me, but he refused to let her acknowledge me as her son. Instead, she was my big sister." He shook his head in disbelief. "What an arrogant bastard. He drove my mother . . . I mean, his wife . . . crazy and turned Louise into a drunk."

"So Louise knew the truth?"

"She found out somehow. Big Jack told her if she said anything to me, he'd tell everyone about her son."

"Louise has a son?" Incredulous, Lael tried to take it all in.

Ashamed, Curtis dropped his voice. "Yes. She was very young. Her husband left her, and she abandoned the boy. Considering all that, it's no wonder she turned to booze."

Lael slipped on her robe and padded over to her husband. "Curtis, why do you think I'd hate you for something that isn't even your fault?"

He turned away, trying to figure out how to explain that everything he thought he had known about himself had just been shattered to pieces. He was not the man Lael had left on their doorstep two scant weeks ago. But he was too scared to give voice to his fears.

"Look at your family," he said ruefully. "Your folks are as fine as they come. Your brothers and sisters are all happy and successful. Now look at mine. My father was a certifiable jackass, his wife was a lunatic, my sister's a drunk, and I'm an illegitimate bastard. Ain't much to write home about."

"Oh, Curtis,"—Lael wrapped her arms around his waist—"I didn't marry your family, I married you. Every family has its skeletons. Yours are just a little more . . . interesting than most."

"Is that right?" he said, cherishing the twinkle he saw in those sage-green eyes he loved so much. "And just what are the Buckley family skeletons, pray tell?"

"Well . . . rumor has it Uncle Charlie sells illegal moonshine," Lael said hopefully.

Curtis threw back his head and laughed. "Quite a sin, by Buckley standards." He drew her back to the bed, and they climbed under the covers, the autumn evening having cooled deliciously. He held her close, letting his hand travel up and down the length of her body.

"Not all the news is bad," he murmured, his lips buried in her hair. "Now that Big Jack's gone, I'll be getting money from the operation of the ranch. I'm not sure how much, yet, but it ought to be enough that you can scale back your rodeoing and stay home more."

Lael stiffened. "You know that's not what I. . . ."

"Calm down," Curtis interrupted. "I didn't say quit altogether. You can still hit all the big shows, but there's no reason now for you to be gone six months a year. With my job at the studio and the money from the ranch, we'll be sitting pretty. We can finally think about starting a family."

"Curtis, I. . . ."

"Shh," he whispered, moving against her slowly. "Just let me take care of everything."

Chapter Twenty

Leaning back against the plush, red velvet seat, Lael watched the Canadian countryside speed by, grateful that she had been enticed to ride in this luxurious Pullman car. When Guy Weadick had called, inviting her to sign on with his tour of Canadian rodeos, he had encouraged her to leave her car and trailer in Los Angeles in favor of this specially chartered train.

"You'll have everything at your beck and call," he had reasoned. "Your own sleeping compartment complete with maid service, porters to bring you meals, and hot water. Why, you can even set your boots out at night and they'll come back the next morning clean and polished. What's more, in almost every town, we'll pull the train onto a spur right next to the rodeo grounds so you can stay in your own Pullman car throughout the show. Door-to-door service, Lael, you can't beat that."

In addition to top-notch accommodations, Weadick had promised a well-run operation with large purses and sizable crowds. So far, he had delivered. Over one hundred thousand spectators had passed through the gates in Winnipeg, and he expected twice that number at Calgary. In between those bookends, the tour stopped in places with names like Stony Indian and Moose Jaw. Lael found she enjoyed the small-town rodeos almost more than the headliner stops. Born and raised on the prairie, she appreciated the simplicity and serenity of these isolated little villages that sprang from the flat earth like cottonwoods near a creek. She allowed herself to relax and revel in the beauty of the wind-swept plains of the far north.

If only Curtis were with her, she would feel truly content. She had asked him to come, but he had declined, citing the demands of his new status as a contract player at Universal. She had not argued with him, although she knew for a fact he could have taken the time to accompany her on at least a portion of this trip. But refusing to go with her was his way of making the point that his job was as important as hers. It was also a protest against her busy schedule which she had refused to alter despite his entreaties. One of these days she would be ready to settle down and start a family, but not yet. Rodeo was in her blood, and, as long as she could rope a steer or sit a broncho, she would be out there where the crowd cheered and the dust flew. A pity Curtis could not understand that elemental fact about his wife.

Slowing down, the train crossed the Saskatchewan River and pulled onto a spur line that dead-ended at the town of Saskatoon's rodeo grounds. Just before the train lurched to a halt, Lael caught some movement out of the corner of her eye. She leaned forward for a better look. Sitting tall in the saddle, a cowboy in battered chaps and faded cotton shirt herded a team of horses toward the stock corral. As she watched, he removed his hat and wiped his forehead on his shirt sleeve. A flash of black hair, a glimpse of strong features—the man was Rafe Callantine.

Lael jerked back from the window, plastering herself against the seat. Just as quickly, she leaned forward again, her hands splayed across the glass, searching for him through the dust and smoke that swirled around the train. There he was, trotting away from her, barely visible now. Had it been a case of mistaken identity like the hundreds of others over the past seven years? Straining to see, she stared intently at the man's broad shoulders, at the dark hair curling over his collar. It was him, all right. It was Rafe.

Not knowing what to do, Lael stood, then sat, then stood again. Her heart pounded, and her breath came in short puffs. All around her, people streamed off the train, eager to stretch their legs, take in their new premises, settle their stock for the night. Still, she stayed inside her walled-off compartment, shaking like a leaf.

Sooner or later, she had been bound to run into Rafe Callantine again. As it happened, it had been later, much later. So much later, in fact, that the way she was reacting now was ridiculous. Ordinarily in complete control of her body, Lael was shocked at the way it was betraying her now, making her feel like a lovesick teenager, instead of the mature, married woman she was.

A knock at the door brought her to her senses. Lorena Trickey stood in the aisle, peering in at Lael. She gave the cowgirl a questioning smile and pointed toward the exit. Shakily Lael grabbed her hat and followed.

Resolved to act as natural as possible, Lael stepped out into the cool Canadian evening. Observing her usual routine, she fetched Dancer from the stock car and led him to the stables. She gathered with some of the other cowboys and cowgirls around the small arena, giving it her customary inspection. But no matter how normal she acted on the outside, on the inside every nerve ending tingled. Her eyes flitted here and there, seeming to see Rafe in every broad back or canted hat.

He was out there somewhere, and sometime in the next two days she would run into him. And when that happened, she would smile politely, say—"Hello, remember me?"—and then go on about her business. Yes, she promised herself, that's what she would do.

Lady Buckaroo

★ ★ ★ ★ ★

Lael's first thought as she rolled out of her berth early the next morning was of Rafe Callantine. Groaning, she peered at her image in the mirror above the compartment's tiny sink. Had she changed much in the seven years since she had last seen him? Back then, at eighteen, she had been young and brash, ready to take on the world, green as the grass that lined the Niobrara River. Now, at twenty-five, she was wiser, more experienced, at the top of her game. She had conquered the world she set out to take on. There was another big difference, of course—she was married now.

"Don't do this, Eulalie Buckley," she muttered, giving herself a stern look. She rang the porter for hot water, then opened her trunk. This morning the entire troupe would parade down the main street of Saskatoon in full cowboy kit. For this tour, Lael had created a new type of outfit that was all the rage with the Canadian crowds. Drawing on a Spanish theme, she wore satin trousers and a matching bolero, both trimmed with elegant brocade.

She took special care with her costume today, fiddling for several minutes with a bright red sash. Trying it first as a headband, then as a scarf around her neck, she finally tied it about her waist. By the time she finished primping, she was running late.

Stepping from the train car, she automatically scanned the busy yard. At any moment she expected to bump into a certain elusive cowboy, and she wanted to be prepared with a neutral smile and a breezy attitude. *My goodness, it's Rafe Callantine, isn't it? Fancy running into you again after all this time. You probably don't remember, but you taught me to ride relay, what, seven years ago? My, how time flies.*

But although her lines were well rehearsed, she never got a chance to recite them, for Rafe did not appear at the parade

183

or for the afternoon's scheduled events. By the end of the day, Lael decided she must have imagined him, just like all the other times. But this time, she had been so sure.

Masking her guilty disappointment, she joined Mabel and Hugh Strickland, Lorena, and several other people for a night out on the town. Saskatoon was just big enough to offer a selection of night spots, and the troupe hit both of them, tearing up the town in their own rambunctious way. Lael laughed and sang and danced along with the others, but it all felt hollow. Finally, about midnight, she slipped out and began walking back to the train.

Although the hour was late, the sky was yet twilight, for at this time of year in northern Canada the sun never completely set. As she wandered down the street, Lael decided this season of the Midnight Sun was a little eerie. It gave her an unfinished feeling, as though she could never put the day to rest. She passed the end of town, noting how the dusky light concealed the edges of things. Squinting, she tried to bring the distant train into focus. Suddenly she heard something behind her, a boot crunching on rocky soil. Turning, she beheld a tall figure cast in the shadow of half-light. The figure stopped and said not a word, but his identity was no mystery to Lael.

The words she had meant to say darted from her brain like a minnow from roiling water. She simply stood there, taking him in. He wore the same dusty clothes he had had on the day before. Over his shoulder was slung a pair of saddlebags that he gripped with one rough-skinned hand. His hat slanted low, obscuring his features, but, by the tilt of his head, she knew he was staring at her.

She said the first words that came into her mind. "Are you following me?"

A pause. "No, ma'am." Like he was a stranger to her.

"Do you remember me?" Lael asked, on tenterhooks.

He made a sound, a sort of ironic chuckle. "I remember you all right. You're famous."

"Not then, I wasn't. Not when you knew me."

Another pause. "I remember you," he repeated.

Lael swung her head toward the train. "I . . . uh . . . I was just going back to my car."

"I'm going that general direction myself," he admitted. They fell into step, separated by a good three feet, the only sound their boots crunching on gravel.

Lael cleared her throat. "What brings you to Saskatoon, of all places?"

"Picking up a string of horses for a friend of mine. Gonna ship 'em down to the States."

"Oh, so you being here's got nothing to do with the rodeo?"

"That's right." He shifted the saddlebags to his other shoulder. The supple smell of leather wafted toward Lael.

"Did you know the rodeo was going to be in town?"

"Yup."

Did you know I'd be here, too? she wanted to ask, but didn't.

Having apparently exhausted all topics of conversation, they covered the remaining distance in silence.

"This is my car," Lael said, stopping in front of one of the Pullmans.

He hesitated, then with a brief—"Good night."—headed off into the twilight. She almost called him back, but she knew, if she did, she would be lost. Besides, what would she say if he did come back? *I barely know you, but I've carried your memory with me for the past seven years, though that didn't stop me from marrying another man.* Impossible for her to say the words, impossible for him to understand them.

Tears filling her eyes, Lael stumbled up the steps of the car and tore open the door to her compartment. A naked man turned to stare at her.

Lael backed up a step, knocking into the door jamb. "What are you doing here?" she demanded.

"Well, now, I might ask you the same thing, little filly," replied the exposed cowboy, reaching calmly for his shirt.

Lael realized she had made a mistake. This was not her compartment; none of her things was here and even the color scheme was different. "Oh, my God," she clapped a hand to her mouth. "Ex-excuse me, I'm sorry."

Back-pedaling furiously, Lael tumbled out of the car, catching her heel on the last step and sprawling unceremoniously in the dirt. Rolling over, she propped up on her elbows and searched for the car's number. Sure enough, this was not her car. Confused, she looked about, studying the landscape. She was certain this was where her car had come to rest.

She heard a crunching sound; Rafe Callantine was returning. Terrific. All she needed now was to look like a fool in front of the one man in the world she wanted to impress. With a groan, she plopped flat on her back and covered her face with her hat.

The crunching came to a stop beside her. Mortified, Lael remained hidden.

A moment passed, then: "I've heard that's the way ostriches hide. In case you were wondering, it doesn't work."

The absurdity of the situation caught up to her. She let out a small chuckle, then another, and before she could stop herself she was laughing out loud.

Rafe lifted her hat brim with the toe of his boot and peered at her, mystified.

Lael rose to a sitting position, wiping tears from her eyes. "I'm sorry," she gasped, still chuckling. "You must think I've gone bananas. But I just got . . . mooned, or whatever the equivalent expression is for frontal exposure."

"Come again?"

She gestured toward the train car. "That isn't my Pullman. I opened the door to what I thought was my compartment and walked in on some guy who was, well, not prepared for company. The funny thing is, I'm sure I know whoever it was, but I was so busy looking . . . elsewhere . . . I didn't get a good look at his face. Now all day tomorrow I'm going to be wondering if every man who looks at me twice is this poor Joe." She laughed again.

Rafe's mouth turned up at the corners. He reached a hand down and hauled her to her feet. "Doesn't every man look at you twice, anyway?" he asked softly.

Still holding his hand, Lael gazed up at him. She loved the way his mouth looked when he smiled, if this could be called a smile.

She gave him a broad grin. "Only when I do something stupid, which is about every other minute. Like right now. I seem to have misplaced my train car."

"That's a mighty big thing to lose," he said, letting go her hand.

Lael did a slow three-sixty. "I could swear this is where it stopped." She shrugged helplessly.

"Don't feel too bad." Rafe shifted the bags hanging over his shoulder. "Sometimes the engineers uncouple the cars and move 'em around."

"Why?"

"Any number of reasons. To do repairs, or maybe they've been adding or subtracting some cars, and yours just got moved to a different spot. It's probably close by."

Lael caught herself staring at him, mesmerized by the way the tiny scar pulled at his lip when he spoke. She jerked to attention, aware that he had stopped talking and was giving her an amused look.

"Right, right," she stammered. "I'll just check up and down the line. It's got to be here. Um, thanks for your help." She started off down the line of cars.

Wordlessly he fell in with her. They checked every car in the line and the few that sat uncoupled in the yard, but could not find hers. By the end of their search, Lael had started laughing again, threatening to break into another car and spend the night there no matter what the state of its inhabitants.

At this, Rafe's mouth turned up again. Lael decided her goal in life would be to get him to laugh, a real laugh, a belly laugh. What on earth had made him so sad? Was it something she could change? Once again, she brought herself up short. These were not proper thoughts for a married woman.

The train yard bordered a little pine-rimmed lake. Someone had built a fishing pier that protruded a few dozen feet over the water. They wandered out on it, their boots rapping woodenly on the weathered planks. At the end of the pier, they stopped and gazed at the lapping surface, still shimmering in the two a.m. twilight.

"I think I could get used to it never turning dark," said Lael, reëvaluating. "I like the unreality of it all. It's like a phantom time of day when anything's possible because it isn't really happening."

Rafe gave her a strange look, but said nothing.

Embarrassed, Lael reverted to more mundane subjects. "So, what have you been doing with yourself since I last saw you?"

Silence. It seemed as though he had to ponder every response, no matter how simple the question. "Nothing worth mentioning," he said.

Lael sighed inwardly. How could she get him to open up? Why should she even want to?

"I never got a chance to thank you for tending to me that night in Amarillo. Remember, when I got in that fight with Maude Kelly? Another stupid mistake of mine."

"No, you're wrong about that. You didn't have any choice. You had to stand up for yourself, show everybody what you're made of."

Lael stood very still, afraid to show the pleasure she felt at his praise. "Well, anyway," she said with a little laugh, "you doctored me up real well. I don't have any scars to show for that particular escapade. 'Course, I've had plenty since."

A long pause. Rafe turned to her slowly. "I know. I heard what happened in Pendleton two years ago. They said you got torn up pretty bad." He raised his hand and lifted her hat from her head. Her hair, mussed and full of bits of grass and twigs from lying on the ground, tumbled about her face. Tipping her chin up, he examined her carefully in the half-light reflected off the lake. He frowned when he saw the scar Sharkey had left on her forehead. Very slowly, he traced it with the tip of his finger. Lael shivered at his touch. He lowered his hand and stepped back. "You're cold. Come on. I'll get you a jacket, and then we'll hunt up the conductor of that blasted train and find out what they did with your car."

She followed him down the pier, past the train yard, and beyond the stables where a number of tents were pitched. He opened the flap to one of them and disappeared inside, lighting a lantern as she stepped in after him. Removing his hat, his face, reflected in the lantern's glow, was completely visible to her for the first time all night.

The main thing, of course, was his eyes. So dark, yet so richly blue, like sapphires on velvet. And so clear, not at all red-rimmed as she remembered them. The lines in his face had deepened, highlighting even more the tiny white scar at the corner of his mouth, and his hair was just showing gray at the temples. But his jaw was still firm and his body lithe and lean. Just looking at him took her breath away.

While Rafe knelt to search through his duffel for a coat, Lael took in the contents of his tent. They were minimal, even spare, consisting of his bedroll and duffel. They did not give the impression of a person who routinely lived on the move, but of someone who was making a quick trip away from home, traveling light. Did he have a home? Where was it, and what did he do there? So many questions, and Lael feared she would never be privy to the answers.

Callantine rose, shaking out a dark oilskin duster. "Here. This'll swallow you up, but it's all I've got."

Lael turned and let him drape the coat across her shoulders. True to its name, it smelled of dust, but also of horse and leather and sun and sweat. She closed her eyes and drew it close around her, engulfed in his scent. Was it her imagination, or had his hands lingered on her shoulders?

Opening her eyes, she noticed for the first time a canvas, fold-up camp chair, partially hidden behind the tent flap. On it sat a tiny, framed photograph. She picked it up. A pretty, dark-haired girl, maybe ten years old, smiled out at her.

"How sweet," Lael said. "Who is it?"

Behind her, Callantine stiffened. "None of your business," he said in a low, even voice. Reaching around, he took the picture from her and buried it in his duffel.

"I'm sorry," said Lael, stung. "I didn't mean to pry."

"Never mind," he said curtly. "We'll go find the conductor now." Jamming his hat on his head, he waited for her to exit the tent.

Wounded and not a little mad at his abrupt dismissal, Lael snapped aside the tent flap and stepped out into the gloomy dusk. But she did not want to leave like this, confused and resentful. She should not care about this rude and enigmatic man or his precious secrets, but she did.

"Rafe," she turned to him plaintively, "I said I was sorry. Don't be angry with me."

He lowered his head, the slope of his hat concealing all but the lower half of his face which was set in lines of tension. Then he looked up, his gaze riveting Lael to the ground.

"She's my daughter," he rasped.

Lael was too scared to breathe. "And your wife?" she whispered, not able to stop herself.

"You ask too many god-damned questions." Grabbing her arm roughly, he began to tow her back to the train yard.

"Stop that! Let me go!" Lael cried, barely able to keep up with him. "You're right, I'm too damned nosy. But why does it bother you so much that somebody cares?"

He stopped in his tracks, still gripping her arm. Lael felt he might slap her or kiss her, and she would not have been surprised at either one. Instead, he turned on his heel and stalked off into the twilight shadows.

Chapter Twenty-One

Misery is a too long train ride that you don't want to end. Too long because there is nothing to do but think. Not long enough because a decision waits at the end of the line.

With the end of summer came the end of Guy Weadick's Canadian Stampede, and Lael headed back to Los Angeles, to her cozy little home that she loved and to the man she had married whom she did not love.

She had come to that conclusion after many sleepless nights, and a part of her still fought it, but it seemed unarguably true. Had it been simply a matter of falling in love with somebody else, somebody who would most likely never enter her life again, Lael might have been able to put it behind her and focus her efforts on being a good wife to Curtis. But it was more than that. Sadly Lael realized her marriage had bigger problems than the reëmergence of Rafe Callantine.

As Weadick's specially chartered locomotive chugged west across Canada and down along the coast, Lael recalled with perfect clarity all the moments of her life with Curtis. They had had good times, had shared a certain happiness, but never had they been soul mates. She had married him because she was tired of being alone and wanted somebody to share the burdens of her nomadic life. But Curtis wanted no part of that existence, preferring a steady job and the same roof over his head at night. Someday, those things would hold an attraction for Lael, too, but for now being on the road was her freedom. If her husband could not deal with that fact, then changes must be made.

When she told Curtis that their marriage was not working and she wanted a divorce, it was the hardest thing she had ever done.

"It's because of the thing with Alice, isn't it?" he accused, his face ashen. "You don't want to have children with an illegitimate bastard like me. And my sister being a lousy drunk. We're not good enough for the sainted Miss Buckley, are we?"

"Oh, Curtis"—Lael shook her head sorrowfully—"don't you know me any better than that? It doesn't matter to me who your parents were, and as for Louise, well, she's one of my heroes and always will be. Our problem is that we don't want the same things in life, and it isn't fair for me to hold onto you when you'd be so much happier with someone else."

"Someone else," Curtis repeated, a light dawning in his injured eyes. "You've found someone else, haven't you? All that time you spend on the road . . . I know men must be after you constantly, but I always trusted you. . . ."

"Don't do this, Curtis. It's beneath you," Lael said sharply. "You know I've never been unfaithful."

He gave her a scathing look of his own. "You're right. I have no reason to think you've cheated on me. No reason except you don't seem to mind being gone from me six months out of the year. No reason except when I take you in my arms, I feel like you're still gone . . . some place where I can't reach you. Maybe you don't love somebody else, but you sure as hell don't love me."

Tears streamed down her face. She had nothing left to say. Angrily, Curtis slammed out the door.

Later that day, he returned, packed a bag, and moved into town.

Lael was never sure how she got through the next few days. She went nowhere and did nothing, aside from caring for the stock. Then one morning as she was cleaning out some old newspapers, a small headline caught her eye: Rodeo Cowgirl Accused of Murder. With shaking hands, Lael read the story. Down in Tucson, Arizona, a young woman, formerly a well-known figure on the ladies' rodeo circuit, had allegedly shot and killed her common-law husband. The woman's name—Fanny Lavelle.

Within the hour, Lael was in her car headed east. Moving automatically, not bothering to analyze her decision, she raced down the highway, keeping the gas pedal as close to the floor as she dared. Fanny was in trouble, big trouble, and it did not matter that they had not seen each other in five years, or that they had parted under unhappy circumstances. Fanny was still her friend and needed her.

The first thing Lael did when she reached Tucson was look up Fanny's lawyer, whose name she had gleaned from the paper. It did not take her long to conclude that the unfortunate man, with his hacking cough and poorly concealed flask in the top desk drawer, was in way over his head. Not the least of her concerns was the fact that he was willing to tell her, a complete stranger, the details of the crime.

According to the lawyer, Fanny had shot her so-called husband, a man named Del Weaver, in self-defense. He had come after her, not for the first time apparently, but on this occasion armed with a knife. He had slashed her a few times before she managed to grab a gun and kill him. A clear-cut case of self-defense, said the lawyer, yet, despite her obvious wounds, the prosecution had charged her with murder. Evidently Del Weaver had had friends in high places, including the sheriff's office, who would testify that such a gentle man, who was crippled to boot, would have never raised his hand to a woman.

The second thing she did was hire a new lawyer, reputedly the finest criminal defense attorney in town, guaranteeing his best efforts by plopping down a hefty retainer. This new lawyer was more than happy to take Lael's money, but he warned her he could not legally represent a client without that client's approval. Lael told him she would be back that afternoon with Fanny's signature on his contract.

She was ready now to visit Fanny, or so she thought until she pulled up at the county jail and suffered a sudden crisis of confidence. What would her gay old friend be like? She had obviously been through hell the last five years. What if she had lost her spunk, her willingness to fight? Or worse, what if she were still so angry with Lael over Curtis that she would refuse to see her?

Oh, for gosh sakes, Lael thought, jerking the car handle impatiently, *you'll never find out sitting here.*

They led her to a tiny, windowless room and made her wait several minutes before bringing the prisoner. Lael's worst fears were confirmed when Fanny, recognizing her visitor, told the deputy to take her back to her cell.

"Shut up and sit!" growled the overweight, smelly guard, pushing Fanny roughly onto the flimsy wooden chair. Lael made note of the name on his shirt pocket—Bromley—so she could later tell Fanny's new lawyer about his client's mistreatment in jail.

Fanny sat, half turned in her seat, facing away from Lael. Bromley hiked up his pants, which immediately settled back underneath his huge belly, and posted himself at the door.

"May Miss Lavelle and I meet alone?" Lael ventured.

"Nope. Only her lawyer can see her by herself. And if you're a lawyer, I'm Jack Sprat."

No chance of that, Lael thought. She tried another tack. "I'm here as a representative of her lawyer. As you can see, I have some documents needing Miss Lavelle's signature." Pulling the lawyer's retainer contract out of her bag, she flashed the letterhead in Bromley's direction.

"So get her to sign and get on outta here," he sniffed.

"I'm afraid these papers will require some explanation before Miss Lavelle can sign them. They involve confidential matters, you understand."

Bromley eyed her suspiciously, then broke into a leering grin. "OK, but I'll have to pat you down. It's the rule if you're left alone with a prisoner."

Swallowing her disgust, Lael stood and held out her arms. Bromley frisked her very slowly, his sweaty hands lingering at her breasts and between her legs. Finally, with a last lascivious chuckle, the deputy left the room.

Shaking with revulsion, Lael sat back down. *Pull yourself together*, she thought. *There are more important matters at hand.*

"That fat bastard always did have wandering hands. That was a neat trick, though, the way you got rid of him." Fanny spoke so quietly, still not facing her, that Lael was not sure she had heard her right.

She took a moment to look her friend over. She was shocked at what she saw. Fanny must have dropped twenty pounds—her cheek bones stuck out in sharp planes, and her skin hung limp and sallow on her once-pretty face. Her lustrous red hair had faded to a dingy brown and hung in clumps around her shoulders. There were no visible scars on the parts of her body that Lael could see, but she knew they must be hidden beneath the drab prison clothes she wore. Even so, those probably were not the worst scars Fanny carried with her.

Reaching into her bag, Lael pulled out a fresh pack of cigarettes and a box of matches and placed them on the table in front of Fanny. The girl looked at them for a moment, then shook one out and lit it, closing her eyes as she exhaled.

"Thanks. I didn't think you approved of smoking."

"I'm relaxing my standards under the circumstances."

Fanny continued to smoke, her bony fingers shaking ever so slightly as she brought the fag to her lips. She still refused to look at Lael.

How much of what happened is my fault, Lael thought miserably. *Why didn't I just get out of the way and let her have Curtis? They both would have been better off.*

Fanny finished her cigarette and crushed the butt on the cement floor. She turned to Lael, a look of resentment in her tired eyes. "I don't know why you're here. If you want to talk about old times, forget it. My memories ain't as good as yours."

"I don't want to talk about old times. The only thing I want to say about that is I was wrong about a lot of things, including the way I felt about Curtis. He and I aren't together any more."

Fanny lit another cigarette and smoked in silence for a while. "I'm sorry," she murmured.

"No you're not. And you shouldn't be. I'm the one who should be apologizing. But we'll have plenty of time to hash that out some day down the road. Right now, we've got to get you out of this mess."

"We?"

"I hope you don't mind, Fanny. I've done a few things on your behalf."

"Like what?"

"Well, I went to see your attorney. Where on earth did you find him? He looks about ready to kick the bucket from drunkenness, if the consumption doesn't get him first. And your case seems to have completely overwhelmed him."

"He's all I could afford," Fanny said defensively. "I don't have jackshit, and he agreed to let me work off his fee after the trial."

"Well, I think we can do better than that." Lael placed the contract before her friend. "I asked around and was told that this man, Thomas Hale, is the best criminal defense lawyer in town. He's willing to take over your case. All you have to do is sign this representation agreement."

Fanny flipped through the document, pausing at the last page. "Says here he requires five hundred dollars up front. I ain't got that kind of money."

"Don't worry. That's been taken care of."

"I get it." Fanny tossed the contract on the table. "You figure if you pay my legal fees that'll make up for having screwed me out of Curtis."

The remark stung, but Lael took it in stride. Fanny had a right to be mad at her. "I do feel bad about the way I treated both of you, but that's not why I want to help you now."

"The hell it ain't!" Fanny pushed away from the table angrily. "Does this make you feel good, Miss Ivy League? Dropping in like an angel on your poor, beat-up, slutty ex-friend and bailing her out of another scrape she's gotten herself into? Does it give you a little thrill to climb down from that pedestal and muck around in the mud with trash like me? Well, I ain't falling for it this time. I don't want your pity, and I don't want your help. Now, get on outta here!"

With an anguished sob, Fanny dropped her head in her hands and cried in great, wrenching heaves. Lael came around the table and held her tightly, shushing her as she would a skittish colt.

After a while, her tears all cried out, Fanny pulled away

and fixed her rival with a look that was no longer hateful but merely melancholy. "I loved him, Lael. He's the only man I ever really loved. But you were so busy trying to convince yourself you felt something for him, you couldn't see that. Not that it mattered. He never loved me anyway. Now look at me, look what I've come to."

"Oh, sweetie"—Lael hugged Fanny again—"how awful these last few years have been for you. When I think of it, I just want to cry."

Fanny wiped her sallow cheeks with the back of her hand. "It wasn't bad at first. The bastard treated me real good for a while. But nothing good ever sticks around for long, not for me."

"Why didn't you leave? How I wish you would have let me know. You could have come to live with me."

"I don't know. I was . . . paralyzed. Convinced I didn't deserve no better in life. Sometimes even now I feel like I should've just let him kill me."

"Don't say that!" Lael cried, grasping Fanny's hands. "Don't talk like your life is over. There's still hope!"

"I ain't the type to get second chances," said Fanny, shrugging back into her hard-bitten exterior. "But maybe this time'll be different. Here, let me sign that."

The next few weeks were busy ones for Lael. Not content to let events unfold, she offered her assistance to Thomas Hale, who suggested she organize a show of support for her beleaguered friend. With abundant enthusiasm, Lael wrote letters, sent telegrams, and made phone calls to anyone she could think of who knew Fanny, either from her movie studio days or from her years of riding the circuit. She received only a handful of responses, so she was shocked when, on the first day of trial, over twenty of Fanny's former acquaintances packed the courtroom, sending an unmistakable message to the judge and jury.

Perhaps most surprising was the appearance of Curtis Morris, whom Lael had been too nervous to contact. Nevertheless, there he was, although it could not have been easy for him to swallow his pride and lend his support not only to the woman he had spurned, but to the woman who had spurned him. Not for the first or last time, Lael reflected on what a fine man she had married and regretted that things could not have turned out differently. But when she saw how Fanny looked at him and the way he smiled back at her with his bashful smile, Lael hoped there might yet be a happy ending.

The trial certainly ended happily, for in the hands of a capable defense attorney the prosecution's witnesses were debunked and the physical evidence presented so as to leave no doubt that Fanny had acted in self-defense. When the verdict of acquittal was read, the courtroom erupted in cheers and applause.

Outside the courthouse, Lael thanked all the people who had responded to her plea for help. She had not realized how popular Fanny was with the rodeo crowd. In fact, she had expected some of the women to hold a grudge against the flashy cowgirl. But in the end, when the chips were down, rodeo folks could be counted on to come through for one of their own.

Lael saw Curtis detach himself from a group and make his way toward her. She took a deep breath, dreading this first confrontation since he had moved out over two months ago.

"Curtis, I want to thank you. . . ."

"That was a fine thing you did. . . ."

They both spoke at the same time, stopped, laughed at their awkwardness.

"Thank you so much for being here," Lael said fervently.

"As much as it meant to me, I think it made all the difference to Fanny. Did you see how she lit up when you entered the courtroom?"

Curtis frowned. "It's a little premature to be playing matchmaker, isn't it? We aren't even formally divorced yet."

Lael blushed and reminded herself that she would have to tread very carefully where Curtis was concerned. "I didn't mean it like that."

He pursed his lips and said nothing.

"Have you thought any more about . . . what I said before I left?" she asked meekly.

"Why, yes, it's crossed my mind once or twice," he sneered.

"Oh, Curtis, don't be like that. Don't you know I'd change things if I could?"

With a deep sigh, he reached out and stroked her cheek. "I love you, Lael. I always will. But I can't make you love me. I'm beat and I know it. Just don't expect me to be happy about it."

Aching inside, for both of them, Lael grabbed his hand where it rested on her cheek.

"You two patching things up, or what?"

They turned to see Fanny, looking gaunt and tense as she sized up the situation.

"Fanny!" Lael pulled her friend close and held on tightly. "Thank God, thank God! I'm so happy for you."

Relaxing a bit, Fanny brought her arms up and patted Lael on the back. "It wouldn't have turned out like it did without you, Lael. I won't forget what you done for me."

Pulling away, Fanny eyed the tall Texan uncertainly. "Thanks for coming, Curtis. You didn't have to."

Smiling, he gave her a big bear hug. "Of course, I did, Fan, of course, I did."

As he set her away gently, Fanny blinked back tears. "Now that I'm a free woman, it just occurred to me I got nowhere to go."

"Yes, you do," said Lael firmly. "You're coming home with me."

Chapter Twenty-Two

Fanny refused Lael's invitation at first, arguing that she was already too much in the champion cowgirl's debt. But the truth of the matter was she desperately needed a place to stay, no one else was offering, and a chance to recuperate at a ranch in the San Fernando Valley sounded like heaven. The deal was sealed when Lael convinced her she needed a roommate to look after things while she was off riding the circuit.

Throughout the rest of that winter, the two women stuck close to home. Lael rode her horses daily, keeping them and herself in shape for the upcoming season. Fanny adjusted to life back in the world she had known before fear and pain had been her constant companions. Under Lael's dutiful care, she regained her shapely figure and the shine returned to her hair, which she left its natural brown color.

"Never thought I'd give up my red hair," she admitted one day.

Lael paused in what she was doing and looked pensively out the window. "I guess we all do things that surprise us, now and then."

Fanny was about to ask what she meant but thought better of it. These days Lael frequently appeared troubled, no doubt due to her pending divorce. Fanny would have liked to provide comfort to her friend, but, given her own interest in the outcome, she was not sure how to go about it. For her part, Lael never brought it up.

Then one day in early spring, Lael asked Fanny to go riding with her. They saddled up and rode leisurely up into the hills, their mounts delicately picking their way along the rocky trail. When they reached an overlook, Lael pulled up and sat her horse. Her gray-green eyes studied the scene below calmly, and the morning sun sparkled on her golden ponytail. Fanny shook her head in wonder. How could she have ever blamed this beautiful girl for anything that happened? Why, Curtis Morris would have been a fool not to fall in love with her.

Leaning forward to stroke Dancer's neck, Lael said in a low voice: "The divorce was final yesterday."

Fanny kept quiet, struggling with a lump in her throat.

"I agreed to buy out Curtis's portion of the ranch. I think I can swing it, just barely, but I'll have to put in a long season and count on winning more often than not."

"That shouldn't be a problem for you," said Fanny, and she meant it.

"You never know. Anything can happen . . . injuries, new competition. There's no guarantees." Lael smiled crookedly. "That's what I love about it. Anyway, there's a couple of early season rodeos in Arizona, one in Texas. I'm going to head out tomorrow and, depending on my schedule, might not be back till the fall, after Pendleton."

"Don't you worry about a thing, doll. I'll look after everything here."

"I'm counting on it." Lael took a deep breath and fixed Fanny with a serious look. "I want you to know it's OK with me if you look Curtis up while I'm gone. I've got no claim on him any more, and it's no secret how you feel about him. I know you think he doesn't feel the same way about you, but I don't think he'd take much convincing. He always had a soft spot for you."

"It's no good, Lael. I'm not in his class and never will be.

204

Especially not now," said Fanny resignedly.

"Class? What are you talking about? Listen, girl, there's a lot you don't know about Curtis Morris, and I'll leave it to him to tell you, if he chooses to, but I guarantee you he doesn't think he's any better than you or me or the man in the moon."

"But he is better than me. He's the finest man I know."

Lael sighed in frustration. "I read something once that stuck with me . . . hitch your wagon to a star. If Curtis is your star, honey, then just hitch a ride. I think he'd like the company."

Fanny remained unconvinced. "Maybe you're right. I'll think about it."

They sat, watching the rising sun bathe the valley in its crystal clear light. Thoughtfully Fanny said: "I know rodeo is your star, Lael, and that's what you've hitched your wagon to. But it's awful lonely, ain't it? I hope there's someone else out there for you . . . someone you can share it with."

Lael raised her face to the warm sunshine. Without meaning to, she sent out a little prayer, wondering if the cool Pacific breezes would blow it . . . where? She did not even know where he was. Reining Dancer around, she headed on up the trail.

True to her word, while Lael rode the circuit that summer of 1928, Fanny took care of the home front. But even after tending to all the chores around the little ranch, she found she was left with time on her hands. Besides, she could not live off of her friend's generosity forever. So she applied for a job at Universal Studios, not as a riding extra, for she had had enough of that rough and tumble existence, but as a make-up artist. Though she was aware that Curtis also worked at Universal—he had been elevated to the position of head wrangler—their paths did not cross, and she did nothing to change that. She had not forgotten Lael's advice, but could not bring herself to follow it.

Then one day she was eating lunch in the studio cafeteria, when Curtis walked over, pulled up a chair, and asked why she had been avoiding him.

"I ain't . . . haven't done any such thing!" she cried, blushing to the roots of her natural brown hair.

"Good, 'cause I was wondering if you'd go out with me Friday night."

So, just like that, all her worries and insecurities about rekindling their relationship were behind her. Curtis had come looking for her, and it soon became clear that, however he might feel about his former wife, he was determined to move on.

When Lael came home in September, after another successful season, the romance between her roommate and ex-husband was in full swing. Just after the first of the year, they married. Lael gave them her blessing, although she had to admit to a small pang of regret. Why couldn't she have found that kind of happiness with Curtis? And a touch of jealousy, too, for when she saw the way Curtis looked at Fanny, so contentedly with none of the uncertainty that used to fill his eyes when he had looked at her, she knew that he was happier now than he had ever been.

Just before Lael was set to head out on the road for the 1929 season, the newlyweds invited her to their house for dinner. Afterwards, they spread a blanket in the back yard and sat under a starry sky. Curtis lit a cigarette, handed it to his wife, and fired up his own.

"Now I know why you divorced me . . . so you wouldn't have to smoke in secret any more," joked Lael.

"Ah, the truth is out," smiled Curtis. "Though I think

you've got that backwards, Miss Buckley. The way I remember it, you divorced me."

"And lucky for me she did," said Fanny, pushing him back on the blanket and planting a fat kiss on his lips. "Say, honey, did you tell Lael the good news about Louise?"

"Not yet." Rolling onto his side, he propped up on one elbow. "We got a letter from Louise the other day. Says she's kicked the bottle and is back running the ranch. Not only that, she plans to bring her son to live with her, if he wants to."

"Oh, how wonderful! I'm so glad!" said Lael happily. "Do you suppose she'll ever get back into rodeo?"

"Not likely. She's a little old for that life."

"It's a young person's sport, that's for sure. I'm starting to feel like the grandam of the rodeo," said Lael wryly.

Fanny looked at her askance. "You're only twenty-seven, doll. You've got lots of good years left."

"A few, maybe," Lael shrugged. "If I don't get hurt. But even if I'm not changing, it seems like rodeo is. It's . . . I don't know . . . different from when I started."

"How so?" asked Curtis.

"I don't know," Lael repeated, "it's just a feeling I have. Back when I started, there weren't a lot of rules. Nobody told you how to do things, or that you couldn't do something if you wanted to. There weren't a lot of women bulldoggers or broncho riders, but nobody said we couldn't do those things. In fact, most places encouraged us to take risks because the crowds loved it. But now, it just feels different. A lot of places don't allow cowgirl bulldogging any more because it's *too dangerous*. Not too dangerous for the men, of course. And this new group, the Rodeo Association of America, worries me some."

"I haven't heard about that," admitted Curtis.

"It's an organization of rodeo producers. Their idea is that all R.A.A.-sanctioned rodeos have to include four events . . . broncho riding, bulldogging, steer roping, and calf roping. They keep track of the scores, and at the end of the season name the world champion. But there's no mention anywhere of any events for women."

"That's not fair!" said Fanny indignantly. "The ladies' events are just as popular as the men's! Someone oughta straighten those fellas out!"

"That's the problem," sighed Lael. "The group's made up of producers. There hasn't been a female producer since Louise got out of the business. Consequently, there's not a soul around to give the women's point of view."

"You two are getting all upset over nothing," scoffed Curtis, rolling onto his back and crossing his arms behind his head. "This R.A.A. thing's going nowhere. Rodeo people are too independent to get organized."

"I hope you're right." Lael stared at the night sky uneasily. "I just hope you're right."

Chapter Twenty-Three

It was eleven o'clock at night when Lael pulled into Frontier Park in Cheyenne. She set the brake and dropped her head on the back of the seat, too tired to get out of the car just yet. Earlier that day, she had performed in Deadwood, South Dakota. Too small to offer women's competitive events, Deadwood had contracted for her trick- riding act. She had hit the road immediately after performing, so as to reach Cheyenne in time for the opening ceremonies of Frontier Days.

Climbing out of her beat-up old Dodge, she unhitched the trailer, stabled Dancer, and pitched her tent. She moved automatically, having set up camp so many umpteen times she could do it in her sleep. Grabbing a five-gallon jug, she headed for the communal water pump. At this time of night, few people were out and about. Most were either asleep in their tents or chasing the night life downtown.

As Lael approached the pump, she could see a figure bent over, water from the spigot running over the back of his neck. Coming closer, she realized the figure was actually that of a woman or teen-aged girl. Sputtering and coughing, the girl sank to her knees, groaning. Long sheets of dark, wet hair plastered her face.

Concerned, Lael stepped nearer and was met with an overpowering stench of regurgitated whisky. She bent over the girl and saw she had been sick all over the front of herself.

"Let me guess," Lael said, not unkindly. "You were celebrating your first time at the Daddy of 'em All."

Miserably the girl nodded.

"A little too much celebrating from the looks of it." Lael pulled a handkerchief from her jeans pocket and offered it to the girl.

With trembling hands, she wiped her face and then held the cloth to her lips, trying to gather herself. Lael narrowed her eyes, straining to make out the girl's features in the dark. Something about her seemed familiar.

Slowly the girl came to her feet, weaving precariously. Lael put out a hand to steady her. "Whoa there, kiddo. Not so fast."

Sinking back down, the girl started to cry silent tears.

"Feels like hell, doesn't it? I wish I could tell you you'll feel better tomorrow, but you may be paying for this for a while. You want to tell me what happened?"

The girl spoke haltingly. "Daddy and I went to the Frontier Nights festival together, but, when we got there, I saw my friend, Adele. He said it would be OK if I went with her, so I did. But then we ran into her big brother and all his friends. They were passing around a jug, and, I don't know, I just wanted to see what it tasted like. They kept handing it back to me, and, before I knew it, I felt dizzy. So I found a place to sit down. Somehow I lost Adele in the crowd, and then all of a sudden, I felt so sick. I tried to make it back to the tent, but. . . ." Embarrassed, the young girl dissolved in tears.

Lael put a hand on her shoulder. "It's OK. Seems like you've learned your lesson. Come on, let's get you back to your tent."

The girl pulled back sharply. "No! I can't go back there. My father will kill me!" Then, the effort of speaking having roiled her stomach, she bent over and was sick again.

Calmly Lael detached her little camp cup from her belt,

filled it at the pump, and offered the girl a sip. "What's your name, hon?"

"Jenny," she moaned, wiping her mouth with Lael's hankie.

"Listen, Jenny, if I know anything about fathers, he will kill you for what you've done tonight. But he'll probably kill you deader, if you don't come home. Sure he'll be mad at you for getting drunk. He'll get over that. But he'll be downright scared, if he thinks you're missing. That's something he might never get over."

"I guess you're right," Jenny groaned.

Helping her up, Lael wrapped an arm around her waist. The girl was as tall as she was, but slim, not yet filled out. She was quite pretty, although her features were not what one would call delicate—dark brows, deep-set eyes, a strong chin. Again, Lael had the nagging feeling they had met.

"Are you entered in the rodeo?" she asked, as the girl pointed in the direction of her tent.

"Not a chance," Jenny replied caustically. "My dad says I'm too young."

"How old are you?"

"Fifteen."

"Well, he's probably right then, at least for Cheyenne. Pretty soon, though, you could try some smaller rodeos just to get your feet wet. That is, if your dad says it's OK."

Jenny made a face, as though the likelihood of that happening were not great.

"What's your favorite event?" Lael tried again.

"Broncho riding," Jenny replied without hesitation.

Lael smiled. "I like that, too. Though I don't get a chance to do it much any more. Frontier Days eliminated ladies' broncho riding last year, you know. But my favorite thing is to race. I love to go fast!"

Jenny grinned weakly. "So does Daddy. That's his specialty, training racehorses."

"Really? What's your father doing here in Cheyenne?"

"He's Mister Jordan's right-hand man."

"Mister Jordan? Deke Jordan, the stock contractor?"

"That's right." Jenny paused as another wave of nausea hit her.

"You OK?"

"Yeah," the girl gasped, "that's our tent over there. But I just can't face Daddy like this. Please, can you take me to your tent, just for a little while?"

"No honey, I can't do that." Lael patted her gently. "Your father would be so worried."

Jenny's shoulders sagged. "Well, thanks anyway, Miss.... Gosh, I don't even know your name!"

Just then, a tall figure appeared out of the shadows. "Jenny? Jenny! Where the hell have you been, girl? I've been tearing this place apart looking for you!"

Lael's stomach flipped. Stepping into the glow of the street lamp was Rafe Callantine. Catching sight of her just as she recognized him, he pulled up short, staring in amazement from her to his daughter and back again.

Of course, she's his daughter, Lael thought. *How could I not have seen it immediately?*

"What . . . ?" Rafe shook his head in confusion. "She was with you?"

"I ran into her at the water pump," Lael explained, her breath coming short. "She needed some help so. . . ."

"Help? What's wrong?" Callantine's eyes narrowed in concern. He grabbed Jenny's arm and caught a whiff of her stained shirt front. Slowly his face darkened, and he got a look in his eye Lael had seen once before, the time she had called him a whisky-head.

"So this is what you've been up to," he said, his voice dangerously quiet. "How could you . . . ?" He cut himself off. Making an obvious effort to remain calm, he turned to Lael. "Thanks for bringing her back. I'm glad it was you found her."

"You two know each other?" Jenny said, amazed.

Rafe gave the golden-haired cowgirl a haunted look. "Yeah, we've seen each other around," he rasped. "Now get inside, young lady. On the double." He pushed his daughter toward their tent.

"But who is she?" Jenny cried.

Lael stared at him, willing him to say her name. She wanted to hear her name on his lips.

"This is Lael Buckley, Jenny." He turned his dark eyes on her once again, and for the millionth time Lael wished she could penetrate their fathomless secrets. "Or is it Lael Morris these days?"

Lael's head came up. "It's Buckley, and always has been. I'm no longer married, though, if that's what you want to know."

Callantine shot her a sharp glance.

"Lael Buckley!" Jenny's jaw dropped. "My gosh, I had no idea. . . ."

"Go inside. Clean yourself up," her father ordered.

With a last look over her shoulder at the famous cowgirl, Jenny disappeared inside the tent.

They stood for a moment, neither knowing what to say.

Lael crossed her arms over her chest, suddenly cold. "Well, I better go. I left my water jug at the pump. I'll see you around, I suppose."

With a curt nod, he bent to enter his tent.

"Rafe!" she called, not wanting him to leave just yet. "I . . . um . . . I just wanted to say I don't think you should be too hard on Jenny. She's young. We all make youthful mistakes."

He turned to scowl at her. "You think this was just a youthful mistake? God only knows what could have happened to her out there." Passing his hand over his eyes, he shuddered. "I don't need your advice on how to deal with my daughter." With a last fierce look, he entered his tent.

Stung by his criticism, Lael retreated to her own shelter, her anger increasing with each step. "Bastard!" she cried, throwing her camp cup against the canvas wall where it made a very unsatisfying *thwop*. With a vicious kick to her mess kit, she sent pots and pans clattering across the ground. "Unfeeling son of a bitch!" Sinking to her knees, she dropped her head in her hands and wept.

Chapter Twenty-Four

" 'Mornin', Lael!"

A cheery Mabel Strickland stuck her head through the tent flap. "My Lord, what happened here?" She surveyed the scattered pots and pans curiously.

Slowly Lael rose from her cot. Her head pounded after a long night of crying. "Took out my frustrations on my mess kit," she muttered.

"Gosh, honey, we gotta find you a man," Mabel declared, hands on hips. "Whenever I feel the need to hit something, I just pop Hugh a good one! He's so big, it don't hurt him none, but it sure makes me feel better!"

Lael considered telling Mabel that a man was the cause of her frustration, but thought better of it. The last thing she needed was camp gossip.

"What are you doing up so early?" she inquired.

"On my way to the pancake breakfast. Come on with me."

"You better go ahead. I look like absolute hell." Lael picked up a mirror and cringed at the sight of her swollen eyes.

"Sweetie, you never look like hell. All us cowgirls hate you for that. Just splash some water on that gorgeous face of yours and pull your hat down low. That'll do the trick."

With a sigh, Lael spruced up as best she could and joined Mabel for the short walk to the center of the park where one of the rodeo's many booster clubs had set up tables and were serving flapjacks and bacon. A hot wind blew in from the west, kicking up dust and trash.

"Where's Hugh?" Lael asked, hunching over to protect her plate from the dust.

"Riding slack," Mabel replied.

Frontier Days had become so popular that cowboys from all over the United States and Canada came to participate—so many that some had to be winnowed out before the competition started. These qualifying rounds were called "slack" rounds.

"Hundreds of cowboys here, and how many of us gals?" Mabel went on. "Maybe a dozen? And some of those are just here for exhibition acts."

Lael pushed her plate away in disgust. "Well, why should a cowgirl show up when she's not allowed to do much of anything? All I'm entered in this year is relay racing and trick riding. Even if I win both events, it barely pays my way here."

"I hear ya," Mabel agreed. "I would've dropped out long ago, if it wasn't for Hugh. I figure as long as I'm tagging along with him, I might as well compete myself. But if I was on my own, I wouldn't be making enough to keep going."

"It's not right! We ought to do something!"

"Nobody'll listen. There's just not enough of us gals to make a difference." Mabel shook her head in resignation.

"Of course not! They drop most of our events so a cowgirl can't afford to travel the circuit, and then, when the number of women contestants declines, they say there aren't enough of us to justify holding a ladies' event. It's a vicious circle."

"Not every place has signed on with the R.A.A.," Mabel pointed out. "There's a lot of rodeos still holding cowgirls' events."

A strong gust of wind battered the picnic area, flapping the red and white tablecloths wildly. "Mark my words," Lael said ominously, "change is coming. And from what I see, it's not going to be good."

Later that afternoon, Lael was behind the arena, checking out the new chutes. Called side delivery chutes, they could hold eight horses or bulls simultaneously, allowing the wranglers to ready more than one animal at a time. Needless to say, this invention had contributed to a smoother, more rapidly progressing show.

"Miss Buckley?"

Lael turned to see Jenny Callantine standing before her, neatly dressed in pressed jeans and a cotton shirt. Her dark hair was pulled back, and aside from a hint of paleness in her cheeks she looked none the worse for the previous night's intemperance.

"Hello, Jenny," Lael smiled. "It appears your father did not kill you, after all."

Chastened, Jenny stared at the ground. "No, but he might as well have. He's never going to let me go anywhere by myself again. I'm supposed to stay in the tent while he's off working, but I wanted to find you and apologize. I'm so embarrassed about last night."

"Now, honey,"—Lael threw an arm around the girl's shoulders—"you don't have to apologize. I'm just glad I was there to help."

"But that's just it . . . you, of all people, found me like that. I mean, you're Lael Buckley, maybe the greatest cowgirl ever, and there I was, heaving my guts out!"

"Here," Lael said, holding her arm out. "Pinch me. Go on, pinch me as hard as you can."

Reluctantly Jenny gave her a little pinch.

"Oh, come on, you can do better than that."

Jenny pinched her hard.

"Ow! See, I'm human, just like everyone else. And humans make mistakes. What counts is learning something from them. My guess is you've learned a lot in the past twenty-four hours. So give yourself a break, sweetie. Don't keep punishing yourself."

Jenny smiled meekly. "OK, I'll try." Sighing, she gazed off into the distance. "I just wish Daddy would take your advice."

"Oh? Why is that?" Lael asked, in spite of herself.

Jenny walked to the nearby bleachers and sat, pressing her hands between her knees. "He just can't forgive himself, even though what happened wasn't his fault, not really."

Lael swallowed hard. "Tell me about it."

"It's been more than ten years now. I was only four. My little brother, Lucas, was just a baby." Jenny paused, her eyes misting. Lael reached over and took her hand. "We lived on a ranch in south Texas, nothing big, I guess, but Daddy raised a few cattle and horses. He was gone a lot, trading horses, he said. It was hard on Mama. My grandma told me Mama never really liked the ranch, wanted to live in town, instead. I can remember terrible arguments when Daddy would come home, both of them shouting and throwing things." A tear escaped and rolled down her pale cheek.

"You don't have to go on, honey," Lael whispered.

Jenny nodded. "It's OK. I want to tell you." She brushed away the tear and continued. "The funny thing is, even though Daddy was gone a lot, and even though he and Mama fought, I knew he loved us. I felt so safe and happy when he was around. He used to lead me around the corral on a little pony . . . I can still remember him showing me how to hold the reins. But those were the good days. On the bad days, he'd come home all dark and angry, and, lots of times, he didn't come home at all. Grandma said he was a no-good drunk. I don't know, maybe he was."

Lael's heart went out to the poor girl, but even beyond sympathy for Jenny she felt a certain anticipation, as though a locked door was about to open.

Jenny took a deep breath. "That night, they had another fight. He left, and I guess Mama must have put me and Lucas to bed. The next thing I knew, I woke up and I couldn't breathe. There was smoke all around. I screamed for Daddy, but he wasn't there. Mama grabbed me and ran with me outside. I turned back to look, and the whole house was in flames. Mama was coughing, and her face was all black, but she put me down and went back for Lucas, back inside the burning house." Jenny turned tortured eyes to Lael. "Neither one of them came back out."

"Oh, Jenny, how awful." Lael hugged the girl tightly.

Jenny rested her chin on Lael's shoulder for a minute before going on. "Daddy never came home that night. The neighbors found me and took care of me. After that, I went to stay with Grandma. I didn't see Daddy or know where he was for two years. And then one day he came to get me. Grandma didn't want him to take me, but he said I was his, and he wanted me. He's been a good father. Not happy and lots of fun like before, but he's taken good care of me. I've never seen him take a drink. That's probably why he got so upset about what I did last night."

Lael looked past the girl in her arms, her heart breaking. "He thinks if he hadn't been out drinking that night your mother and brother might still be alive?"

"Yes. I used to hate him sometimes, because maybe he's right. Maybe he could have saved them. But I couldn't go on thinking like that. He's all I have. I can't help loving him."

"No," Lael said, more to herself than to Jenny. "No, you can't."

Chapter Twenty-Five

So now she knew the dark secret of Rafe Callantine's past, but the knowledge was less than comforting. On the one hand, Jenny's story confirmed what had seemed obvious about the man from the beginning—that he was a drunken cad, a rake, and a loner. On the other hand, how could one feel anything but compassion for a man who had lost his wife and baby so tragically, especially since, by all accounts, he had reformed his ways?

Over the years, Lael had imagined thousands of different reasons for his churlishness, but never this. When she had first met him, it would have been less than two years since he had lost his family. He had still been running then, still drowning his sorrows in the bottle. But something, who knew what, had halted his flight, because soon after he gave up drinking and returned for his daughter.

At the Canadian rodeo, when she had seen Jenny's picture in his tent and inquired about his wife, his refusal to answer had fueled her worst suspicions—that he had never married and the child was illegitimate, or that he had abandoned both wife and child. Never had she guessed the truth—that he had lost his wife in a tragic accident and was raising his daughter on his own. Lael felt that she had misjudged him all this time and desperately wanted to tell him that she now knew the truth and still . . . loved him?

Yes, loved him. For what else could it be when a person lived inside of you, occupying your every waking and sleeping thought for nine years? What else could it be when you carried the memory of a face with you for so long and over so many miles and yet it stayed as clear and vivid in your mind as if you had seen the person yesterday? Yes, she loved Rafe Callantine. But could she tell him that?

For days, Lael struggled with her thoughts, one minute clear about what to do, the next uncertain and confused. Although it was inevitable that she would see him during the rodeo performances—as the stock contractor's number one assistant, he would be a ubiquitous presence back of the chutes—she did her best to steer away from him.

Only once did they come into contact; dashing from the arena on Dancer, she exited just where Rafe was helping load some bronchos into one of the chutes. Exhilarated and out of breath, she spotted him and spontaneously laughed, all the joy and freedom she felt whenever she rode bursting out of her unchecked. Rafe acknowledged her with a nod, his twilight blue eyes lingering on her face no more than a second. Even so, it sent her heart racing.

At night, she stayed close to her tent, purposely avoiding the celebrations in Frontier Park. Until she knew what she wanted to say to him, she did not want to risk a chance encounter.

On the last night of the rodeo, Lael was in her tent, nursing a bruised shoulder. Somehow, during one of her stunts on Dancer, she had come down hard on the cantle, almost dislocating her shoulder. Despite the pain, she had finished the routine, posting the highest score of the day. Now she sat, tired, aching, and melancholy as she contemplated breaking camp and heading for the next spot on the map. And she still had not confronted Rafe.

"The hell with this!" she cried. "Moping around here won't solve a darn' thing." Resolutely adjusting the sling she had fashioned from one of her bandannas, she made her way toward the center of Frontier Park, where the nighttime entertainment was in full swing.

This year there was a new night show, featuring an open air dance hall and gambling casino. Both attractions were astonishingly popular. Rodeo participants and spectators alike jammed the hall, using fake money for games of blackjack, roulette, faro, dice, and poker.

Lael tried her hand at roulette but had to give it up when people crowding around the table kept bumping into her sore shoulder. Dancing was too painful even to attempt. Discouraged, she wandered down the row of concessionaires, stopping at one to buy an ice cream cone.

Holding the cone in her immobilized right hand, she delved into her skirt pocket with her left hand, searching for some coins to pay the vendor. Nothing there. Awkwardly she reached across her body, trying to get her left hand into her right pocket.

"I'll pay for the lady's cone," came a voice behind her. "And one of my own."

"Rafe! I didn't see you there!" Startled, Lael stepped back clumsily, brushing against him with her right hand, the hand that held the cone. Vanilla ice cream smeared the front of his shirt.

"Oh, gosh, look what I've done," she blushed. "I'm sorry."

"Don't worry about it." He took out his handkerchief and dabbed at the spot.

"Well, anyway, thanks for the cone. I do have some money. I just can't seem to get to it." With a helpless look, Lael indicated her self-doctored shoulder.

"I'm always happy to come to the aid of a damsel in distress," he said lightly.

Stunned, Lael stared at him as he steered her down the lane. Was this the same Rafe Callantine—being friendly, making polite banter? What was it she had meant to say to him? After days of agonizing, one would think she would remember, but he had so astounded her with his sudden appearance and pleasant demeanor, she was rendered speechless.

But it didn't matter. It was enough just to be with him. To walk down the row of vendors' stalls as they noisily hawked their wares, to hear the band music drifting over from the dance hall, to see the pretty lights strung throughout the park. To feel the pull of his magnetism as they strolled along, licking their cones.

The night was warm, however, and Lael couldn't lick fast enough to keep up with the dripping cream. Tossing the unfinished treat away, she held up her sticky hand for inspection. "Oh, dear," she said ruefully. "I'm afraid the only handkerchief I've got is wrapped around my bum arm."

"Hmm, mine is hardly fit, seeing as it's already mopped up one mess tonight. But this ought to do." Tugging at his shirt, Rafe pulled the tails out of his trousers and held one out to Lael.

"You want me to use your shirt?" she grinned.

"Why not? You've already christened it once tonight." And then he smiled at her, a real smile that made the tiny scar at the corner of his mouth almost disappear inside a deep dimple.

Lael caught her breath. "You're smiling!"

The smile faded, but his eyes still glistened with amusement. Reaching for her hand, he wiped it with his shirt.

Suddenly the words she wanted to say came to her. "Rafe . . . ," she began.

"Shh." He cocked his head, listening. "Indian drums. Hear 'em? Come on."

Still holding her hand, he led her in the direction of the sound until they found its source—the Indian camp at the edge of the park. Among the teepees and bonfires, several Indians were engaged in an impromptu dance, their bodies gyrating to the rhythmic beat of their drums. Standing just outside the circle of light, the two of them watched, captivated by the elemental spectacle.

After a while, Lael turned and found Rafe staring at her, an odd, torn expression on his rugged face. The firelight flickered in his eyes.

"I want to tell you something, but I'm afraid you'll be angry," she said.

"Try me."

"Jenny came to see me a few days ago."

"I know. She told me."

"Did she tell you what we talked about?"

His eyes narrowed. "No. Just that she apologized to you."

"Well, yes, she did. She's such a sweet girl, Rafe. You should be proud of her."

"What did she tell you?"

Lael gathered herself. "She told me about the fire."

He looked at her, then turned to stare at the dancing Indians. "She shouldn't have done that," he said quietly.

"Why not?" Lael challenged. "I'm glad she did. It . . . it makes me feel closer to you to know what you've gone through. And I don't hold anything against you. It was an accident, for God's sake. Jenny told me how you came for her and raised her all these years. How hard that must have been, all on your own. My God, how I admire you!"

He turned to her, a quizzical look on his face. "Admire me?"

"Yes. For refusing to wallow in self-pity. For making something of your life."

Suddenly he was at her side, so close she could feel his body heat and smell that dusty, leathery smell that was uniquely his. He grabbed her arms and shook her, oblivious to the pain in her injured shoulder.

"Listen to me, Lael. I let my wife and baby son burn to death in that fire! I killed them as sure as if I'd lit the match myself. Not a day goes by that I don't have visions of them crying out for me, screaming for me to save them. And where was I while they died that hellish death? Drunker than shit, in bed with a whore! Is that the kind of man you admire?"

"You stopped running!" she cried. "You came back for your daughter. You aren't that man any more!"

Rafe let her go. "I'll always be that man," he said bitterly. He left her then, moving quickly out of the circle of firelight.

Grasping her throbbing shoulder, Lael let the sound of the Indian music wash over her, sinking deeper into despair with each beat of the drums.

Chapter Twenty-Six

A hot, gritty wind blew across the Texas plains, buffeting the lone cowgirl as she stood uncertainly before the huge oak door. Although she had heard enough about this place to describe it right down to the welcome mat under her feet, this was her first time here. She raised the horseshoe knocker and let it fall.

Louise Morris answered the door. "Hello, Lael. It's good to see you."

"You, too, Louise. You're looking fine."

And, indeed, she was. At forty-five years of age, the famous rodeo star was thinner than in her youth, and her sun-baked face was lined with wrinkles. But she held herself erect, and her eyes were clear and bright.

"Bet you're ready to wet your whistle," Louise said, ushering her guest into the kitchen. "One thing we got plenty of around here is dust, and it all seems to be rearranging itself today. Looks like some of it found a home on you."

"It was a long drive from the train station," Lael admitted. "The last few miles were the worst. I could see the house in the distance, but I kept driving and driving, and it never seemed to get any closer."

Louise poured her a glass of ice water. "Hard to tell distances in this heat. I do believe this is the hottest fall we've ever had. If we don't get some rain soon, the winter grazing's going to be mighty slim pickings."

Lael sipped her water, eyeing the older woman over the rim of her glass. Louise was in charge of the ranch now, re-

226

sponsible for all the myriad details involved in running a several thousand acre operation. Would she be too busy to help Lael?

"How's that brother of mine?" Louise asked.

Lael smiled, grateful that her former sister-in-law had broached the subject of Curtis. She had thought there might be hard feelings among his family because of the divorce, but apparently Louise was willing to let bygones be bygones.

"I saw him just before I came out here. He and Fanny are doing great, and that little one of theirs is a real pistol!"

"So I heard. I'd love to see him, but it's hard for me to leave the ranch. I wish they'd come here for a visit, but Curtis just doesn't seem to have much interest in the old place." Louise sighed.

"That is a shame," Lael mused. "This house is the perfect place for a growing family."

"But a bit too much for two old ladies like Alice and me?" Louise smiled.

Lael blushed. "Oh, no. I didn't mean it like that."

The kitchen door swung open. In walked an extraordinarily handsome young man. "Sorry, Ma. Didn't know you had company."

"Come on in, Son. I'd like you to meet a true star of the rodeo, Lael Buckley. Lael, my son, Cory O'Sullivan."

"It's a pleasure, Cory." Lael shook his hand warmly.

"Oh, the pleasure's all mine!" The young man's blue eyes shone. "Gosh, I saw you perform at Fort Worth earlier this summer. You were terrific!"

"Why, thank you. Of course, I couldn't hold a candle to what your mother used to do."

"Don't believe a word she says, Son," Louise chuckled. "This gal does tricks I've never even dreamed of."

"Well, it sure is an honor to meet you." He tipped his hat.

"Listen, Ma, I came to tell you I'm heading out for the north section to repair some broken fence. Probably won't be back for a day or two."

"That's fine, Son. Be careful." With a final nod to Lael, Cory clomped out of the kitchen, his spurs jingling. "You'd never know that boy spent the first nineteen years of his life on the south side of Chicago," Louise said proudly. "He's taken to the ranch like a rattler to the underside of a rock."

"I'd heard that he moved in with you."

"Two years ago, and, if you want to know the truth of it, I think he's here for good. You know, Lael, it's no secret I wasted a lot of years of my life. Time I could have spent with my son. One morning I woke up, my head aching, my stomach heaving, my mouth so foul-tasting it felt like I'd swallowed a gallon of piss, and I realized something . . . in life, there's only one go-round. You only get one shot at it. I stopped drinking, then and there. Now I'm living for one thing . . . to keep this place intact so I can leave it to my son. It isn't going to be easy . . . this damn' Depression has wiped out a lot of my neighbors, good people who just couldn't hang onto their land. But I'm determined to come through it all in one piece. The day I sign this ranch over to Cory is the day I can finally thumb my nose at Big Jack!" Louise pulled out a chair and sat triumphantly.

"I hope it works out for you," Lael said kindly, even though her heart was sinking. With Louise being so wrapped up in the ranch, how likely was it she would agree to Lael's plan?

"So," Louise eyed her curiously, "when you wrote me you were coming, I thought there might be more to it than a social visit. Not that I'm not happy to entertain my ex-sister-in-law, but it did seem a bit unusual."

Lael cleared her throat nervously. "Yes, well, I did want to ask you something or, rather, get your advice about something."

"Shoot."

"Well, Louise, I know you've been busy on the ranch the last few years, but surely you can't have missed what's been going on with rodeo, with women's rodeo, that is."

The older woman nodded grimly. "It's been bad ever since Bonnie McCarroll got trampled to death. I never could understand why they didn't outlaw those damned hobbles!"

"Bonnie's death just made it worse. All of a sudden, rodeo committees everywhere are saying broncho riding is too dangerous for women, even though plenty of men get injured. When Pendleton dropped it after Bonnie's accident, the others did, too. I've written I don't know how many letters asking them to change their minds, but nobody wants the bad publicity of a cowgirl getting seriously hurt."

Louise's eyes flashed. "Don't you believe it! The crowd loves it when somebody gets thrown or trampled. That's part of the thrill."

"That may be true for cowboys, but not cowgirls, at least that's what the R.A.A. says. But it's more than just the elimination of ladies' broncho riding. Even the events we're still allowed to participate in have been downgraded. Like trick riding. Nowadays, it's strictly an exhibition act. And racing and roping? Sure, we still compete, but the scores are based on who's the prettiest, or who has the most attractive riding outfit, for God's sake!"

"I heard about that," said Louise somberly. "They're called sponsor contests, if I'm not mistaken."

"It's awful!" Lael paced the room. "We're becoming props, nothing but decoration! Nobody cares how well you ride any more, it's all about glamour."

"It's always been show business," Louise reminded her.

"People always wanted to see a pretty cowgirl."

"But they wanted to see her ride a broncho, or rope a steer, or climb under the belly of a horse! Not just parade around looking pretty."

"It's a shame, no doubt about it. But rodeo's always been a man's world. I found that out the hard way."

"Well, I want to do something about it," said Lael intently. "That's why I'm here, Louise. I need your help."

The older woman raised her eyebrows. "I can't promise anything, but go on."

"I want to produce an all-women's rodeo," Lael announced. "Invite all the top cowgirls but open it up to any woman who wants to compete. We'll have all the events . . . broncho riding, steer riding, bulldogging, relay racing . . . everything! I think the R.A.A. is wrong. I think people do want to see talented cowgirls competing, especially in the rough-stock events. So let's prove it!"

Louise held up a cautionary hand. "Excuse me, did I hear you say *let's?* As in, you and me?"

Lael drew up a chair and leaned forward, excitement and enthusiasm lighting her face. "I've never produced a rodeo. I don't know how to go about it. I could learn, I suppose, but it would take time, and I'd make rookie mistakes. But you, Louise, you're an expert. It'd be like falling off a log for you! With your brains and expertise and my legwork, we couldn't fail!"

Shaking her head, Louise sat back in her chair. "I'd like to help, I really would. But I've got a ranch to run. That's a full-time job."

"I'll do most of the work," Lael pleaded. "I just need you to help me plan, give me ideas, steer me in the right direction. Please, Louise!"

"I don't know. . . ."

"This might be our last chance to show 'em what we can do!"

The older woman wavered. "Where were you planning to hold this rodeo?"

"Right here in Tom Green County."

"What?"

"That's right. The San Angelo fairgrounds."

"That's a long way from nowhere. Why not somewhere more populated?"

Lael shrugged. "I wanted to make it easy for you to say yes. I figured if we held it in your own back yard, you wouldn't have to be gone from the ranch that much. And I'm betting people will be willing to come a long way to see the line-up of top stars we're going to get. What do you say?"

Louise sighed. "You aren't making it easy for me to say yes, but you are making it hard to say no. OK, I'll do it, on one condition . . . the ranch comes first."

"Deal!"

"What are you going to call this rodeo, anyway?"

"The San Angelo Cowgirl Reunion of Nineteen Thirty-One!"

Chapter Twenty-Seven

With Louise on board, however reluctantly, Lael returned to California, where she set about the difficult task of raising money. Investors were impossible to find; not only were times tough, but no one was willing to bet on the success of an all-female rodeo. Lael was confident she could cover her costs once she collected the entry fees and ticket receipts, but that would not happen until next June, when the rodeo took place. Yet she needed up-front money for things like advertising, producing promotional items, hiring judges, pick-up men, and hazers. Before the month was out, she had used up her meager savings and had taken a second mortgage on her house. Ironically the business courses her parents had forced her to take were finally paying off now that she was in charge of her own production company.

Louise kept in close touch, writing or phoning often to offer guidance. At Christmas time, she invited Lael back to the ranch so they could go over their plans in person.

West Texas was a different place in late December than it had been in the glory of autumn. What green there had been had faded to brown, the color of dried earth as far as the eye could see, and the ever-present wind carried a sharp sting. But the Morris house was warm and welcoming, its fireplaces blazing and its mantels festooned with holiday garland. The four inhabitants made for an odd group: Alice, getting on in years and as plump as St. Nicholas himself; Louise, still fighting Big Jack although he had gone to his grave; Cory, a newcomer to the family but perhaps more at home than any of

232

them; and Lael, a dropout from the family who had temporarily rejoined the fold.

After dinner one dark, blustery evening, Louise suggested everyone finish their cups of hot chocolate before the fire in the study.

"Tomorrow we'll drive over to San Angelo," she said, settling in comfortably. "I'll introduce you to the committee members who've signed on. You need to give them a little pep talk, let them know you've already registered a lot of big stars, that sort of thing."

"You did a great job lining up the committee," Lael said. "The bank president, the owner of the mercantile . . . that's terrific community support."

"It wasn't all that easy," Louise admitted. "These aren't the greatest times to be asking people to put their money and reputation on the line for a rodeo. But I'm owed a few favors around here and figured it was time to call them in." She sipped her hot chocolate thoughtfully. "Incidentally, did I tell you I asked a fella to come over here this evening who I'm thinking about hiring to be the stock contractor? If you approve of him, that is."

"No. Tell me about him."

"He's a local guy, owns a horse ranch on the other side of the river. He's only been at it about a year, but I hear he's got a background in rodeo. Cory's been over to meet him, says his stock looks first-rate."

Down the hall, the door knocker boomed loudly.

"That's probably him now." Louise rose to answer the door.

"I'll leave you all to your business," the portly Alice said pushing out of her chair. "Good night, Lael."

"I've got to be going, too," said Cory. "Time to put th horses to bed. 'Evenin', Miss Buckley."

233

Lael bade them good night and rose to tend the fire. Out in the hallway, she could hear the front door open and Louise greeting the newcomer.

"So, you're my new neighbor. Well, not all that new, I guess. I feel bad I haven't been over to meet you yet. I hope my son's been making you feel welcome."

"He has at that, ma'am. I should tell you that even though we've never actually met, I've seen you a few times, back when you were riding the circuit. It's quite an honor to finally meet Louise Morris."

The iron poker Lael held clattered to the floor. Whirling around, she brought her hand to her mouth. That voice . . . she would know it anywhere.

"How's Jenny doing?" Cory was saying.

"She's doing fine, thanks," came the answer, a bit brusquely.

"Glad to hear it. Well, good night, sir. Good night, Ma." The door opened and closed.

"Come this way, won't you?" Footsteps approached the study. Lael stood by the fireplace, frozen. "I can't honestly remember if I mentioned to you that I have a partner in this endeavor, but she's here this evening to meet you. Right through here. Lael, this is the man I was telling you about, Rafe Callantine. Mister Callantine, meet Lael Buckley, one of the premier cowgirls in rodeo. Of course, you probably know that, seeing as you follow the sport."

He stopped, stared at the petite figure dwarfed by the huge fireplace. His indigo eyes seemed to glow darkly, although perhaps that was just the reflection from the fire.

"We've met," he rasped.

"Is that right? Well, that's not surprising, I suppose," Louise prattled on, offering him a drink, that he declined, and a seat, which he also declined. She described Lael's idea for an

all-female rodeo, explaining that they were looking for a stock contractor willing to supply animals that had plenty of buck to them.

Lael heard nothing. She was back in Cheyenne, on the outskirts of an Indian camp, reliving the last time she had seen Rafe Callantine. A year and a half ago. Why did he keep popping up in her life like this? Just when she thought she had put his memory behind her, or, at least, decided she must carry on even if she could never forget him.

"Isn't that right, Lael?"

"What?" She jerked back to the present.

"I was telling Mister Callantine you've lined up all the great female rodeo stars for our show."

"Yes, most of them." Lael wrenched her eyes away from Rafe. "Louise, could we talk privately for a moment?"

Louise looked startled. "Is something wrong?"

"Yes . . . well, not really . . . but. . . ."

"I think I'll be going now."

The two women turned to stare. Rafe buttoned his heavy overcoat and tipped his hat at Louise.

"Pleasure to meet you, Miss Morris. I appreciate you calling me over here, but I'm afraid I'm not the right man for the job. Good night, now." With a quick nod, he headed toward the door, Louise trailing him, trying to coax him back. The door slammed.

Louise returned to the study, looking peeved. "What was that all about?"

Lael sank into a chair, her head in her hands. "I'm sorry. I hope I didn't embarrass you. It's just . . . I can't work with Rafe Callantine."

"Why not? Is he a crook, a bad actor?"

"No, no, nothing like that. Rafe and I . . . we just don't get along."

Suzanne Lyon

Louise regarded her for a moment, hands on hips. "You had a thing for each other, didn't you?"

"No," Lael murmured, "no, I can't really say that."

"Well, then, what for God's sake? Come on, Lael, spill the beans. I want to know why we can't hire this guy. He's perfect . . . got a great reputation, and he's close. It'll double our costs if we have to go to Amarillo or Fort Worth to get somebody."

Suddenly Lael burst into tears, all the frustration, anger, need, and desire of the last eleven years spewing forth in a hot gush. Ashamed, she tried to stop the onslaught, catching her breath in stuttering gasps, only to burst out anew. When she could cry no more, she wiped at her tear-streaked face, drained of all emotion.

Louise sat on the sofa, waiting patiently. "Tell me, honey."

Exhausted, Lael leaned back in her chair. Her eyes glimmered like nuggets of jade in deep pools of water. "I've loved Rafe Callantine since the day I met him, eleven years ago. I married Curtis, lived with Curtis, slept with Curtis, and all the time I loved Rafe Callantine. I barely know the man, and I still love him." She squeezed her eyes shut, forcing out more tears. "But he doesn't think any more of me than he would a bug on the sidewalk. You saw him just now . . . couldn't wait to get out of here."

"I saw him, all right. I saw him look at you so hungry-like I thought he might take you right there on the floor!"

Lael's jaw dropped. She stared at the older woman, stunned.

"You heard me right. That man's a goner for you, head over heels, plumb loco about one little blonde cowgirl or I ain't Big Jack Morris's daughter. It appears to me you two have been working at cross-purposes. But you know what?"

236

Louise leaned forward, elbows on her knees, and fixed Lael with a look of consternation. "I don't give two hoots about any of that! You're a grown woman, Lael, so act like it. If you want to produce a successful rodeo, then march on over to Rafe Callantine's place tomorrow, apologize for acting like a god-damned debutante, and hire yourself a first-rate contractor! The rest will just have to work itself out." With that, she rose to leave. At the door, she turned back. "I won't expect you back tomorrow until supper."

"I thought we were meeting the rodeo committee tomorrow," Lael sniffled.

"It'll wait. You've got more important things to do."

Chapter Twenty-Eight

Lael rose early the next morning and headed out to the barn. Needing to clear her head, and not knowing a better place to do it than on the back of a horse, she had decided to ride over to Rafe Callantine's place, instead of taking the car. Cory saddled her up and offered to go with her to show the way. Gratefully she accepted, hoping the young man's company would keep her spirits up.

He did not disappoint, carrying on a running commentary throughout their ride. He told her of his upbringing in Chicago, how he had followed the exploits of his famous mother, how thrilled he had been when she asked him to come live with her. This ranch was in his blood, he said, even if he had never laid eyes on it until he was nineteen years old.

Lael smiled, knowing just how he felt. It was like her and rodeo—a connection so strong that you did not talk about it in terms of what you do, but who you are.

They clomped over the hard earth, regenerating itself for spring. A band of Herefords milled beside the river, lazily nudging each other aside. *What a peaceful place*, Lael thought. *Every season has its particular beauty and special purpose.*

"Mister Callantine sure runs a good operation," Cory was saying. "He only bought the place about a year ago from the Hendersons. They went bust, couldn't pay their taxes. Everybody was sorry to see them go, and not a little put out with Mister Callantine, I guess, for getting the place so cheap. But he's proved himself, all right. Why, just last summer, old man

Strook came down sick, and Mister Callantine was over there most everyday, helping out until the old guy got back on his feet. And, of course, everybody thinks the world of Jenny."

Lael cast him a sideways glance, her mouth turned up in a sly smile. "Maybe you in particular?"

The young man blushed. "Reckon so. But I'm not getting too far in that department, her daddy's seeing to that."

They came to a gate with a wooden sign hanging above it: **Starbuck Ranch.**

"This is it?" Lael asked.

"Yes, ma'am."

"Starbuck," she murmured. "What a lovely name."

Cory leaned over his horse and lifted the wire loop that held the gate closed, followed Lael through, and slid the loop back over the fence post. In the distance, Lael could see the ranch buildings. She squared her shoulders, preparing herself to eat some serious crow.

They rode up to the main house and dismounted. The front door banged open. Jenny Callantine bounded down the steps, her dark hair flying. "Miss Buckley! My gosh, I can't believe it's you!"

Lael grinned, surprised at the way her heart leapt at the sight of the girl. At seventeen, Jenny had matured into a beautiful young woman, graceful where she had once been gawky.

The door slammed again, and Lael looked up to see Rafe standing on the verandah, his hands jammed in his back pockets, a wary look on his face.

"Daddy!" Jenny cried. "Look who's here!"

He nodded, then shifted his gaze to Cory, frowning slightly.

" 'Mornin', sir." The young man touched the brim of his hat.

Rafe did not respond.

Jenny turned to Lael, talking quickly to cover up her father's rude behavior. "What brings you all the way out here, Miss Buckley? Didn't I read somewhere you usually spend your winters in California?"

"I guess your dad didn't tell you?" She caught Rafe's eye for a split second. "I'm producing a rodeo in San Angelo next summer. An all-female rodeo. I've come to talk business with your dad."

"Daddy, I can't believe you didn't tell me!" Jenny turned an excited face toward Lael. "An all-female rodeo! What a great idea! Can anybody enter?"

"As long as she's a she and not a he." Lael smiled.

"Jenny," Rafe said sternly, "go back in the house, now. You can visit with Miss Buckley later."

"Oh, Daddy, don't send me away. We almost never have visitors." She ran up the steps and linked her arm through her father's. "Tell you what! I'll take Cory down to the barn to show him that new stallion you bought while you and Miss Buckley talk shop, OK?"

Before Rafe could say no, she hopped over to a delighted Cory, took his hand, and sprinted toward the barn, laughing gaily.

"Can you bottle that?" Lael smiled tentatively.

He looked at her for a moment, then reached behind him and opened the door, standing aside to let her enter. He followed her in and turned toward the kitchen, yanking out a wooden chair as he passed it.

Guessing that was an invitation to sit, she sat.

"Coffee?" he asked.

"Sure, if you've got some."

He picked up two cups from the drainboard and lifted the pot from the stove. With his back to her, Lael felt free to study him. In eleven years time, she had seen him on only three occasions, not counting yesterday and today, yet he never seemed to change. His body was still rock hard—a cowboy's body, lean through the hips, strong in the back and thighs. His hair still grew thick and full, and was only just beginning to show streaks of gray. His hands were a workman's hands, rough and scarred, but the fingers were surprisingly long. She watched the fine bones move under his skin as he filled her cup and set it in front of her. He filled his own cup and leaned against the drainboard, waiting for her to begin.

She had meant to leap right into it, get it over with, but the way he was looking at her made her nervous. Sipping her coffee, her eyes traveled around the kitchen as she tried to think of something to say.

"Nice spread you've got here," *God, how stupid did that sound?*

"Thanks."

"How'd you come by it?"

"How's that?"

"Well, I mean, a rodeo wrangler usually doesn't have a whole lot of extra cash . . . ," she trailed off. *Lord, this wasn't what she had meant to say.*

He set his cup down hard. "I robbed a bank," he said dryly.

"Oh, God, Rafe, I'm sorry. I shouldn't be asking questions that are none of my business. But I never know what to say to you. You . . . fluster me." She went to stand next to him, facing the opposite way so she was looking out the window over the sink.

He tilted his head toward her. A muscle in his jaw jumped as his eyes raked over her blushing cheeks and full lips.

She sighed deeply and crossed her arms over her chest. "Nevertheless"—she made her voice light—"I've been informed I need to grow up. To that end, I've swallowed my pride and am here, begging on my knees. Please forgive me for my foolish behavior last night, and please reconsider about the rodeo. I promise that, if you come to work for me, I'll treat you in a business-like fashion at all times."

"Damn." He knit his brow. "Ain't sure the job's worth taking now."

Lael laughed uncertainly. Was he making a joke? A barely detectable grin tugged at the scar on his mouth. She felt a twinge of disappointment; he was joking. Well, then, fine. If he wanted it to be all business, then that's how it would be.

"OK, then. We estimate we'll need forty broncs, maybe half that many steers, a few calves for roping. None of these tired-out old nags a lot of contractors want to pass off on the ladies. I want them fresh and ready to buck! I'll pay you ten dollars a head."

"Fifteen."

She narrowed her eyes at him. *It's just business.* "Twelve and a half."

"Done."

She extended her hand, and he took it, his long fingers grazing the soft underside of her wrist. She gazed into his sapphire eyes and saw something there—Louise had called it hunger. No, on second thought, she was wrong. She was seeing things because she wanted to see them, not because they were really there.

Letting go his hand, she settled her hat on her head decisively. "I'll be in touch."

Chapter Twenty-Nine

God must have been saving up to create this day. Lael Buckley nudged Dancer into a high-step as she rounded the corner and headed down the main street of San Angelo, Texas. A rare northerly breeze had wafted across the plains, chasing away the normally insufferable heat of June. The sky was blue as Wedgwood, the grass grew unusually green, thanks to abundant spring rains, and the town of San Angelo, despite its Depression woes, had risen to the occasion, draping its main street with flags and bunting and hanging pots full of colorful flowers and trailing ivy.

Riding at the front of the procession, Louise Morris on her right, Jenny Callantine on her left proudly bearing the stars and stripes, the golden-haired cowgirl had never felt such a sense of accomplishment. All these people lining the street, all the women mounted behind her in their fringed leather and pretty silks, were here because of her. She had recruited the best of the best: Mabel Strickland, Lorena Trickey, Fox Hastings, Tad Lucas. But perhaps her more important achievement was the number of younger cowgirls, around twenty in all, who had come from throughout the West to compete. They were the future of women's rodeo.

"Don't forget to smile for the camera," Lael reminded Jenny, unnecessarily since the dark-haired girl had been beaming all morning long.

At Curtis's suggestion, Lael had talked Universal Studios into sending a camera crew to record all the rodeo action.

The director planned to make a short documentary out of the footage. Not only would this provide excellent publicity for women's rodeo, but the fee it paid had considerably eased Lael's financial concerns. Following her own advice, she turned the famous Buckley grin toward the movie camera that was mounted in the bed of a pickup truck that inched along just ahead of the parade.

"Oh, I see Curtis in the crowd!" Louise edged her mount over to the sidewalk. Lael followed.

Curtis stood with his son in the crook of one arm, the other wrapped around Fanny's waist. Hovering near the baby was Alice, aglow with grandmotherly pride.

The perfect family tableau, thought Lael a little wistfully. But in truth, she was happy for the Morrises—all of them. They had come to terms with the past and each other. Curtis's return to the ranch, his first since Big Jack's death and finding out the truth about his parentage, was a concession to the significance of his roots. This is where he was from, damn it, where his sister and mother still lived, and he did not intend for his son to grow up ignorant of those roots. He and Fanny were perfectly happy living in Los Angeles, and wholeheartedly approved of Louise's plan to turn the ranch over to Cory one of these years, but no longer would they be strangers to the big house on the hill.

"Congratulations, doll!" cried Fanny happily. "Everything looks terrific!"

"Thanks. I just wish you were riding with us."

"Like I said . . . I hung up my spurs." Fanny grinned and reached over to cluck her baby under the chin.

In fact, when Lael had invited Fanny to join the competition, she had been surprised by her friend's refusal. "I'm a mother now, sweetie, I can't be climbing on the back of some crazed animal."

244

"You sound just like the R.A.A.," Lael had said, not a little put out.

"Don't get me wrong," Fanny had replied. "I ain't sure daddies oughta be rodeoing, either. Thank God Curtis ain't interested in it any more."

Now, as the champion cowgirl watched the new mother fondle her baby, a feeling very close to envy crept over her. Maybe Fanny had it right, after all. Maybe she had missed the boat by not having children when she could. *What a ridiculous thought!* She was only twenty-nine years old; there was still plenty of time for motherhood. Unconsciously she turned to look over her shoulder at Jenny Callantine, smartly leading the parade.

"Curtis, hand that boy of yours up here," Louise demanded. "It's time he learned what it felt like to sit a horse."

"You want him to ride with you now, in the parade?"

"Sure, why not? Crowds love babies."

"Have you forgotten this baby's of the male persuasion?" said Fanny.

" 'Course not!" Louise reached for the child and settled him on the saddle before her. "He's just what we need to break up this hen party."

Proudly bearing her nephew, Louise returned to her spot at the head of the line. Lael fell in beside her.

"Wave at the camera, sweetie." Louise picked up a tiny hand and waved it in the direction of the rolling movie camera. She turned to Lael. "This is perfect, don't you think? People watching this film won't see just a bunch of cowgirls riding down the street. They'll look at this baby, and they'll see us as women and mothers, grandmothers even. I'm old enough to be this little tike's grandma." She paused. When she spoke again, she looked straight ahead, but Lael could tell the words were meant especially for her. "You know, being

245

successful means doing one thing really well. Being happy is all about what you do with the rest of your life."

By afternoon, the unusual northern breeze had blown in banks of tall, puffy clouds. Thunderheads building in the distance presaged a stormy evening, even though it looked like the rain would hold off until the show was over.

Lael was far too busy to notice the weather. When the parade was over, she gave an interview to a reporter from *Hoofs and Horns*, took the film crew out to the arena to show them the best camera angles, added a few details to the announcer's notes, and checked with Rafe on the stock. The last task was not something she really needed to do, but she did it anyway; it always made her feel better to see the tall, quiet cowboy.

Not unexpectedly, Rafe had everything under control. Clipboard in hand, he directed the movement of several steers toward the arena for the first event, bulldogging. In a surprising move, he had hired Cory O'Sullivan to assist him with the stock. When Lael had asked Cory how that came about, given Rafe's undisguised antipathy toward him, the young man had grinned sheepishly and replied: "He told me as long as I was going to hang around his place so much, he might as well give me something useful to do."

Lael had not been able to resist teasing her contractor, telling him he was losing his famously gruff touch. He had responded with a look that said: "Don't be too sure about that." So Lael had backed off, hiding her disappointment that he insisted on keeping her at arm's length. *It's just business*, she told herself over and over again.

Only once had he broken out of his shell, and that was to show anger. Contrary to his wishes, Jenny had registered to compete in the broncho riding. When her father found out, he stormed over to the Morrises and read Lael the riot act, accusing her of encouraging his daughter to become a rodeo cowgirl like herself. When she finally could get a word in, Lael informed him she had done no such thing and, in fact, did not even know Jenny had registered. She hotly suggested he straighten things out with his daughter before blaming other people and slammed the door in his face. She had no idea what type of battle ensued when he did confront the girl, but it was obvious who had prevailed; Jenny was competing this very afternoon.

"Everything OK here?" she asked, slapping the haunches of a balky steer.

"So far, so good," Callantine replied. "We had to round up a few more beeves after this last batch of new entries, but we got it covered."

"Well, then"—Lael adjusted her hat nervously—"guess I'll get mounted up. Jenny's going to present the colors in a few minutes and then it'll be time to get started." She gave a last look around the crowded pen before heading for the gate.

"Lael." She turned around. "Good luck." He gave her a crooked grin. Smiling back, she walked away with a new spring in her step. What could possibly go wrong on this beautiful summer day in West Texas?

Taking her place on the arena fence, beneath the announcer's elevated platform, she surveyed the scene. The stands were full, thanks to Louise's promotional efforts, and the crowd buzzed with anticipation. The scratch and hiss of a recording blared over the loudspeaker, and the announcer invited the spectators to rise for the national anthem, just recently adopted by an act of Congress. Jenny Callantine entered the arena to the strains of "The Star Spangled Banner," pausing directly in front of the film crew as Lael had instructed her to do. Her high-spirited horse pranced nervously, but Jenny kept him firmly under control, her smile never wavering.

Then the action began. First came bulldogging, followed by relay racing, and then steer roping. The trick riding, led by Lael's own performance, had the crowd on its feet. Then Louise gave an exhibition in fancy roping, tossing the lariat over the horns of seven steers at once. People had never seen anything like it; they cheered and stomped their feet enthusiastically. The camera caught it all on film.

At last, it was time for the final event: broncho riding. This is what everyone had been waiting for—the event deemed too dangerous for women by the R.A.A. Through the luck of the draw, Jenny Callantine was scheduled to ride first, followed by Lael, Mabel Strickland, Fox Hastings, and six more contestants. The remaining ten entrants would compete in tomorrow's go-round.

The announcer went into his spiel, playing up the perilous nature of the event. Lael had forbidden him to mention Bonnie McCarroll's death, but she did not mind a certain amount of alarmist talk—it helped keep the spectators on the edge of their seats.

Jenny was perched on the side of the chute, watching Rafe saddle her broncho. Lael climbed up next to her. "Who'd you draw?"

"Black Magic."

"What's the word on him?"

"Daddy says he's only been ridden one other time, and that the man who sold him to us called him a spinner."

Lael sighed inwardly, secretly wishing Jenny had drawn a veteran rodeo horse, one whose moves were more predictable. "Well, you know what to do. Keep those toes pointed out for balance."

The young girl nodded. Frowning, she turned her head

first one way, then the other. "Where's Cory? He said he'd be here to see me ride."

"I told him to stay with the stock," Rafe growled. "Don't you be worrying about things like that now, young lady. You got to concentrate on this horse and nothing but this horse, understand? Go ahead and climb on . . . let's measure the rein."

Slowly Jenny lowered herself onto the animal's back. It shifted uneasily beneath her. "Easy. Easy now." She patted Black Magic's powerful neck.

Rafe adjusted the length of braided hemp and handed it to her. The announcer wound up his introduction, reminding everyone that the next performer had been the rodeo's flag-bearer. Jenny's eyes found a point at the base of the horse's neck and honed in on it.

"Ready when you are," called the cowboy manning the gate.

"Go!"

The gate crashed open. Black Magic shot out of the chute, leaping six feet into the air. He kicked out savagely, jolting Jenny's head until it practically collided with his spine. She hung on gamely, sweeping her spurs down the animal's shoulders.

"Go Jenny, go!" Lael shouted, clutching the fence rail tightly. She was aware of Rafe next to her, barely breathing.

Suddenly Black Magic stopped kicking and ran for the center of the arena. He began his fabled spins, twisting first one way, then the other. "Three, two, one . . . ," the crowd chanted. The buzzer sounded. She had done it!

From the sides of the arena, the pick-up men headed out to help the rider dismount, but, before they got close, Black Magic took one last, terrifying leap. Jenny started to slip off. The pick-up men were almost there. Then, before the crowd's unbelieving eyes, Black Magic lost his footing and crashed to the ground, rolling in the dust all the way over on his back, all the way on top of Jenny.

"Oh, God, oh, God," Lael whispered. Beside her, Rafe made a strangled sound. The arena was deathly silent.

Black Magic regained his feet. One of the pick-up men steered him away from the crumpled form on the ground. The other leaped from his horse and bent over Jenny. Rafe sprang from the fence and ran to his daughter, Lael right behind him.

"Jenny! Jenny!" He knelt beside her, started to roll her over.

"Best not to move her, sir," warned the pick-up man. "Wait for the doc."

Rafe looked at him like he wanted to kill him but gently let her shoulders fall back to the ground. He brushed the hair from her cheek. Her face was pale, her mouth ajar. Blood seeped from her nose.

Lael whirled around, searching for the stretcher-bearers. She caught sight of the movie studio camera, rolling, rolling, rolling, every detail being recorded in all its horror.

"Hurry, hurry!" she screamed as the doctor shuffled through the gate. Grimly he felt for a pulse, explored the girl's battered body for broken bones. Rafe peered at him from beneath dark brows, willing him to say something good. But the doctor just shook his head and directed she be loaded onto the stretcher.

Meanwhile the announcer kept up a steady patter, assuring the crowd that everything was fine, that this kind of thing happened all the time in rodeo, and it was never as bad as it looked. Not a soul believed him.

Louise met them at the gate, her face ashen. She grabbed the doctor's arm. "How bad is it?"

"Don't know yet. She's alive . . . that's about all I can say right now. Load her into the ambulance, boys."

The stretcher-bearers started off, Rafe and Lael flanking them.

"Where do you think you're going?"

Lael turned, not certain whom Louise was addressing. America's Cowgirl stared straight at her.

"To the hospital, of course."

"I don't think so. You're up next."

"What?" Lael shook her head, confused. "No, no. The rodeo's canceled. It's over, all over."

"I'll be damned, if it's over! There's ten thousand people out there waiting to see how you carry on. You can't send them home with the last image in their brain being that poor girl getting crushed."

"Louise, I can't ride right now. I've got to stay with Jenny." Lael sprinted to catch up with the stretcher.

Louise trailed her, arms pumping furiously. "Listen to me, Lael Buckley. I pray with all my might that sweet young thing will be fine. But whether she will or won't doesn't depend on you being there to hold her hand. She's got her pa with her to do that. In the meantime, you've got a show to put on. If you call it quits now, tomorrow's lead story in every newspaper in this state will be about the failure of Lael Buckley's all-female rodeo. Is that what you want?"

Lael hesitated, watching them shift Jenny into the back of a converted touring car. She turned to her partner with a tortured expression. "I don't care what they say. I just care about Jenny!"

"That's bullshit, Lael!" Rafe Callantine was at her side, gripping her arm painfully. "This rodeo means more to you than anything you've ever done. Why do you think I . . . ?" He cut himself off. "If you really care about Jenny, you'll go out there and ride. Ride for her, dammit!"

She stared into his agonized eyes and felt her own fill with tears.

The doctor leaned out the car's window. "Let's go."

Rafe turned and leaped into the back of the ambulance. It sped off in a cloud of dust.

Lael stood rooted to her spot. Behind her, she could hear the announcer's voice crackling over the loudspeaker, sounding desperate as he tried to fill time. The restless crowd hummed and buzzed. An image of the rolling camera flashed before her.

Suddenly, she jerked to attention. "Louise, have the announcer tell everyone that Jenny's injuries aren't serious and the show will resume immediately."

"Atta girl!" Louise marched off.

"Cory!" She caught sight of Rafe's assistant. "Are we ready to go?"

Cory turned to her with grief-stricken eyes. "Miss Buckley, what about Jenny? I just heard what happened."

She placed a sympathetic hand on his shoulder. "I won't lie to you, Cory. It doesn't look good. But Rafe's with her, and all we can do now is pray. I need your help. You're the only one left who knows how to handle the stock. Will you help me finish the show?"

He dropped his head, struggling to bring himself under control. "Yes, ma'am."

"Good." She slapped him on the back. "Is my broncho in the chute?"

"Yes, ma'am. You drew Devil's Brew."

Indeed, I did, she thought. *Indeed, I did.*

Chapter Thirty

She gave the performance of her life, although, afterwards, she could not recall one detail of those ten seconds. Inspired by her gutsy ride, Mabel, Lorena, Fox, and the others followed suit, all posting scores in the eighties. Later, when the dust had settled, it was generally agreed that the finest display of cowgirl broncho riding ever seen had occurred at the San Angelo Cowgirl Reunion of 1931. But that was only the asterisk. The headline story was how, once again, a cowgirl had gotten seriously injured while busting a broncho.

Lael did her best to change the focus of the reporting, but there was not much she could do. Every time she pointed out the championship caliber of the assembled cowgirls, she was met with questions about Jenny.

"How is the injured girl doing?"

"Will she survive?"

"Was she too young to be competing?"

And worst of all: "People say Bonnie McCarroll died because she got hung up in her hobbled stirrups. But this girl was riding slick. Does that mean that it's never safe for a woman to ride a broncho?"

Lael got fed up and left Louise to handle the unruly pack. Enough was enough. She had done her duty; her place now was with Jenny and Rafe. But when she arrived at San Angelo's tiny hospital, she was told they had transferred Jenny to a larger facility in Abilene, seventy-five miles away. No, they said, they could not reveal the patient's condition, but the doctor had deemed her strong enough to make the journey which was a good sign. She momentarily considered driving to Abilene herself but then rejected the idea. There was nothing she could do there besides provide comfort to Rafe, and he had made it all too clear that was not what he expected from her. *It's just business.*

So she returned to the rodeo and, when her work was done there, to the Morris ranch, hoping he would at least think to telephone with Jenny's condition. But he did not, and the evening dragged until, finally, Lael excused herself and went up to bed.

Not surprisingly, sleep would not come. The thunderheads that had been building all day had ushered in a new round of hot, ozone-laden temperatures. Sticking to the limp sheets, Lael stared out the window and watched heat lightning illuminate the horizon.

It was very late when she rose from the bed, dressed, and quietly left the house. Working in the dark, she saddled up her favorite mare, Delilah, and led her out of the stables. Mounting up, she kept the horse at an easy gait. She would have liked to turn Delilah loose and race across the shadowy plains at a full gallop, but the night was too black except for the occasional flash of lightning.

Although she had had no particular destination in mind when she had risen from her bed, she found herself pointing Delilah in the direction of Starbuck Ranch. She told herself she just wanted to check on things, make sure someone had tended the stock in Rafe's absence. Of course, she knew Cory had undoubtedly done so.

By the time she reached the ranch, the coming storm had intensified. Judging by the thunderclaps, lightning was less than ten miles away, and the wind had picked up, whipping tumbleweeds against her horse's legs. Heading for the barn, she confirmed that the stock had been fed and bedded. Now with that concern satisfied, she ought to head back to the Morrises before the storm broke. Instead, she left Delilah in the barn and headed for the house. *I probably wouldn't make it back in time*, she told herself. *I'll just wait it out here on the front porch.*

She sat down on the porch swing, watching and waiting as the storm moved across the plains. The electrified air lifted the hair off the back of her neck. Her heart pounded, and her breath came short. What was wrong with her? It was only a thunderstorm, no different from countless others she had witnessed.

But when it broke, it proved fierce, indeed. It took only a moment to realize that the verandah would not provide adequate shelter from the wind-driven raindrops. She rose from the swing and pressed herself against the wall of the house, but still the rain pelted her, depositing large, wet blotches on her clothes. Perhaps she should run for the shelter of the barn, but in the time it would take to reach it she would be drenched. She stood there a moment longer, hoping the storm would abate. Instead, the wind shifted, blowing the rain in from a new direction and soaking what had been her dry side.

Well, there was nothing for it. Much as she hated to intrude, she must get out of this weather. Rafe would understand, if, indeed, he ever knew about it. She tried the door; naturally, it was unlocked. Nobody in Tom Green County locked their doors. Pushing it shut behind her, she leaned against it, listening to the rain battering the walls and windows.

From conversations with Jenny, she knew that the Hendersons had not been able to afford electricity and that Rafe had not yet gotten around to putting it in. There was really no reason for a light—her eyes were perfectly accustomed to the dark—but something in her wanted the cheeriness of a glowing lantern. Spotting one next to the fireplace, she lit it, noticing as she did so a framed photograph adorning the mantel. It was the same picture she had seen years ago in Rafe's tent: Jenny as a little girl, smiling innocently for the photographer. Holding the frame to her chest, Lael fought back tears. *Dear God*, she prayed, *let her be all right, please let her be all right.*

A gust of wind sprayed the window with hard pellets of rain. Shivering, Lael pulled her wet shirt away from her skin. Picking up the lantern, she scouted around until she found Jenny's bedroom. Choosing a warm, flannel shirt from the wardrobe, she removed her own and put on Jenny's, rolling the too-long sleeves up a cuff-length or two.

Back out in the hallway, she paused before a closed door—Rafe's bedroom she guessed. She hesitated. Whatever was behind that door was none of her business. If she went in, she would be the worst kind of snoop. But what would it hurt? Nobody would ever have to know.

Her fingers grazed the knob; she pulled them back and touched them to her lips. *Eulalie Buckley, what have you come to?* But her hand reached out again, almost as if it operated independently from the rest of her body, and twisted the knob. The door swung open, and she entered the room, holding the lantern before her. Leaping into the light were a few nondescript pieces of furniture—a bed, a chest of drawers, a straight-back chair—and nothing else. No pictures, no books, nothing but the most basic personal items. The only thing that gave any indication this room was actually occupied by Rafe Callantine was a discarded shirt casually draped over the foot of the bed.

A hot wave of shame flooded her chilled body. What had

she expected to see, for God's sake? Pictures of his dead wife lining the walls? She turned to leave. The sound of the front door crashing open froze her to the spot.

"Who's there?" shouted a rough voice.

Lael gasped. It was Rafe. She would almost rather it be an intruder. How could she explain being in his bedroom?

Footsteps came nearer, and she realized she would have to declare herself. Squaring her shoulders, she stepped out into the hallway—and found herself looking down the barrel of a shotgun.

"Jesus!" Callantine fell back a step and lowered the gun. His face, lit by the lantern's glow, looked fearsome as he stared at her from beneath his dripping black hat. "What the hell are you doing here? I just about took your head off."

Lael looked at him meekly. "I . . . I couldn't sleep so I decided to come check on your stock."

His eyes strayed behind her to his open bedroom door. She hurried on to prevent him from asking the obvious question. "The rain caught me so I came inside to get dry. I hope you don't mind."

Leaning the shotgun against the wall, he passed his hand over his stubbled chin. "No, I don't mind. It's just . . . I drove up and saw a light moving around inside and thought somebody was up to no good. I guess I overreacted . . . my nerves are a mite frayed."

Lael stepped toward him, wanting to lay a comforting hand on his arm, but holding back. "Of course, they are. Is Jenny . . . is she better?"

His shoulders sagged. Bracing himself against the wall, he stooped over, his hands on his knees. "They don't know yet. They say she'll live, but whether she ever walks again. . . ." He trailed off.

The need to console him overcame her reticence. Setting

257

the lantern down, she clutched both his arms and peered at him intently. "She'll be fine. I know she will."

He shook his head, exhausted. "I wish I could be so sure. All I know is that I failed her, just like I failed. . . ." He could not go on.

"Stop it, Rafe! Stop doing this to yourself." She shook him, furious with him and yet grieving for him at the same time. "Sometimes bad things happen. They aren't anybody's fault . . . they just happen!"

Hardly knowing what he was doing, he turned on her, breaking her grip on his arms by grabbing her own. "You don't understand!" he shouted, his dark eyes flashing. "What if I lost her? I'd have nothing, no one."

Lael threw herself into his arms, burying her face in his chest. "You'd have me,"—the words came out part whisper, part sob—"if you wanted me."

She could feel his arms close around her, his hand in her hair, pulling her head back. He looked at her mouth for what seemed like an eternity, then bent his head and touched it with his own, gently at first, then harder and harder, devouring her. She answered with equal passion, savoring the taste of him, the smell of him, redolent of earth and rain.

Holding her tightly, he stroked her face, her hair, her body, and gazed at her with haunted eyes. "I've wanted you since the first time I saw you, when that damned hat of yours spooked my horse. I wanted you so badly when you got in that fight and I brought you back to the barn to doctor you up that I liked to die. But I was a drunk, just like you said . . . a whisky-head . . . and you, my God, you were so young and innocent and beautiful. And talented. I knew the first time I saw you ride . . . remember, when you ran down that runaway palomino . . . I knew then that you were going to be a star. I couldn't stand to watch you, knowing that I could never have you, not the way I was."

"Oh, Rafe"—Lael brought her hand up to caress the scar on his mouth—"couldn't you see I wanted you, too?"

"Maybe, a little. I saw something that gave me a shred of hope. That's why I left. I figured if I went away, got myself cleaned up, took care of my responsibilities, maybe I'd have a chance of winning you."

A tear slid down her cheek. Lifting her in his strong arms, he carried her back to the main room and sat with her in his lap, cradling her like a child. The rain had slackened and beat a soothing drumbeat on the roof.

After a while, Lael turned to him with a questioning glance. "But you did all those things. You stopped drinking and started taking care of Jenny. Why didn't you come for me then?"

"One small problem . . . you'd gotten married. When I heard that, I figured I'd been wrong before, that you really didn't feel anything for me." He gazed past her, lost in the memory. "It was almost enough to start me drinking again. But I had Jenny to think of. She saved me." He gave a little start. "I've got to get back to Abilene. I didn't think I'd be gone this long."

"Why did you leave anyway?"

"Jenny came to once we got to Abilene, started babbling a bunch of gibberish. The one thing she kept mentioning over and over was . . . her mother's locket." His eyes filled with pain. "It's the only thing she has left that was hers. I decided to come get it for her. Maybe it'll help somehow. The doctor gave her a shot, said she'd be out for a few hours. Just enough time to drive here and back. He lent me his car."

Reluctantly Lael climbed off his lap. Of course, his place was with his daughter, but that did not make it any easier to let him leave. Especially now that he had finally opened up to her. There was something nagging at her, though, something he had said that did not ring true. But the spell was broken. His thoughts were with Jenny now, not her.

He disappeared into Jenny's room and came out tucking the locket into his shirt pocket. Awkwardly he paused in front of Lael. She wanted to go to him, put her arms around him, and kiss that special place on his mouth. After what they had just shared, it should have been the most natural thing in the world to do. But even now, she could sense him holding her at arm's length.

"Maybe I should drive you back to the Morrises," he offered, rather half-heartedly.

"No, don't be ridiculous," she said. "That would add an hour to your drive. Sounds like the rain's about stopped. I'll be able to ride back just fine."

"Well, then. . . ." He strode to the door, pulled it open, then hesitated. "How'd the rest of the bronc' riding go? Was it a good show?"

Lael grinned mirthlessly. "The best ever. It'll go down in history."

"I'm glad for you," he rasped, and pulled the door shut behind him.

Chapter Thirty-One

"Miss Buckley?"

"Oh, for heaven's sake, Cory, call me Lael. This Miss Buckley business makes me feel a hundred years old."

The two of them rode across the plains, on their way to Starbuck Ranch. After a month in the hospital, Jenny Callantine was coming home today. She had asked them to be there to meet her.

"Sorry, ma'am."

Lael rolled her eyes—*ma'am* was not much of an improvement.

"I was just wondering if I could ask your advice."

"I'm not an expert on much of anything, but go ahead." Halting by the river, she let the reins go slack.

"Well," Cory began shyly, "I guess it's no secret how I feel about Jenny."

Lael smiled. "No, it isn't."

"And I'd like to think she feels the same way about me." The young man reached down and stroked his horse's neck, anxiously avoiding Lael's eyes.

"Jenny thinks a lot of you, I can tell."

"Well, what I was wondering is, do you think I ought to ask her to marry me?"

Lael blinked in surprise. "Gosh, Cory, I . . . she's only seventeen."

"I know, but I'm twenty-one, and Ma pays me a decent salary, and one day, well, let's just say I plan to be ranching in these parts for the rest of my life. What I'm trying to say is . . . I've got good prospects and God knows I love her."

Lael's heart swelled. What a fine young man was Cory O'Sullivan and how precious was young love. "In that case, this is a conversation you ought to be having with Jenny and her father. It's not for me to tell you what to do. All I can say is . . . follow your heart. Nine times out of ten, it'll take you in the right direction."

They crossed the river, no more than a stream in the middle of July, and rode side by side through the grama grass. "I'm not worried about what Jenny will say," Cory sighed. "It's the conversation with her father I'm not looking forward to."

"He's not as tough as he seems," Lael said, not at all certain she spoke the truth. "One thing I'm pretty sure of . . . if he thinks you'll make Jenny happy, he won't stand in your way."

Cory shot her a grateful look as they rode up to the Callantine spread. "Look, there she is!" he cried.

Narrowing her eyes, Lael could make out a figure on the front porch waving at them. Spurring his horse, Cory raced to the foot of the steps, leaped down, and stood before Jenny awkwardly, not certain how to circumnavigate her crutches.

"Come here, you big lug," Jenny laughed. "I'd rather lean on you than these stupid things."

With a huge grin, Cory encircled the pretty girl with his arms. Letting the crutches fall to the ground, Jenny twined her hands behind his neck and let him take her full weight. "Don't let go," she whispered.

"Never," he replied, and gave her a long kiss.

Lael came trotting up on Delilah just as Rafe emerged from the house. Both of them took in the young lovers, and then glanced at each other. She winked at him as though to say: "Better get used to it, Pa." He cleared his throat.

Disengaging his lips but still holding Jenny tightly, Cory nodded at Rafe. " 'Afternoon, sir."

Rafe acknowledged him with a pursed mouth. "You aren't supposed to be standing on that leg yet, young lady," he grumbled.

Jenny smiled at him sweetly. "Whatever you say, Daddy. Here, Cory, help me sit down."

The young cowboy assisted her to the porch swing and sat next to her, stretching an arm out behind her. Jenny gave him an angelic look, then turned to greet Lael.

"Thanks for coming over, Miss Buckley. I sure do appreciate all the flowers you sent, and that story they did about me in the San Angelo paper . . . thanks for sending that, too."

"It was the least I could do," Lael said. "Looks like you're feeling pretty good."

Indeed, for a girl who a month ago had been near death, Jenny Callantine looked remarkably fine. The only visible remnant of her injuries was the cast on her broken leg.

"I'm feeling great!" Jenny declared. Once more, she turned to gaze at the handsome young man beside her. With his free hand, Cory reached over and took hers, interlacing their fingers. Behind them, her father shifted uneasily.

"Say, Rafe," Lael said, dismounting quickly. "It seemed like Delilah might have caught a burr in her hoof on the way over. Would you mind checking it for me?"

"Uh, no, I guess not." He stomped down the steps and started to raise the horse's leg.

"Let's take her down to the barn," she suggested, smiling at the young couple behind his back. "She's pretty thirsty."

Straightening up, he gave her a look but, without a word, took the reins and started leading Delilah toward the barn.

Lael followed, leading Cory's horse. Glancing at him from the corner of her eye, she wondered what he was thinking. Did he remember the last time they had been together, the night of the storm? Nothing in his demeanor indicated he had given it a second thought.

They stopped at the water trough and let the horses drink. Sliding his hand down Delilah's leg, he started to lift it.

"Oh, I just made that up about the burr," Lael said, grinning.

"What?"

"She doesn't have anything wrong with her. That was just an excuse to get you away from your daughter."

He propped an elbow on Delilah's saddle and stared across the horse's back at Lael. "Why would you want to do that?"

She laughed. "Come on, Rafe. It can't have escaped your attention that those two are sweet on each other. It's been a whole month since they were together . . . they didn't need you and me breathing down their necks."

He tipped his hat forward on his brow, a puzzled look on his face. "I'll be god-damned," he muttered.

Laughing again, she strolled over to the corral fence. Hooking one boot over the bottom rung, she surveyed his beautiful herd of horses. "Don't you just love the way they look at each other," she mused, "as though the whole earth and sky was right there in the other person's eyes."

He came up behind her. "Why are you still here?" he asked softly. "Why haven't you gone back to California, or gone out on the circuit?"

"Oh, I had a few odds and ends to take care of after the rodeo, you know, bills to pay and. . . ." Taking a deep breath, she turned around to face him. "Actually, the truth of it is, I like it here. I don't really want to leave and . . . and . . . I feel like you and I haven't really settled things yet." *There, it was out.* She stared at him apprehensively, her heart thudding in her chest.

He dropped his head, letting his hat hide all but the lower half of his face from view. "If you're talking about the night Jenny got hurt . . . I wasn't myself that night."

Stunned, she clutched the fence tightly, afraid she would fall to the ground if she let go. Was it true? Had he not meant all those things he said that night? She could not believe he had been lying to her. Still, there was the question she had been left with, the one she had not been able to ask him before he had rushed out to return to Jenny's bedside.

"Rafe," her voice trembled, "you told me you straightened yourself out so you could try and win me, but then you found out I'd gotten married. I admire you for staying away from me then, never mind that I'd married for all the wrong reasons and was still in love with you. But when we met again in Cheyenne, I told you I had been divorced. You knew then there was no longer any reason why we couldn't be together . . . and still you stayed away. Why? Is it because of what happened before . . . the fire and everything? Because I told you what happened in the past doesn't matter to me. I love you for the man you are now."

"Oh, God, Lael, that isn't it." He looked at her with eyes full of pain. Leaning against the fence, he let his gaze travel across his land, down to the cottonwoods that lined the river. "I think about the fire, my wife and son, every single day of my life, and I always will. That's not something you get over. But I've learned to live with it, and I know it doesn't have anything to do with you, or how I feel about you." He turned his head and looked at her intently. "The reason I haven't gone after you, Lael, is because you belong to somebody else. Somebody called rodeo."

She stared at him in shocked surprise. "What are you talking about?"

"You heard me. You say you love me, and I believe you think you do. Well, maybe you can kid yourself, but you can't kid me. Your heart belongs to rodeo, Lael. Riding the circuit, busting bronchos, racing fast horses, cheering crowds, rising dust, your hair flying in the wind. . . ." He reached out and stroked her wheat-colored ponytail. "That's what you really love. I'm not so selfish that I'd ask you to give it up. But I am selfish enough that I can't share you with it. I want you more today, this very moment"—he swallowed hard—"than I ever have. But I want all of you, here, with me, all the time. I want to roll over in bed every morning and see that gorgeous face of yours next to me. I want to fall asleep at night holding you close. I just can't share you." He shrugged helplessly.

"I've thought about whether I could give all this up"—he glanced around his ranch—"and go with you on the road, but I can't do that, either. First of all, there's Jenny to think of, though it appears she won't be holding me back for long. But it's more than just wanting to provide a home for Jenny." He knit his brow and looked deep into Lael's eyes, needing her to understand what he said next. "I've sunk my blood, sweat, heart, and soul into this place. All I've ever wanted to do is raise horses, and this is where I want to do it. This is my little piece of paradise, and I can't give it up. Not even for you, God help me."

Suddenly, it all seemed so clear to her. She felt her spirits soar with the realization that what she was about to say would truly set her free. "You're right about me and rodeo . . . I do love it, and that will never change. But rodeo is changing. It's not the same as it used to be, and the way it is now"—she shook her head—"it's just not worth it any more. I tried to fight the R.A.A., and I got nowhere. I tried to produce my own rodeo and look what happened . . . with the help of Universal Studios, I produced a bang-up advertisement for shutting down all of women's rodeo."

"That wasn't your fault," Rafe argued.

"Of course, it wasn't. None of it is my fault, but what does that matter? The fact is . . . women's rodeo as I know it is finished, done with. So I have two choices. Either I accept the changes and participate in it in the limited fashion it allows, or I bow out. Frankly, that's not a real difficult decision." She looked at him shyly. "Truth be told, you're doing exactly what I always said I'd do when I retired from the circuit . . . raising horses. How 'bout it, cowboy . . . need a partner? I'm real good at keeping the books."

"Are you saying you're quitting rodeo?"

Lael bowed her head for a moment, fighting back the sudden prick of tears. God, it wasn't easy. But she knew she was right, and being able to spend the rest of her life with the man beside her was only one of many reasons why that was so.

"I choose to think of it more as refusing to lend my name to the sham they call women's rodeo these days. I suppose I'll always keep my hand in, but, yes, I'm quitting the circuit. I've got other dreams now." She looked at him with liquid, sage-green eyes.

Gently he reached for her hand and pulled her to him, enveloping her in his sturdy arms. "You know I named this place for you, don't you?"

"Starbuck Ranch?" she asked, wishing he would shut up and kiss her.

"That's right. You're my star, Lael Buckley." He obliged her with a sweet, lingering kiss. "Welcome home."

About the Author

Raised in the Midwest, Suzanne Lyon moved to Colorado at seventeen to attend The Colorado College. She worked as a lawyer for, among others, the National Park Service before turning her talents to writing. Lured by the landscapes and legends of the West, Lyon's interest is in Western historical fiction. She resides near Denver with her husband and two children. Her first **Five Star Western** was BANDIT INVINCIBLE: BUTCH CASSIDY. She will continue the story begun in this novel in EL DESCONOCIDO: BUTCH CASSIDY, her next **Five Star Western**.

Suzanne Lyon was born in Des Moines, Iowa. She attended The Colorado College and graduated with a Bachelor's degree. She later said: "I came to Colorado to go to school at the foot of Pike's Peak. Like so many others before me, that landmark drew me in and took hold." She went on to earn a degree in law at the University of Colorado School of Law. She has worked as a lawyer for, among others, the National Park Service. She grew up listening to stories handed down in her family from a precursor who was the first white woman settler west of the Mississippi. Lured by the landscapes and legends of the American West, Suzanne Lyon became intrigued with the life of the legendary bandit, Butch Cassidy, and made him the subject of her first historical novel. She is keenly interested in bringing to life the times and the people who went West and to tell their stories. "Out West," she has said, "the land refuses to be taken for granted. Everything is bigger, taller, windier, sunnier, drier, harsher, farther. You can love it, or you can hate it, but you can't be complacent about it. The same could be said of the men and women who settled the West. Whether of noble character, or base, their stories take on almost mythic proportions. They require our attention." *Lady Buckaroo* is a narrative based on the lives of female rodeo stars in the 1920s. Her most recent novel is *A Heart for any Fate*. She is married with two children and lives in Broomfield, Colorado.